WILD IRISH

A PREQUEL TO VICIOUS IRISH

&

WITHDRAWN

VICIOUS IRISH BOOK ONE

BY VI CARTER

Other Books by VI Carter

A BROKEN HEART SERIES

SAVING GRACE

CLAIMING AMBER

TAKING LAURA

WILD IRISH SERIES

WILD IRISH (PREQUEL)

VISIOUS #1

RUTHLESS #2

FEARLESS #3

MERCILESS #4

HEARTLESS #5

CHAPTER NINETEEN **336**

    UNA 336

CHAPTER TWENTY..**351**

    SHANE...351

CHAPTER TWENTY ONE **363**

    UNA 363

CHAPTER TWENTY TWO **377**

    UNA 377

CHAPTER TWENTY THREE..**388**

    SHANE...388

CHAPTER TWENTY FOUR **403**

    UNA 403

CHAPTER TWENTY FIVE **414**

    SHANE...414

ABOUT THE AUTHOR..**427**

CHAPTER ONE

FINN

"Where is your brother?" My father bends over a map that takes up the top of the table. His index finger has stopped moving as I enter. He doesn't look up at me. Shane stands firmly beside him, arms folded across his wide chest. I scratch my eyebrow in annoyance.

There is so much I want to say, like, 'Just because we are twins doesn't mean we keep tabs on each other.' Or 'Do I look like a fucking slave?' But our motto is carved into the wood that hangs over the dining table that is mostly used for meetings.

The Irish word 'Chlann' has been carved into that piece of wood by our father's, father, and it is carved into all of us. The family comes first, no matter what. My eyes flicker back to Shane who still stares at me, a shadow of a grin on his face.

"Probably in bed with a whore," I rattle off, and that gets my father's attention. His finger slightly curls.

"Watch your mouth, Finn." He speaks but doesn't look at me. Is he fucking kidding? His mouth spews poison half the time.

I flicker a glance at Shane, expecting the grin to be visible, but it isn't, instead, his head tilts slightly towards our father, his way of telling me to shut the fuck up and go and get our brother.

"I'll get him now." With a sigh, I close the door behind me and take the stairs two at a time, slowing down once I reach the landing. I can hear the undercurrent of a beat. Darragh never switches his music off. In his life, the party never seems to stop. I can smell the cigarette smoke before I even open his door, and once I do, a lot of other smells follow.

"Darragh, get up." I kick the base of the bed, where three sets of legs hang out. The alcohol fumes in the room have me wanting to open a window. My steel toe boot connects with the bed frame again. A blond pops up like a blow-up doll, mumbling as she looks around the room. Her eyes settle on me, and she slowly grins.

"Good morning." A polish accent or maybe Russian—I can't tell the difference—coats her words.

"Get out," I tell her. Her brows furrow as she looks down at sleeping beauty, who I am tempted to kick the shit out of if he doesn't wake up soon.

"Darragh, get the fuck up." This time he does, and the second blow-up doll inflates. Topless. She does a double take to me and then Darragh. "Twins."

"You're a genius. Now, get out," I say slowly for her. This time they both get out of the bed. The second one yelps as Darragh lands a slap to her arse. I wonder sometimes how we are related. The idea that we shared the same womb is baffling.

"Da is waiting, Darragh, and he's pissed." I don't blatantly watch the girls as they get dressed, but I can't help the occasional glance; they are fit, a little too thin for my likings, but still nice. I light a fag as Darragh finally gets off the bed and pulls on a white t-shirt.

"Pick a different color," I tell him. I am wearing a white t-shirt, and I'll be fucked if we are dressing the same.

"You know who you are like?" Darragh asks while pulling the t-shirt off. I don't acknowledge him but smoke my fag, hoping by the time I am finished, that Darragh will be ready. "You're like Da."

I snort because I am the furthest from our father, and Darragh knows it. I don't respond as each girl moves past me and out the door. Darragh promises to ring them later, and they believe him. Our front door has become a rotating one with all of Darragh's women. None are ever brought back for seconds. He pulls on jeans, and I want to tell him to change them. I'm wearing jeans, but I don't want to sound whiny.

"What does he want?" Darragh slaps his face twice, and I am glad that he shaves daily. I'm growing a beard just so we look different. Being identical twins is a pain in the ass.

"I don't know. Shane's with him," I say as we make our way downstairs and return to the dining room with my brother, like a good little doggy.

"Close the door," Dad barks, and Darragh does. Once we all stand around the map on the table, he finally looks up, blue eyes snapping from me to Darragh. My father is a man that many admire.

For me, I hate him and love him. I hate how he sees me as someone to take care of Darragh, I hate how he treats Connor, my brother. I hate the control.

My mind moves back to the meeting as Shane kicks it off.

"Land close by has come up for sale." Normally Shane doesn't speak unless father has asked him too, but I can see the irritation in our father's stance.

The smell of alcohol off Darragh is wafting through the room, and he looks like he smells. Bloodshot eyes blink several times as he slaps himself across the face again. If he keeps it up, he won't have to slap himself anymore; Dad is ready to flitter him.

Shane jabs a finger at a patch of green fields circled with a red marker on the map. "11.86 acres has come up. Seven of it is bog land." We all stare at the green patch that Shane points at.

"Darragh, I want you to convince the new landowner to sell it to you," Father cuts in, and Darragh folds his arms across his chest while nodding.

"She's only moved back here, she has no family or attachment to the land, and it should be an easy sell." Shane sits down at the table, his black shirt and slacks make him look like he is going to a funeral. Maybe he is.

"You go with him," my father says, cutting me with his sharp eye. Once again I try to hide my irritation at being Darragh's babysitter.

"How much?" Darragh widens his eyes, and I wonder if he's high. I want to kick him and tell him to get his shit together.

"Offer her a hundred thousand."

Darragh nods.

"For *bog* land? That's worth like what, two or three an acre, the good land no more than ten." I can't for a second understand why he is over paying.

"I didn't realize you were my financial adviser." Darragh shifts beside me, and I clench my jaw at my father's words. If Shane gave his opinion it wouldn't be shot down, but the moment I do, I get a smart fucking answer

"You both tidy yourselves up. You leave in an hour." My father dismisses us with a wave of his hand. I am out of there and taking the stairs two at a time. My mind, for some reason, begins conjuring up images of Conor. It's weird how much you can miss a person. I hate him for abandoning me. But he has always been there for me. Now I feel so out of place in our dysfunctional family.

Slamming my door feels pretty juvenile, but I need to release some of my anger. I also need to get showered and ready to go and purchase bog land, land that is only good for one thing.

Dumping bodies.

SIOBHAN

'Death. It comes to us all.' That line is from Gladiator, one of my all-time favorite films, and it rings true to me.. Right now, it's on a loop as I look down at my father. All the wasted time, all the what if's and why's. Now they no longer matter. All that matters is saying goodbye and hoping the next time I meet him, we might spend some time together. I might actually get to know my father.

"Ah, Siobhan I'm so sorry for your loss." Another farmer who I don't know takes my hand in his. His other holds a hat that he takes from his balding head. His tweed jacket is worn and looks like if you'd slap it, dust mites would fill the air. But this is their Sunday clothes, funeral clothes. Irish Farmers have their own unique style.

"Thank you." I don't know his name, and there is a pause, like he is waiting for me to say it. His hand tightens on mine. "Michael," I say. The other part of me wants to say Patrick, but I am wrong either way.

"Peter."

I exhale a breath. "Ah, yeah, Peter."

"Peter, you are holding up the line." Olive, bless her heart, leans in across my shoulder. Peter is a big man, nearly seven foot tall, so being told off by a woman who is small and round is funny. But he moves along the line that just isn't stopping. The room is now filled with men, mostly farmers, all chatting about how great my dad was.

My eyes flicker once again to his corpse. Each story I hear makes me wish I had known him. I don't feel sad, or upset like any normal daughter would. No tears come, I even try to force them by thinking back to burying my mother when I was only fifteen. But I have nada.

The wake is to last three nights. Three long nights. Honestly, I don't understand why we have to wait so long, but it's a tradition, in case he wakes up, but my father isn't waking up. He's dead. For sure. "Olive. I'm going to take a break." I needed to get out of this room of strangers.

Olive nods, each nod sharp. "Don't you worry, Siobhan. I'll keep this show on the road." I suppress a smile that threatens to appear. She pats me three times on the arm. "You take a wee break. Come back when you're ready." I don't delay. Instead, I move through the house quickly and out into the small backyard, which is walled in.

Opening the gate I move out into the farmyard. The large slatted shed that housed eighty cattle is now silent. It's an odd sound. Spending most of my childhood listening to the wails of the cattle, the silence is another reminder that everyone here is gone.

Swallowing the first sign of tears, I tighten my arms across my chest. It's freezing outside, my breaths form small white puffs in front of me. The light black dress in't doing anything to fight off the cold. The wind prickles my skin, making me feel, and I allow it. Standing still with my eyes closed brings back so many memories.

My mother wasn't a conventional mother by any means. She would roll up her sleeves and come out and help Dad with the cattle. She would shovel dung, feed them silage, a pair of overalls was something she owned.

A small laugh bubbles from my lips, accompanied by my first cry. Dad loved her so much. I remember watching him…watching her, thinking one day I hope someone looks at me like that. That is the before. Before she got cancer, before everything changed then, he changed. Our home changed.

"Siobhan?" My name spoken softly and like a question, which has me wiping my eyes quickly. Two young men—brothers—are standing in the yard. Both are not farmers, and they look out of place in my yard. Like when city slickers arrive and stumble upon our house, either looking to buy it or looking for directions.

The one who is closer has a soft smile on his face. His black suit fits him snuggly. His freshly shaven face gives him that city slick feel. Blond hair brushed to the side finishes off the look.

My eyes move to the brother who stands a few paces back. He doesn't wear black. His jeans and white t-shirt is finished off with a black suit jacket. His wild beard and wild blue eyes do funny things to my stomach. They are both attractive, *what an odd thing to think of when my father was laid out a few feet away.*

"Yes, I'm Siobhan," I finally answer on an exhale.

"Darragh O'Reagan. Knew your father. He was mighty." The closest one says, and I take his large, and surprisingly soft, outstretched hand.

"Thank you." I feel he is smiling too hard, and the smell of alcohol emitting off him has my eyes flickering to his brother.

"Sorry for your loss." His voice is deep, and I find myself nodding at him. Darragh still holds my hand, my eyes snapping back to him. "We wanted to know if you had a minute for a chat."

It is my father's wake. But sure why not?

"What about?" I remove my hand from his and take a step sideways just to put a bit of space between us. Folding my arms across my chest doesn't do anything to fight off the cold biting into me now.

"We want to buy your land."

Anger that I didn't expect ripples through me. I unfold my arms and refold them while shifting on my feet I look at both brothers; waiting for what? I'm unsure. Darragh is still smiling while the other is looking around him, like he wants to find somewhere to hide. The fact that he reacts like that makes me like him a small bit more, yet these two brothers have arrived to my father's funeral to buy stupid land. I push down my anger not wanting to create a stir. "I'm not sure what I'm doing with it." There is a time and place for everything, and this isn't either.

"Thank you for coming," I add while moving past both men before the second one with the beard stops me with his words.

"Your father was a good man." I look at him now. Really look at him, because he sounds so sincere, so honest.

"Was he?" I find myself questioning. I am sick of hearing what a good man he was. I want to scream that I don't know the man that was left after my mother died and took him with her. Leaving a shell. Well, not a shell, apparently. Everyone else seems to think he was great.

His brows pull down and I don't blame him, he is a stranger, and he doesn't need to know about our family problems. "Sorry, yeah he was." I leave quickly and go back into the house. I don't go to the sitting room that my father is laid out in. Instead, I make my way into the kitchen that also holds a group of farmers eating sandwiches and drinking tea. A big pot of stew sits on the stove. The kitchen is warm and cozy after the cold outside. I settle into an armchair that faces the window and let the room warm me up.

"Siobhan, sweetheart, will you have a bowl of stew?" I smile now at Teresa. She is a neighbor. Our home is down what is known as the black lane. It sits at the end by itself. Teresa is the closest, and her house is across the road from the lane. I don't know her, but when I got back, she was there taking over, and I didn't mind.

Everyone in the area is here to help, united in their love for my father. Teresa wears a woolly cream Aran jumper and has red rosy cheeks. Sleeves rolled up to her elbows couldn't cool her down. That wool is thick; I used to own a few of them. Once I moved to Dublin, I left it all behind. Just like the life I knew before.

Sandie settles at my feet, another thing I am trying to adjust to. She is my father's sheepdog, one he had gotten after I'd left. She follows me around like she knows I am her owner's daughter. I wasn't exactly an animal lover, and I don't want to get attached. I couldn't take a sheepdog back to my apartment in Dublin.

"I'm fine, Teresa," I tell her. My stomach grumbles, but the thought of eating makes my mouth water.

"Just a small bowl." She had kind grey eyes that smile, even when her lips don't. "A small one then," I tell her, and her smile spreads fast across her face.

"A bowl over here wouldn't go astray," Peter speaks up from the group of farmers, and a few of them follow suit. Teresa is quick to dish out bowls of stew and smiles as they start to dig in. Compliments on the stew are passed around the kitchen making Teresa's face redden and her laughther deepen, and it was in that moment that I find this sense of peace. In my family's kitchen surrounded by strangers, with a dog I don't own at my feet. The heat of the bowl is warming my hands, but the love of these people is going deeper.

Then silence descends on the room, and the shift is immediate. I look up to find the brothers standing in my doorway.

CHAPTER TWO

FINN

"Her father's *wake*?" I lean in towards Darragh the moment Siobhan is out of earshot. I feel so shit now. One thing I don't like is messing with the dead.

"Dad said she'd be vulnerable, make it an easy job." He stuffs his hands in his trouser pockets as we both watch Siobhan disappear inside.

"Clearly Dad isn't always right," I say, and Darragh looks at me with a grin on his face.

"It ain't over yet, brother." He moves towards the house, and I follow quickly on his heels.

"You're not going in?" I ask, waiting for him to turn away from the house and toward the car, but no, instead, I follow him under the arch of the front door. This isn't right, but it will be worse if I'm not there, just in case it gets out of hand. Darragh on a good day can't control his mouth. This morning, with so much alcohol still fuelling his body, anything is liable to come out of his mouth.

I've been to lots of wakes, for lots of ages, and most daughters would be devastated about the death of a parent. Siobhan seemed lost; in a way that I wanted to help her find whatever it was she was searching for. I scratch my eyebrow, not meeting the eye of the men who line the hall. Silence already fills the house, but a new silence follows us all the way into the kitchen, where we find Siobhan.

Sitting in an armchair, a sheepdog at her feet. Its head lifts slightly as it takes me and Darragh in before settling back down between its paws. Siobhan holds a bowl of steaming food, and the look on her face appears to me to be contentment, which is unexpected compared to the girl I saw outside. The guilt that had being gnawing at me lifts now. The silence in the kitchen has her looking at us. Big brown eyes meet mine, and her nostrils flare slightly.

"Ah, Teresa, I'll have a bowl of stew there." I didn't think my brother would be able to stoop any lower, but yet, he does.

Teresa, who we all know as the area's gossip mill, takes a bowl and fills it for Darragh, who accepts it and manages to squeeze in on a bench with the other men. The only noise is of him eating. and I don't know whether to admire his brazenness or kick him.

"Would you like a bowl, Finn." My attention is drawn to Teresa, I shake my head.

"No thank you." Scanning the room I meet Siobhan's eye again. She has been watching me. Now that she has my attention, she lets the silky curtain of long black hair cover her face. My lips twitch but stop as Darragh starts talking.

"Teresa, you have a mighty pair of hands on you. Another bowl would be nice." He holds his bowl in the air, and Teresa looks like she might pour the stew on his head. That I wouldn't stop. I move towards Siobhan, noticing the way her hands tighten on the bowl and spoon she holds. It's the only tell that she knows I'm approaching. She looks so slight in the armchair. But outside, when she had been standing in the yard, she was curves and womanly.

The woman Darragh brought home, had that look in their eyes, like they had seen too much of the world. The bad part. But with Siobhan there was an innocence that I found myself drawn to.

I sit beside her and immediately rub the dog behind the ears. "What's her name?"

She turns her head while tucking her hair behind her ear and up this close I can see that she is indeed beautiful. Her lips are slightly red from the hot food, they are distracting, but what's captured me since I saw her in the yard, is her eyes. Brown eyes that are deep and rich. Her eyes hold her emotions, and now, she's nervous.

"Sandie." Her pink tongue flicks out to lick her lips. I follow her movements.

"Beautiful," I find myself saying, mesmerized.

"Excuse me?" She seems surprised, and I stop looking at her lips and focus on her eyes instead. "Sandie, she's a beautiful Sheepdog." She looks down at the dog as if it's her first time seeing it. My hand still rubs behind the dog's ears.

"Yeah, I suppose she is." From her face and tone, I can see she has no attachment to the dog. A part of her has no attachment to this moment.

"Jesus, Teresa, that is a mighty stew." I clench my jaw at how loud Darragh is being. He is normally a little more discreet. He must be still pretty hungover to not give a shit at a wake. I look across at him, but Teresa is filling his bowl for the third time. At least that will keep him quiet.

"I'm sorry about him," I say to Siobhan.

She shakes her head slightly. "You are twins, not the same person."

"Yeah. Identical twins." I rhyme it off like I have a million times.

"Oh no, you are so different." I'm smiling at her.

"We are identical, same blond hair, blue eyes, same facial structure. It's the beard, isn't it?" I say in a joking manner. But she's shaking her head.

"No you might both have blue eyes but yours are different from his." Her words trail off like she might have said too much.

"How so?" I ask wanting to know, like really know. Hearing someone see me and Darragh as different people makes my stomach tighten. It's all I've ever wanted to hear. With my family, they see us as one, and I hate it.

She frowns now. "I don't know. You are different but the same." Her cheeks color now, making her more beautiful. "Now I sound silly." She sits up straighter, and I can see the strain on her face.

"No, you don't." It was nice to hear that she didn't see us as the same. We were mirrors of each other, yet she saw something different in me, and that made my heart pound a little harder.

The conversation has picked back up in the room, but as Darragh stands up dragging his chair with such fucking disrespect that I even wanted to hit him, the room grows silent again. "Teresa you're a gem." He tells her, handing her his bowl like she is here to pick up after him. I can see the tightness around her eyes, but she just nods, taking the bowl from him. Each step Darragh takes towards Siobhan, I find myself leaning closer to her, wanting to protect her from him. He pulls up a small stool sitting in front of her.

"Me and Teresa go way back." He tells Siobhan with a smile on his face. The smile I know that breaks so many hearts. I remove my hand from Sandie and sit straighter. "I won't keep you, Siobhan, I can see you have your hands full." He waves around the room like she is having a fucking party. I can't stare at him any harder, yet his focus is solely on Siobhan. "I just want to make one final offer." He hands her a piece of paper from his pocket, something he must have prepared before we came here. Something I wasn't informed about. Siobhan reluctantly takes the piece of paper and opens it, I can see what's scrawled across it.

Darragh is smiling like he just won. "Now that's a mighty number, Siobhan."

I can see the side of her face and it looks like she is holding her breath. Her delicate fingers move swiftly as she tears the piece of paper in two. "No," she says and I don't know why, but I'm so fucking proud.

SIOBHAN

My heart is racing in my chest for more than one reason. My emotions were already a jumble before Finn and Darragh, but now I feel like instead of walking, I'm crawling.

"I want you to leave," I find myself saying.

The room is deadly silent. Finn is the first to move. "Darragh, now," he says, his voice deeper. His words are quick, quiet, words his brother obeys.

Darragh gets up. He is no longer smiling, a shiver snakes its way down my spine at how he looks at me. His eyes are hard and narrowed. He doesn't like being told no or told what to do. That's obvious. But right now, I'm not afraid of him, so I don't look away from his hard eyes.

"I'm sorry, Siobhan." I don't look at Finn as he speaks, I don't take my eyes from Darragh until he turns away. Finn walks behind him and leaves my kitchen. I can nearly tell when they have vacated the house as the noise level around us starts to rise again to normal conversation.

"Are you okay?" Teresa sits down where Finn had been sitting, and I find myself rubbing Sandie where he had.

"I'm not sure," I tell her honestly.

"They are bad news. Darragh is a pup." Yeah, I can tell that already. But she doesn't mention Finn. She's silent. I'm silent, I hate silence.

"What about Finn?" I ask stupidly, and Teresa is smiling.

"He's not the worst." I'm not sure how I feel about that. It's good because she says it softly, but 'not the worst' isn't the best.

"Yeah well, they are gone now," I say wanting to wipe the smile from Teresa's face. I didn't want her getting any ideas.

"They'll be back. The O'Reagans don't give up that easy." My pulse spikes, and I bit my lip to stop the smile which threatens to spread across my face. There was something seriously wrong with me that I was happy about seeing Finn O'Reagan again. I got out of the chair feeling silly.

"I better go back in." Teresa is no longer smiling but squeezes my hand as I leave and take my place beside my father's coffin. Olive hasn't moved from where I'd left her, like she had promised, and I resume the senseless motion of shaking hands and making small talk while I listen to a room full of strangers talking about my dad.

***

My room is the same. Posters of Boyzone and Westlife are still on the wall. I'm shaking my head as I scan the room. The pine shelf over my bed holds a dozen books and a Mickey Mouse alarm clock that I refused to get rid of. The bed has been freshly made. The cream floral quilt cover isn't mine; it's from my parents' bed. Someone had pressed it, and the smell of the fabric softener has taken over my room. Sandie jumps up on the bed that I'm admiring.

"Just one night," I tell her firmly, and she lies down, with her head between her paws.

But that's not what happens. One night turns into four. Sandie stays with me through the three nights that Dad is waked in the house and the night after I bury him. I still haven't cried, and each moment here in this place makes me feel more lost than I have ever felt before. Lost in a sense that I know that this is where I came from, but I feel like I don't belong. I want to. The more I'm around these people, the more I want to fit in. In Dublin, it's fight for yourself. It's a city and busy, and everyone is rushing with their heads down, but here, they look out for each other, know each other. It's nice.

***

I wake up to an empty house and make myself a tea before sitting at the table. I miss the noise of the people. The tile floor is freezing, but the fluffy socks that I put on help keep some of the cold away. I've switched my phone off since arriving here and know I have to turn it on soon and let my life come back in. I have so many decisions to make and a small amount of time to make them. Darragh's crazy offer plays around in my mind, but I did the right thing. He was being disrespectful, but on the other hand, that kind of money was life-changing.

I needed a distraction, so I decided to finally turn on my phone. Immediately it started to bleep, and it didn't stop as I topped up my tea. Sitting back down, I scroll through messages from friends and work. I have only four more days of leave from work before I have to go back. My stomach tightens at the idea of returning to Dublin. A part of me doesn't want to, but I push the feeling aside.

Sandie's bark lifts me out of the chair as the house phone rings loudly. It feels out of place after the intense, empty silence in the house. I picked up the phone quickly.

"Hello."

"I'm looking for Siobhan Walsh." The man's voice is very formal, but I recognize it. I try to remember the name of the familiar voice.

"Speaking. How can I help you?"

"It's Brian Harris," Ah yes that's how I knew him. He was my father's solicitor, the one who had told me that my father had left everything to me. I was his only child, and with no other family and with mother gone, I was the only option.

"Hi, Brian. How can I help you." Sandie rubs against my bare leg like a cat would, and I shoo her away.

"We have run into a complication." He says, and I stop focusing on Sandie.

"What kind of complication?"

"Your father's sister is contesting the will." I sigh. Great. Just what I need.

CHAPTER THREE

FINN

Darragh turns around in his seat, looking through the back window. "Are we being chased?"

I lift my foot off the pedal slowing the car down slightly. My hands sting from the grip I have on the steering wheel, so I loosen them.

"Finn, is there something you aren't telling me?" I glance at Darragh as he lights a fag in my new car.

"Don't smoke in here," I tell him, but he shrugs his shoulders while rolling down the window slightly.

"Oops," he says as he blows smoke out the window.

"You are so fucking disrespectful." I want to take my anger out on the pedal and slam it to the floor, but the winding roads won't allow it, and breaking every two seconds is taking the joy out of speeding. That is one of the downsides of where we live. The roads are only good for one car, and the bends are pretty severe. You can't open the car up here.

"I'll get your car valeted, okay." Darragh blows smoke through the crack in the window again. It wasn't just about the car. It was about Darragh being Darragh and yeah, I also didn't want smoking in my new S Class Mercedes. She's my baby, and he's polluting her and not with just his smoke. He had been drinking last night, and he still reeks of whiskey. His crumpled shirt and slacks are the result of falling out of bed. I have just picked him up from a house party and am taking him home.

"So now that we aren't going to crash, can you tell me what's going on?" Darragh flicks the cigarette out the window, and I can't stop my mind from wondering if it has hit the shiny silver exterior. Paying 90K for a car isn't worth it when you have a brother who disrespects everything, including money. "You're not still mad over the chick with the land."

Now I glance at Darragh, and he smirks.

"You know, her name is *Siobhan*, and yeah, I'm still pissed." He rolls his eyes at me before lowering himself in the seat and putting on sunglasses. The sun is hiding behind the clouds but his headspace couldn't have been great. He looks like shit.

A moment of silence passes, and I slow down as we enter the small town of Kingscourt. It's dark and depressing, one long strip of shops that sells a little bit of everything, yet nothing at the same time.

"What did Da say?" Darragh sounds serious now, but I can't tell for sure with the sunglasses on. I can never really tell with Darragh. He often smiles when he's serious and smiles when he isn't. Most people think that because we are twins that we finish each other's sentences. That makes me fucking laugh. I have no clue of what goes on in his screwed-up mind.

"That we should use scare tactics." My hands clench around the steering wheel again. The thought of doing that to Siobhan seems almost barbaric, and I am lucky enough that I have talked him into letting me handle it, but once the funeral is over, that was my proposal. He surprised me by giving me a week to obtain the land.

"We should. She thinks she's playing smart, holding out for more money." Darragh slides out his phone and checks it before lifting himself up slightly and stuffing it back in his pocket. Irritation grows on me at Darragh's words.

"She was angry because you did it at her father's wake. Are you that thick, Darragh?"

"Let it all out, Finn." I hadn't spoken to him in the last few days, so yeah, it was all bottled up inside, ready to pour out of me. After we left Siobhan's house, I had driven home and hadn't spoken to him for a few days. Every time I thought about his behaviour at the wake, I wanted to find him and punch him. Each time I did see him, he was drinking, drunk, or with a woman. I told myself it was a sign to stay away from her.

"What you did was a dickhead move," I tell him, putting my foot down. We are on a straight road now that leads towards our home.

"Are you going to start rooting and tipping at that?" he asks while lowering his glasses, and I want so very much to punch him in the face.

"I'm going to go like a normal person and make an offer on the land. I waited until today when the funeral was over." I slow down as we approach our house. Most days, I didn't notice it, but sometimes I could see the house that looked like a hotel. With twenty four bedrooms, a gym, library and even our own bar, it was a monster of a house, but it was home to us.

The sensors on the garage doors kick in, and the door opens slowly, four cars already take up most of it, but two spots are still available. I don't have the car turned off when Darragh jumps out.

"Mind my fucking door," I say as he nearly connects with Shane's Audi.

"You need to get laid." That's his departing words. I sit in the car knowing that going inside and seeing if Dad or Shane are looking for me would be wise, but I restart the car and pull out of the garage, leaving Whitewood house in the rear-view mirror.

I was going to see Siobhan and convince her to sell the land.

SIOBHAN

"Sandie." I've been calling her for the last ten minutes. Normally, she would appear, but right now she is a no-show. It's not like her, and the worry I'm feeling makes me realise I am getting way too attached to a dog I can't keep. I return to the house and grab a woolly hat and my long black coat. It is freezing outside, and my Aran jumper which normally fends off the cold isn't working today. I hate that Sandie is missing, and also, talking to the solicitor and finding out my dad's eighty-year-old sister is contesting the will isn't helping my mood either. My father didn't speak to her, and I'd never met her, but my mother had told me she was very wicked to my father and to the world.

"Sandie." I tuck my hands into my jacket pockets as I leave the front yard and decide to check the lane. Turning the bend from my small farmhouse, I see someone bent down, petting Sandie. My stomach flips as Finn looks up. He's too far away to talk to unless we shout, but he gives me a wave, and I can't stop the smile that tugs at my lips or the butterflies that erupt in my stomach.

He rotates from looking at Sandie and then me.

"Hi, I've been looking for her," I say as I finally reach them just as Sandie the traitor jumps up and starts licking Finn's face. He laughs, and heat rushes to my cheeks at the sound.

"She likes me," he declares, looking at me from under his lashes.

"She likes everyone," I say it without thinking, and Finn rises still smiling, still causing my heart to pound.

"Does she now? And here I thought I was special."

A small laugh escapes my lips. "Sorry to disappoint you," I tell him. He's wearing jeans again but with a red jumper, and his grey jacket is open but the collar sits up. *He could model*, I tell myself.

"I was wondering if we could chat." The uncertainty in his voice has me agreeing. A part of me is wondering if he felt the pull that I feel towards him, but the more rational part of me is telling me this is about land.

"Let's go back to the house." He smiles with a nod, and Sandie follows us back.

"How have you been?" His question is sincere.

"Honestly, a little lost. I didn't know my dad." I tell him as we step into the house. "He was great when I was a kid, but...then my mum died." I remove the jacket, not looking at Finn. "Everything changed." I pull off the hat and try and compose myself as I turn to him. Finn has a way of making me say what I think. It's odd and refreshing.

"Woah." He moves back out of my personal space as my nose brushes his chest; he had been standing that close.

"Sorry, I was just going to hang up my jacket." He holds his grey coat in his hand. The red jumper hugs him, and my stomach tightens again. He definitely works out.

"What happened to your mother?" We haven't moved, and I look up at him, his eyes stare at me intensely.

"Cancer, it was a long time ago. Sometimes, it doesn't feel that long."

"I'm so sorry, Siobhan." His kindness is going to make me cry. I sidestep so he can hang up his coat.

"Thanks." I make my way into the kitchen where Sandie lies in front of the fire and put the water on the stove.

"Tea," I ask as Finn enters the kitchen, making the room feel tiny, with his presence.

He sits down across from me. "Yes, please."

I smile at him. "He has manners," I say jokingly.

"I make up for the lack of Darragh's." I can see the regret the moment he mentions his brother's name. It changes, and the relaxed atmosphere disappears.

"So you wanted to chat," I say, getting to it as I place a cup of tea in front of him. Milk and sugar have already been set on the table from this morning.

He shifts in his seat while scratching his eyebrow. "About the land, I wanted you to reconsider the offer."

I take a sip of the tea. "To you, Finn, I would sell it." His blue eyes light up with surprise. I didn't want the land. I had no intentions of farming it, so selling it was the only option, and to someone as nice as Finn seemed like a good choice.

"Great." He smiles now, but I don't.

"But I can't. An aunt has contested the will. Otherwise, it would be yours."

Finn seems quiet as he sips his tea. "Is she from the area?"

I'm shaking my head, but I can't stop the smile. "What are you going to do, send Darragh to talk to her?"

He's smiling now. "No, I would talk to her."

"Finn the charmer," I say, and my cheeks heat. Words jump from my mouth without my approval, but I like the spark that they set in Finn's eyes.

"You think I'm charming?" he asks, leaning in slightly.

I hug my cup closer to give my hands something to do. "I didn't say that. I said, charmer. There is a difference."

"There's that word again." He looks intense, and, I find my own smile slipping.

"What word?" I'm starting to feel warm and want to take off the Aran jumper.

"Different. You said I was different from Darragh." He's so serious now, like me saying it means more to him than he wants me to know, and I want to give him an honest and open answer.

"You have a stillness in you that he doesn't. You're like…a tree." It's coming out all wrong. One side of his lip lifts up into a grin.

"A tree," he repeats with amusement in his voice.

"Yeah," I say on a small laugh. It sounds daft, even to my ears, but that's what he is. Strong and tall and sturdy like a tree.

"I'll take it as a compliment," he says, and I pray for my cheeks to cool.

"It was." The room grows serious, and I wonder if I am flirting with him without knowing. Was that possible? Could you be doing something unconsciously?

"I'm not very romantic, so I don't know what to compare you to."

"You think I'm being romantic by calling you a tree." I drink my tea, but he can see the smile in my eyes. He's smiling now, and it's doing crazy things to my stomach.

"I don't get out much," he says on a laugh.

"Me neither," I admit. Even in Dublin, all I did was work. I was a career in Connelly's hospital and took every shift I could. I had been saving for a home. It wasn't important now as I had inherited one. I still wasn't sure what do about the house. Selling it seemed wrong since I was raised here, but moving here wasn't an option. I wasn't going to commute such a longer journey.

"Maybe we should go out sometime. It will get both of us out?" His question pulls me out of my thoughts.

"Yes," I answer way too quickly, and he smiles again. My heart feels ready to explode now. He just asked me out on a date, and I just accepted.

He takes a large drink from his cup before standing. "Perfect, I'll see you tonight then."

I stumble after him, shock at his words. Tonight? It seems too sudden. I don't feel ready. I stand silent in turmoil as he gets his coat on, wondering if I should cancel.

"What should I wear?" *Nice Siobhan, you don't sound desperate or anything*, I tell myself.

"I was thinking dinner." I'm nodding now because his jacket is on; there is no more distractions as he faces me. "Is eight okay?" he asks, and I find my voice this time.

"Perfect," I tell him, and he grins.

"Perfect," he repeats before leaving.

Sandie appears at my leg and I bend down rubbing her behind the ear. "I have a date with Finn O'Reagan," I tell her while smiling.

VI CARTER

CHAPTER FOUR

FINN

"He's not here?" I ask as Liam looks up from his laptop.

"He's out with Shane." I had wanted to get this over and done with. I hated waiting to hear what his decision would be once he found out that Siobhan's aunt had contested the will. Liam is still looking at me. He's the next in line once Father steps down. He never says much, but he's a dark horse in our family. His suits and slicked back hair make people think his appearance means too much to him. But it is a control thing. I've never seen him lose control. His hair always sits perfectly, his skin is always clear, his hands always clean, and that is to the naked eye only.

Liam isn't one for words, but he gets things done, behind the scenes. He doesn't like working with any of us.

I make a decision and close the door behind me. "I'm in a bit of a situation."

Liam sits back and joins his hands together on the table. The laptop is still open, a soft glow shining on his face. Sometimes, he's like a fucking robot, and I falter, wondering if I should just wait for Shane and Dad to get back. At least with Dad and Shane, they will just say it as it is.

"I have to get land signed over for Dad."

"I'm aware of that," Liam says while I pull out a chair and sit down.

"An aunt is contesting the will, otherwise I would have bought it today. She's seventy and a woman…"

Liam cuts me off with a quick wave of his hand. "You are giving the situation too much... life. When something gets in your way, it's an object that needs to be removed. Not a he or she but an object."

So clinical. "Okay, so this 'object...' what do I do?" I ask, hoping he has an answer for me.

"I don't know. But you have to consider the cost of moving the object, will it disturb what it surrounds, you must deal with it at the lowest cost and with the lowest impact." *Great. That's some fucking riddle.*

"Anyone know where Da is?" I don't look at Darragh as he enters the room; I focus on my fist that rests on the table.

"He's out with Shane." Liam gives Darragh the same answer that he's given me.

Darragh eyes me with a smirk. "Did I interrupt something here?"

"What, you've never seen us sit in the same room?" I ask him, his stupid grin and his shirt are irritating me. "What are you wearing?"

"This is my new lucky shirt." He's smiling while he pulls out a chair. His shirt is bright yellow with palm trees on it.

"You look like a moron," I tell him, and he isn't fazed at all, instead he turns to Liam.

"So Stony, what have I missed?" He's the only one who can get away with giving Liam a nickname. Right now, Liam isn't smiling or showing any indication that he likes Darragh, but we all know he's the favorite brother.

"Finn has a problem with his most recent job. An aunt has contested the will, and he isn't sure what to do."

"I got this." Darragh cracks his knuckles while Liam looks at me. "Problem solved."

Problem solved. Problem fucking doubled. Send Darragh to do a job, and he creates a problem that I somehow become responsible for.

"No," I tell Darragh and get up.

"He is the lowest price tag." Liam reminds me.

"He's the highest."

"Why do I have a price on me?" Darragh asks confused.

"This is personal?" Now Liam looks intrigued as he speaks.

I want to hit Darragh as he smirks. "Yeah, he's banging the landowner."

"Shut up, Darragh, I just have a conscience." I can hear the half-truth in my answer. Yeah, I don't feel comfortable scaring a woman into stepping away. A man I wouldn't think twice, but an old lady? That just doesn't feel right.

"And a dick." He's hooting with laughter at his own joke, and even though he is pissing me off, maybe letting him deal with the old woman would be the best. That way I would have clean hands.

"Fine, you do it," I tell him with a grin, and he narrows his eyes.

"Is this a trick?"

"Is it?" I ask him back, just to confuse the fuck out of him as I leave the room and start to get ready for my date.

SIOBHAN

Sandie barks as a car pulls into the drive, and my stomach tightens. Standing up, I fix my red dress. It's tight fitted and goes to my knee, so I get that sexy yet not too revealing look. The doorbell makes my pulse spike, and with one deep breath, I open it.

Finn's eyes roam my body, and I feel each place his eyes touch. I shift, not able to hold still, and his eyes snap to mine. Closing the door behind him, I notice he is holding something.

"Wow, you are stunning," he says with a smile as he takes a bunch of roses from behind his back. Holding them out to me, I take them and smell them like they do in the movies. Now I know why women do that. It isn't because we care about the smell of the flowers, but because it gives us a moment to gather ourselves.

I lift my head from the roses to find him still watching me.

"Thank you. You look great," I tell him with a huge smile that I can't seem to control. His red, black and grey striped shirt, along with a pair of black jeans, looks so good on him.

"People will think we are trying to match," I add out of nerves, and he grins.

"People will think we are a couple." His lip tugs slightly ,and I shift on my feet as his eyes darken.

My stomach tightens, and I give myself a moment to think about what it would be like to be a couple. My heart starts to race, so I push the thought away. "Let me just grab my bag and jacket." I bit my lip trying to keep some of my emotions hidden, but from the smile on his face, I'm not doing a good job.

"We could always just stay here?" The boldness in his eyes has me laughing, but staying here sounded like the perfect idea.

"Finn O'Reagan, what do you take me for?"

His smile is gone now. "It's not you. It's me. I'm not sure I'll be able to control myself." And I'm laughing again. When I look at him, I suck in a large breath. He's looking at me in a way I have always hoped someone would look at me. It's the way my father looked at my mother. But I don't know Finn, Finn doesn't know me.

"What's wrong?" He's in my personal space now. "I'm sorry if I offended you." Stuffing his hands in his pockets, he ducks his head, looking at me with furrowed brows.

"No, you didn't do anything wrong. It's not you. It's me." There is something that draws me in with Finn, I feel like I know him, like he sees me. I close the distance, and I can see the uncertainty in his eyes. He hasn't a clue what just happened.

"My parents loved each other so much, and I remember as a kid when he would look at her, I always hoped one day someone would like at me like that." My throat tightens from the emotion the memory evocates surprises me.

Finn takes my face in his large hands. "Whoever gets you, Siobhan, will never stop looking at you." His eyes roam my face, his thumb strokes away a stray falling tear. "Can I kiss you?" His breath brushes my lips, and my eyes flutter close as my tongue flicks out and wets my lips in anticipation of the kiss.

"Yes," I whisper the single word, and his lips touch mine, and I'm on my toes, my fingers bury themselves into his hair before running along his beard. The bristle of hairs send electricity through my hands. His hands are still holding my face, his tongue flicks out and touches my lips.

Sucking in another deep breath from the sensation, I allow him entry into my mouth. I push my body harder against his, and I can feel the full length of him. He moves me carefully against the wall, one hand now on my waist. But it's not enough for me, so I break the kiss. Both of us are breathless. I'm inhaling his cologne and that manly scent that has me squeezing my legs closer together.

"Too fast. I'm sorry." He's apologizing, but, if he could see inside my head, he might think me very wicked. I smile now, taking his hand as I lead him to my bedroom. Flicking on the light, all my posters look bigger. I turn to him, and he's smirking, one side of his mouth tugging.

"Didn't take you for a Boyzone fan."

I don't release his hand as we look at the posters. "What kind of fan did you take me for?" I bit my lip because I don't care about bands or music; all I wanted was Finn in my bed.

"Not sure, but not Boyzone. Maybe Steps?" I'm laughing as I pull him to my bed, and his eyes narrow before they darken.

"Are you trying to seduce me?"

I bit my lip again as I sit him on my bed. "Would Finn O'Reagan like to be seduced?" I ask as I reach back and unzip my dress. I feel empowered when he swallows.

"Yes, please," he says as I let the dress slip to the ground.

Stepping out of it, I kick it to the side. He reaches out, touching my bare thighs, and pulls me towards him. I sit on him now, my hands around his neck. He's still fully clothed, his eyes roaming my face. I'm not normally this forward, but I know my time here is limited, and if I let this opportunity go, I would never forgive myself.

Finn pulls me into a kiss, and I shimmy closer to him, he moans as his bulge rubs against me, and I sink deeper into the kiss, moving my hips, which causes our breathing to increase faster and unsteady until I want the fabric between us gone.

Sliding off his lap, I pull at his jeans, letting him know what I want. He stands up, stripping them off along with his boxers. His erection makes my heart pound. He doesn't unbutton his shirt but pulls it off over his head, he's perfect. His lean body is toned but not too much. Gold hairs coat his chest, and I like it.

As we stare at each other, I reach back and remove my bra and then my underwear. I've never been naked like this in front of guy, especially with the lights on. I'm more of a light's off kind of girl. But since opening the door and seeing how Finn looked at me, it made me feel not just beautiful but empowered. It was like I wanted to keep feeding the hunger inside of him, with each piece of my body.

"Sit down," I tell him, and he does slowly. He looks good naked on my bed. He helps me position himself at my opening, and when I sit down fully, we both gasp. I can feel of him inside me, and it makes me grip his shoulders as I move up and down, and it's the most vulnerable I have ever felt.

Staring into Finn's eyes, seeing the ecstasy that I am feeling, but behind it all, I see his vulnerability, the mark this world has left on him. Closing my eyes, I only allow the feel of Finn inside of me to consume me as I move faster and faster. His pants and moans make me come fast, and he follows shortly after.

CHAPTER FIVE

SIOBHAN

I'm lying in Finn's arms, both of us still naked under the quilt. My fingers play with his chest hair as we chat. "That's a lot of brothers, who's your favourite," I ask after he lists off his four brothers.

"Connor." There's a sadness to his answer, and I look up at him. His eyes are half closed, and his lips tug down slightly in the corners. I want to erase the look of sadness from his handsome face.

"You want to talk about it?" I kiss his shoulder.

"Conor gets overwhelmed with our family and likes to take a break every once in a while. I just miss him when he goes. " Right now, his eyes look so haunted, and I wonder why. But a part of me doesn't want to pry too much. I don't want to scare him away.

"Your family sounds intense."

He looks at me and smiles. "They can be."

"Any sisters?"

"My dad has been married three times, so we have one-half brother and sister, and his second wife had a daughter from a previous marriage. But we don't see any of them." I nod. It sounds so nice to have such a big family.

"I wish I had siblings," I say honestly, and Finn kisses me on the forehead.

"Sometimes I wish I had none." We smile at each other now just as Finn's phone rings. *Highway to Hell* blares in my room, and I raise both eyebrows in question to the ringtone.

"I took you for a Nokia ringtone kind of guy."

He scratches his eyebrow. "That's the ringtone I have assigned to my family members only." I'm laughing, and Finn lets the phone ring out. Pulling me against his body causes electricity to spark between us. I move my body over his and feel him come to life.

"I'm thinking we should skip the meal and just hang out here," I suggest seductively, and he laughs. "Our reservation was two hours ago, maybe more. So we have definitely skipped the meal." I kiss him again just as *Highway to Hell* blares again.

Finn groans. "I have to get it," he tells me as he gets out of bed, and I admire his backside as he gets his phone out of his jeans pockets. I love how his bum is full and muscly but not too hard to touch.

Taking the phone, he goes out into the hallway naked. His voice is low, but I can hear what's been said from his side. "What? I'm busy." The irritation in his voice makes me smile. "What has he done now?" Silence follows as the caller speaks. "I'll be there in twenty."

My heart deflates at his words. He's leaving. I try to pretend that I wasn't just eavesdropping on his conversation as he comes back into the bedroom. Picking up his boxers he puts them on. "Siobhan, I'm so sorry, but I have to go." I can hear the regret in his voice but it doesn't' stop the disappointment I'm feeling.

"Is everything okay?" I ask as he buttons up his jeans, he pauses briefly and looks at me. I can see the turmoil in his eyes. "Yeah, it's just Darragh being Darragh." I want to ask why one of his brothers can't take care of it. But I bite my tongue. "I don't want to go." Pulling on his shirt, he sits back on the bed with a soft sigh and kisses me gently on the cheek.

"I don't want you to go either," I say, and he kisses my hand before getting up and putting on his socks and boots.

"I might get back, but give me your number, and I will let you know." That makes me feel a bit better, so I rhyme my number off. I get one more kiss before Finn leaves.

The house is too quiet, and it's weird that I miss him already. *What would I be like when I go back to Dublin?* My stomach tightens at the thought. That was sooner then I wanted it to be. I had a few more days before I had to return to work. My phone beeps from the kitchen. Getting up, I wrap myself in my dressing gown. Sandie opens one eye and looks at me from where she is lying in front of the fire. I refill her water dish before checking my phone.

I miss you already. I'm smiling at the message. The number is new, so I know its Finn. He's too sweet. I save his number to my phone before I quickly fired a message back. *I miss you too. Hope you get to come back soon.*

FINN

I arrive at the location that Liam gave me and park down a lane. He told me to go the rest of the way on foot. My stomach won't settle. I'm dreading what I am going to find. Liam was brief as usual on the phone, just that Darragh's in trouble, and they need me. Darragh's always in trouble, but this felt different. Liam being present was the first thing, then during the phone call, I could hear Shane in the background, so I knew this situation was serious.

I hadn't put on a jacket, and the cold had me stuffing my hands in my pockets. The road was dark. Liam said to walk for five minutes, and on my left-hand side, I would see a small bungalow. He was right. I stopped at a bungalow but no lights were on. The gate which was a large black farm gate was half open.

The gravel under my feet sounded too loud. No lights came on as I moved closer to the gray dashed house. I opted to walk on the lawn. It would be less noise. I did once small jump across the small hedge that acted as curbing around the lawn before I approached the side of the house. Liam martialized out from the wall and nearly gave me a fucking heart attack.

"Watch where you step." He turns, and I follow him into the house. We walk into the utility room that's neat and tidy, nothing out of the ordinary.

"What's going on, Liam?" I wish he would just tell me instead of playing the fucking silent game. But we step into the kitchen, and I can see the problem now. A small light in the corner is lighting up the scene for me.

My eyes snap from Liam to Shane to Darragh before settling on the body that we all stand around.

"What happened?" I ask, feeling sick. The woman isn't dead, she's like a fish out of water, her body is jerking as she tries to breathe. But it looks like her neck is broken, her face is covered in blood, and a pool of it is growing around her head.

No one answers me. Shane and Liam look down at her like someone spilled milk, and now they were wondering how to clean it up. On the other hand, Darragh was freaking out. On his hunches, he kept looking at the body and then shooting looks around at us all. A fag was burning away in his hand.

"What did you do?"

"She attacked me. I panicked." He stands up, his eyes wild. He's high.

"You fucking bashed her head in. Is this Siobhan's aunt?" I ask, but I know it is. My stomach twists. Oh, god, this was the last thing I wanted. Real fear crawls down my spine at the thought of Siobhan finding out.

"Man, she was crazy, scrapping me, telling me to get out." He babbles as if he's not hearing me, so I look to Liam.

"What do we do?"

Liam doesn't look away from the body. "Kill her and bury her." I'm nodding, but inside I want to say no, that this isn't right. That maybe we can help her.

I run my hands through my hair and step away from this madness. "Or we could ring an ambulance." I know that's not going to happen but for Siobhan, I feel I should try.

"I'll get the stuff out of my car," Shane says, ignoring my comment, and Liam nods at him.

"Pick up the cigarette butt," Liam tells Darragh who's lighting up another one.

"Are you fucking stupid. They'll take your DNA off that." I growl. I want to strangle him as I pick up the butt and take the fag out of his mouth before running it under the tap, then I put both in my pocket.

The woman is still twitching, and I want someone to put her out of her misery. Rubbing my face, I turn away from the scene again, hating what my family can do to another human being.

"I'm sorry, Finn." Darragh is beside me. The smell of drink emanating off him has me closing my eyes. "I fucked up." He's nearly crying, and I hate that, I hate what he has done, but I don't like to see Darragh hurting either. I know behind all this, he is a good person.

"It's fine, Darragh. Just try not to touch anything." I tell him as Shane arrives back. I notice Liam has been watching us with interest in his eyes. But he says nothing. Now he helps Shane lay down heavy plastic.

"Grab her legs," Shane tells me, and I do as he asks as he takes the top part of her body. I try not to think about the flesh that is in my hands. I try not to think about the fact I am helping kill someone.

I try to just do as my brother asks and not think too much about it. We lift her onto the plastic. We have just laid her down, when Liam kneels down in a suit, and covers her mouth with a cloth. I can't take my eyes off her, and she twitches and fights, but she has no chance. We wait until her body stops jerking, before I look away.

"Is she dead?" Darragh asks, kneeling down again and staring at her. Having him here is pointless.

"Me and Shane will bury her and clean up here. You take Darragh home, and in the morning call the gardai and report his car stolen. We'll burn it." I'm nodding, feeling a sense of relief of getting out of here.

"Darragh," Liam says his name harsher then I have ever heard, and we all stop and wait for him to speak again. "You were partying all night." Darragh nods. "Burn your clothes too."

"We will," I tell Liam. I just want to get away from here.

"I'm sorry," Darragh pleads with Liam, but he's already rolling up the body. I take him by the arm and out of the house.

CHAPTER SIX

FINN

I'm staring into the fire as the last fibres of our clothes go up. Darragh's asleep in bed. Tomorrow, this will all feel like a bad dream to him. For me, it's a waking nightmare. My phone sits on the mantelpiece as I poke the fire while drinking straight from a bottle of whiskey.

I want to ring Siobhan, and I want to ring Connor, but I don't for two different reasons. With Siobhan, it's the guilt of knowing what I know. Knowing that my family is responsible for her aunt's death. With Connor, I feel hearing his voice will push me over the edge. He's the one who beat up the bullies in school. He's the one who dusted off my clothes when I fell.

He told me I was a good person, worthy of a happy ever after. He told me I always had him, but as we grew up, he disappeared more and more.

"Finn." I turn as my father enters the empty room. Once it was a ballroom, now it's empty. I chose this room so no one would come near me.

My father stands near the fireplace; his head held high, he isn't looking at me

"What you did today for your brother, he will always be grateful." Well, that was a load of horse shit, but I nod my head like I agree. "You don't believe me?" the question surprises me. He never asks my opinion or thoughts on things.

"No. I don't," I tell him honestly. "He will do it again because, like all things with Darragh, there are no consequences. You taught us that sometimes blood has to be taken. But never from an innocent or a woman."

Father nods his acknowledgment at that statement, lines appear on his forehead like he is really thinking. "But how many times has he broken that rule? How much more blood will he spill before he's either caught or worse, someone else gets to him first."

My father nods again before he starts to speak. I fold my arms across my chest, trying to push down the anger that is growing inside me.

"When I was a kid, my brother and I were playing in a farm shed along with the farmer's son." I'm glued to each word, him talking about his childhood rarely happens. Hearing him talk about a past makes my father seem more human. Maybe that's why he never speaks of his past. I unfold my arms now and stuff my hands into my pockets.

"The farmer had left a double barrel shotgun lying around. He had gone out that day to shoot crows that had been picking holes in his cover for the silage, but by tea time, none had arrived. So he left the gun in the shed. Loaded." Father unbuttons his suit jacket, like a man who is getting ready to sit down, yet he stays standing.

The door opens, and Shane looks in. Once again Shane is dressed in all black. His dark brown eyes reminds me of trying to see the bottom of a well and you're just not sure you're seeing the end. "Come in, Shane, I'm just telling Finn a story." Shane doesn't blink but comes in and stands around the dwindling fire. Shane looks from me to Father but doesn't speak. Father waits until the room settled again. I want to ask Shane whether it is done, is the body gone. But I know better than to interrupt our father.

"The farmer's son was mine and Tom's best friend. Anyway, Tom found the gun and was playing with it. We didn't know it was loaded, but Patrick told him to stop waving the gun around. When Tom went to lower it, he hit the trigger by accident and blew a hole in Patrick. It was a mess ; we were only sixteen. He was dead within minutes. He was innocent. It was an accident. But I knew no one would believe us. Everyone saw my brother, Tom, as someone evil. He liked to torture small animals, that didn't make him a serial killer." My father's gaze falls on the bottle of whiskey.

"Give me that," he says, and it takes me a second to realize he is talking about the bottle.

I hand it over, and he takes a deep swallow. I want to ask what happened, but Father hands me the bottle. I take a quick drink, letting some of it drip down my chin before handing it to Shane, who declines and places it back on the fireplace.

"So we drag him over to the silage pit and placed him slightly under the cover. We wash away the blood and spread fresh straw, burn the bloodied ones and wipe down the gun before placing it where we had found it." I feel sick at his story. But covering up a crime at the age of sixteen does explain how my father can now do it so easily, and like with everything this family does, he justifies it.

Father indicates to Shane to pass him the whiskey again, and Shane does. The bottle goes around again. Shane drinks this time, and from the look on his face, this is his first time hearing this story too.

"When all was said and done, the farmer had a drinking problem, so he thought he had done it. That bit of information we actually hadn't known. It was pure luck. But me and Tom walked away from it all. The farmer, however, went down for ten years. Wasn't really that long of a sentence."

This time I take the whiskey, because that was not the end I was expecting. The man served time for a crime he hadn't committed. But it wasn't that part that messed people up; it was living with the knowledge that he had killed his son when he hadn't. There might be a wife or other siblings that would think their dad took their brother's life.

"The reason, Finn, I am telling you this is because Tom is like Darragh, and just like I stood beside Tom, you stood beside Darragh, and right now, he might not appreciate it, but one day he will." He squeezes my shoulder as he goes to leave the room.

"Did Tom appreciate what you did?" I ask.

"Yes." Father sounds distant, and I want to see his face, but his back is still to me.

"Why have I never heard of Tom?"

When my father turns around, his eyes have hardened.. "That's a story for another day." I'm left with Shane now, and I honestly don't want to be alone in his presence. He unsettles me in a way I can't explain, but I want to ask about Siobhan's aunt.

"So you and Liam finished that," I say and he nods. "Where?" I ask, and he folds his arms across his chest. His tattooed arm is a reminder of why I don't like being around him. He has twelve black bands now that are thickly inked, each time I see a new one, my stomach heaves, and I find it hard to hold eye contact with him. Each band is for a life that he took.

"Do you really want to know?" he asks.

"I'm off to bed," I tell him. I don't want to know. Now he's staring into the glow of the fire. Taking my phone off the mantelpiece, I leave the room that will now forever remind me of a woman we killed, and Patrick. This house was filling with ghosts, fast.

SIOBHAN

It's odd. The smell of the farmyard is giving me peace right now. Whereas before, If I ever got a hint of farmland in Dublin, it used to remind me of home and that would put me in a foul humor. But now it smells like freedom, hope, and is filled with memories. Now I wish I had known my father. I wish I had grown up here and known Finn. I know I'm only twenty-six, but already I feel as though I wasted years not knowing him. How can I feel this way about someone who I just met? I'm smiling as Sandie follows me around the yard.

I'm wearing my Da's size ten wellies, so I'm swimming in them. But I don't care, I want this to become a memory, and I want this to be that little girl who wore her daddy's wellies out into the farmyard.

"You look good." Finn's voice sends butterflies erupting in my stomach. It takes all my will not to look at him. After not coming back to me last night, I do feel a bit of punishement is due. So I keep walking slowly, but I can't not look and find myself taking quick glances at Finn, who sends my heart pounding.

"So this is what you country boys are into?" I tease, and Finn smiles walking with me but not beside me.

"I like the boots and all, but it depends who's standing in them."

I stop walking and smile at Finn. "Is that so?" He's freshly showered. His blond hair is still damp. The red t-shirt and jeans hug his slim body, and I let myself admire it for a moment.

"You can leave them on if you want to," he says taking a step towards me.

"There my dad's," I say honestly, and the horror on his face has me laughing.

"I'm so sorry, Siobhan." I can hear him, but the laughter isn't easing up and soon he joins me. Sandie starts to whine, and I pull myself together.

"Not exactly sure why that was so funny," I tell him, and he nudges me.

"I'm sorry for not coming back last night. Did you get my text?"

I had. He had apologized, saying Darragh had gotten sick everywhere, and he was covered in it. He had to shower, and it was way too late to come back. But still I felt disappointed and hurt. Hoping The idea of Darragh always coming first didn't sit well with me.

"I did." I kick a pebble with my huge boots and watch it roll towards a slurry pit.

"I got you something." Finn sounds nervous, and that's what makes me look at him more than the box he holds out to me.

I take it slowly, looking from the box to him. "You didn't have to," I tell him.

"Open it." He's smiling, and I open it to see a gorgeous slim bracelet, Finn removes it from the box and puts it on my wrist.

"Do you like it?" My throat closes as I move my wrist, the light catching it.

"It's beautiful, Finn." I'm looking from him to bracelet. It's perfect, and he's perfect, and this moment is perfect and it's making my throat tighten.

"Why do you look so sad?" He lifts my chin up making me look at him.

"I'm not staying, Finn." I whisper the words that lodge themselves in my throat, not wanting to come out.

"Staying here?" he questions, and I nod.

"I have to go back tomorrow to Dublin. To my job, to my life." What life? An empty apartment. Twelve hour shifts at the hospital. For the first time, I feel like I am living. But I can't run away again. I did it once and swore I would never run again.

I want to remove the bracelet, because now it doesn't feel right, but he stops me. I've never seen his face so serious. "I got it with you in mind. It's yours, no matter what." My throat burns, and I have to look away. I hate the silence.

"Maybe a cup of tea would be nice," I ask, and when I look at him, he finally smiles again. It's not one of his full-on smiles, but I'll take it.

"Is that code for something else?" he asks, and just like that, the tension is lifted, and I laugh andtry to look sexy as I shuffle in my dad's wellies back into the house.

I'm in the back door when his arms wrap around me, stopping me in the tracks. Sandie zooms past us and goes to her usual spot beside the fire. I'm lifted slowly out of the wellies, and Finn doesn't put me down until we are standing in the kitchen. His breath is hot on my neck, and I close my eyes and inhale him. As he spins me around, I wrap my arms around his neck, I look into his heavy blue eyes, and I feel so much is said between us. This isn't love; it's not there yet, but it's so close, that it's scary when I think of it. Once again, I don't want to go back to Dublin not when I have so much standing in front of me.

"This time I'm taking the lead," Finn informs me, and I don't disagree.

VI CARTER

CHAPTER SEVEN

SIOBHAN

This time, it's *my* phone that keeps ringing. I'm so cozy in bed with Finn that I don't want to come back to the real world. He pulls the blankets off my head; I've been hiding out down here, lying on his chest of man hair as I just enjoy the feel of him under me. The smell of him surrounds me, and I'm pretending that this is normal. That this is mine forever.

"Your phone is ringing," he says with a smirk, and I know I should answer it.

"Fine," I mumble and reluctantly get out of bed. Throwing on my dressing gown, I make my way to the kitchen where I left my phone. Each step away from Finn makes me want to run back to bed and curl up with him. I need to get a grip of myself. I'm leaving tomorrow. That thought fills me with dread.

I reach for the phone, wanting to stop my thoughts. "Hello."

"Siobhan, it's Brian Harris." I sat down, waiting for what could only be more bad news.

"Hi Brian, I hope you have some good news for me?"

"Actually, I do." I'm sitting up straighter now and rub Sandie behind the ears as she lays her head on my lap.

"Your aunt is no longer contesting the will. Everything is yours." This news should have caused me a sense of relief, but It made me feel unsettled.

"Just like that?" I ask, and Brian clears his throat before answering. "Yes. Her reasoning was false and, after been advised by another solicitor, she withdrew."

"What reasoning?" I wanted to be happy, but I don't know what I was really asking. I thought to the man in my bed, the one who wanted this land, the one who was going to talk with my auntie. He must have, and this was the real reason she had withdrawn. I wonder now if he had paid her off? Now I wonder if he was sleeping with me to get the land. I tell myself no. I had told him the land was his already, only for my aunt who contested the will.

"That, I am unsure of, Siobhan. It could be for a lot of reasons. But it's good news, right?" I didn't blame Brian for sounding so unsure. I was sounding very ungrateful right now.

"Of course it is. Thanks for letting me know."

"No problem at all. Have you decided what you are doing with the land?" Once again my mind wanders to the man in my bed. The one wanted the land, and I hoped him being here wasn't just about the land.

"Not yet," I lie. I don't want a hundred phone calls about land. Right now, I just wanted to digest this bit of information.

After hanging up, I give Sandie a final rub before returning to the bedroom where I find Finn dressed. His pulling on a boot when I walk in, and he pauses, looking up at me. My stomach twists, as my thoughts won't slow down and stop with the idea that I'm being used.

"Everything okay?"

It must be written on my face, so I just jump in with both feet. "Did you talk to my aunt?"

He pauses again before he pulls on his boot. Then he answers me. "No, I didn't. Why?" As he looks at me, I can't see any deceit in his eyes, and I relax slightly. I don't know what I was thinking, and even if he had spoken to her, that wasn't such a bad thing. But I could tell he wasn't lying.

"She's no longer contesting the will." I still watch him for signs.

"You don't look happy about that."

"I am. I am, it's just…odd. But Brian did say she spoke to a solicitor, and he had advised her against proceeding."

Finn stands up and walks to me. "You should be happy Siobhan." He takes my arms and gives me a kiss to the cheek that relaxes me further.

"Yeah, I am." I'm smiling now, letting my stupid worry float away.

"So what are you doing for the rest of the day?" Finn's hands linger on my hips, and I entwine my arms around his neck. I step into the smell of him, and it's so good. My bracelet shines and sparkles as the lights hit it, and it captured my attention. It's really beautiful.

"Thank you so much for my bracelet. It's beautiful," I tell him, looking from the bracelet and then back to his smiling eyes.

"A beautiful bracelet for a beautiful woman."

"You're such a charmer, Finn O'Reagan." I'm smiling now. Really smiling.

"You're calling me 'charming' again," he says before capturing my lips with his, cutting off the short laugh that threatens to spill from my mouth. His kiss this time is soft and tender like he's savoring our final time together. My stomach twists again. I'm not ready to leave him. Maybe he is ready to leave me.

When we break the kiss and look at each other, I wonder would I ever be ready to leave him. It surprises me how quickly I feel so much for him. But there's also the voice in the back of my head that's telling me this is all about land, and once I sell it to him, he will be gone. Wham bam, thank you, mam.

He hasn't mentioned the land since our last discussion, not since he said he would speak to my aunt. I can't hold his gaze as mixed feelings rush through me so I focus on my bracelet again.

"What's going through your mind?" he questions, and for the first time with him, I don't want to share my insecurities, because they are about him, so I remove my arms from around his neck and step out of his hold.

"That I have so much to pack before tomorrow," I say instead, giving him a quick glance his lashes flutter down, not allowing me to see what he is feeling but I notice a muscle twitches in his jaw.

"Do you want me to give you some space?" he sounds unsure, and his brows furrow.

I wonder if he wants to leave. I'm nodding as I start to gather my clothes off the floor. I don't' want to look at him. My heart is pounding out a tune, and my head is screaming at me to tell him not to leave.

FINN

My heart's ready to come out of my chest. I want to leave so badly. Standing in this room with her and knowing what we did to her aunt is torture, but leaving her feels worse. So I stand still as I watch her gather her clothes. I have so much I want to say, but I can't seem to find the right words.

"Don't leave," I settle on, and she snaps around to face me, her eyes wide.

"What?" She sounds breathless, and I haven't a fucking clue what's going through her mind. Maybe I was a bit of amusement while she was here, but I can't help how I feel about her. I know I can't just walk away and not try to make this work. But what we did to her aunt is eating away at me. I know I should walk away, that secret is huge, but I love her.

"Maybe you could stay longer." I stuff my hands into my pockets to give them something to do. I'm not normally nervous and I've never asked a girl to stay before, so I'm feeling out of my depth here.

She's clutching her clothes tightly to her chest; the look on her face is conflicted. I want to know what's going through her head. I want to know what she is thinking. "You want me to stay?"

Why does she sound so unsure? Each step I take towards her has her clutching her clothes tighter, and I loosen her hands and remove them, letting the clothing fall to the floor.

"I know we haven't known each other that long, but I'm going to put all my cards on the table, even though my dad told me never to do that." I smile briefly because he would think I was a fool right now. Actually, so would all my brothers. I push my family out of my mind and focus on Siobhan. "I don't want you to go. I want you to stay here with me."

"Here? With you?" The way she says it has me smiling.

"Yes. *Here* with *me*. I think we have something strong here. And I know you feel it too." My heart is pounding, being this honest.

She's in my arms now and her lips touch mine. I kiss her back.

"I don't want to go either; I want to stay here with you." My pulse spikes at her words, and my body wants her. The adrenaline from her words has my blood pumping all to the one place. I push my body against hers and deepen the kiss, moving us back towards the bed. I have her nightgown off within seconds, and it falls to the floor. My hand goes to the warmth between her legs, and she moans as I easily slip a finger in. She's as pumped as I am. She makes me feel powerful.

I trail kisses slowly down her jawline, and she throws her head back, offering me her neck that I kiss. Her moans are growing, and I want nothing more than for her to come in my hand. I move faster as I bend and take one of her nipples in my mouth, sucking it slowly before releasing it. "Oh God, Finn, I'm going to come!"

I increased my movements as I suck harder on her nipple, and then she releases. Her warm fluid coats my fingers, and it nearly makes *me* come. My jeans have shrunk several sizes to the point of being painful.

"You're so beautiful," I tell Siobhan as she opens her brown eyes and smiles at me. The bliss on her face makes me feel ten feet tall. Her fingers move to the band of my jeans, and my erection jumps. I need to release.

She opens them and pulls them down, along with my boxers. Looking down at Siobhan on her knees is the best sight I have ever seen in my fucking life, and when she takes me in her mouth, I nearly lose it, but instead, I hold back. I want to savor *every second* of this. Her tongue flicks out, hitting the head, and it jumps again in her mouth, telling me this might actually only be seconds long.

"I can't hold it much longer," I moan honestly, and she starts a quick rhythm that has me sinking my hands into her hair as she releases me into her mouth. "Wow." I'm breathless as Siobhan releases me, and when she looks up at me, my heart beats faster. She's everything I could want.

"Give me a moment," she says, leaving the room with her dressing gown. I sit down on the bed until I hear the shower running and decide I could do with a shower too.

The bathroom that I walk into is small and made to look even smaller as it's covered in wooden pine from floor to ceiling. Even the toilet seat is pine, the bathroom hasn't been updated in a long time. My eyes snap to the white shower curtain, and I smile as I pull it back and step in.

"Finn, what are you doing?" With a gasp, Siobhan runs her hand over her face, pushing water away so she can see me.

"I need a wash," I tell her, and she smiles.

"Since you're here, you can wash my back." She hands me a bar of soap, and I grin.

"Let's hope I don't let it drop." She's laughing, and it's music to my ears.

"If you drop it, *you* are picking it up," she says once I have started to wash her back.

"Oh, you'd like that, would you?"

She glances at me over her shoulder, the grin on her face has my body coming alive again. She turns back around, and I take a moment to admire her perfect backside. She turns around again and speaks. "My back is clean." She has a look in her eyes, one I recognize, and one I would never ignore.

Lathering up the soap, I start with her breasts before making my way down to her sensitive area. "You're a very bad girl, Siobhan," I tell her.

"Then punish me." The answer is unexpected, and I give her what she wants.

CHAPTER EIGHT

SIOBHAN

"So are you still interested in buying my land?" I ask Finn as we take Sandie for a walk. It's cold outside, but it always is. The cream jacket I am wearing has fur on the inside and is waterproof on the outside–perfect for walking in. Leaves fall from the trees. The orange, and green, and yellows are so beautiful. I'm so used to inhaling car fumes in Dublin that the crisp fresh air is nice. It's really nice. It's another reminder of why I don't want to go back to Dublin.

"Are you still willing to sell it?" He kicks a falling twig. The lane is scattered with them. Any kind of wind that blows causes the pass to be coated in leaves and twigs.

"Yes, if the price is right." I glance at him, trying not to smile.

"I feel like you are using me for money." He's teasing; the smirk on his face has my stomach tightening.

"So what am I worth to you, Finn O'Reagan?" We stop walking and stare at each other. His smile slowly fades.

"You are priceless. But the offer of 100,000 for the land still stands."

Priceless, I'm smiling at the word. He thinks I'm priceless. He's watching me closely now, "That's a crazy amount of money. We should get it valued correctly. I know you're overpaying." And the money sounds nice, but I really didn't want to have Finn overpay for it. It just didn't seem fair.

He removes the few feet between us and pulls me into his arms, surprising me with a kiss to the nose. "You're so moral, and I love that." The word love has my stomach flipping. I know we are not fully there yet, but we are so close. Before I can answer he places a kiss on my lips. "But take it, it's my father's money, not mine, so take it."

He's so serious, and I can hear resentment in his voice. I nod as he takes my hand, and we continue walking down the pass. I hope one day he will tell me his story. I can see he has one to tell.

"Okay, I'll take your father's money," I tell him, and he snorts a laugh. The recent tension leaves, and I'm glad. I hate seeing him upset. It's crazy to care this much for a person in such a short time. But I do.

"How did work take you not going back yet?"

The change in topic has my stomach tightening, and I chew on my lip, I had worked so hard to get that job. After doing night courses as I worked in a clothes shop, to get into a nursing home where I wasn't happy, I continued to do courses and waited until a job came up in the HSE. Then factoring in the time it took to get my Garda vetting form, to lose it wasn't a nice feeling. But leaving Finn was even worse.

"Yeah, they are fine, but I hate not going back. I mean, it's a state job so you know, it comes with perks that a private nursing home wouldn't provide..." We are silent for a few more minutes when we reach the end of the pass. I can see Teresa's house, she lives across the road, her bungalow stands proudly by itself.

"I can put in a word so you can be transferred to Cavan." I stop walking pulling my jacket tighter around me.

"Are you serious? You could really do that?"

Finn is smiling again. "It would come at a price." I'm smiling now, too, my mind going to one place only.

"Name your price."

"We could do it in IOU's." Finn takes my hand as we walk back down the pass, Sandie follows close.

"What kind of IOU's?" I actually don't care, I just love when Finn teases. His blue eyes become so alive, and that cheeky grin does funny things to my stomach.

"Breakfast in bed."

"That's easy," I say.

"Massage my feet."

I laugh a little. "Okay, I could do that." His lips tug on one side.

"You would have to tell me I am very well endowed." I snort a laugh.

"You want me to tell you that you are well hung." I ask incredulously, trying not to giggle.

Now Finn laughs. "You have a way with words, but yes, basically that."

"That's it?" I ask, and his eyes darken.

"Not even close."

"You want to cash in on your IOU's now?" I ask as everything starts to tingle, and I wonder how I could do it again, but I can. With Finn, I can.

"I would like that very much." His serious tone has me walking faster to the house.

"You better live up to your word, Finn," I tell him, and he tugs on my hand.

"Consider the job in Cavan yours."

I haven't a clue if he's serious or not, but the idea that it might be remotely possible marks today as the best day of my life, and as we enter my house, I knew this will be the cherry on top.

FINN

I don't know why I am hesitating outside the dining room. My dad is in there alone so this is the perfect opportunity to talk to him.

After leaving Siobhan's, I got Shane to call in a favor at the hospital, making sure Siobhan had a job to start in the next few weeks. When I rang her, she was on cloud nine, and my heart squeezed with pride that I had done that. Shane hadn't asked any questions; he had done it for me without hesitation. H

im doing it so easily had me wanting to back away, but for Siobhan I it was worth it. No doubt I would owe him in the future, but for Siobhan, I didn't mind. I suppose our family could be useful at times. I wasn't sure what Shane had done to call in the favour, but I was glad of it.

I knew Liam was the one who had spoken to Brian Harris, he took care of any official business like that. A stuffed envelope was never passed up, and as much as I hated the bullshit of politics, I was glad for it now.

I had one last thing to do, and that was to tell my dad the land was ours. I had wanted him to be proud of me, but now I don't know, because it was Siobhan's land, and I just didn't feel that way anymore.

"If you want to speak with him alone, I will wait five more minutes," Liam speaks from behind me, and I turn to see him in a new suit, his eyes skim over me like he actually doesn't see me. His brown eyes are almost black, and I wonder about the saying that the eyes are the door to the soul. If it's true, his soul is a very dark place.

"Yeah, thanks," I tell him and go into the dining room. My father doesn't look up from a file in front of him. He keeps flicking until I'm close enough to see. It's then that he closes it.

"Finn, your week is almost up," he tells me with a gleam in his eyes, one that warns me not to disappoint him.

"We have the land." He doesn't smile just nods.

"Good. Now don't forget we are all having dinner here tonight." I groan internally. I had completely forgotten. We celebrated the anniversary of our mother's death every year by all coming together and having a meal. It's painful, and I hate it.

"Of course. I can't wait." I tell him, and he gives me a second nod. He's not one to show too much emotion, but his nods are a really good sign and would normally have me feeling ten feet tall, but now the only person who seemed to have the power over me was Siobhan. Maybe I should be grateful to my father. If only for him wanting the land, otherwise I would never have met Siobhan.

I leave as he returns to his file and pass Liam as he goes in. I used to wonder what they got up to, but as I grew older, the thoughts of being involved in their meetings made me uncomfortable. I think the depth they were involved in criminal activity was far too deep for me. I often thought that me and Darragh only ever saw the surface.

"What's the jazz?" Darragh arrives at the front door, and he doesn't look hungover. This is a surprise.

"We have the family meal tonight." That gets a string of curses from Darragh, and I smile at how inventive he is.

I go into the kitchen to get a bowl of cereal today; Mary isn't in. I'm not sure why, but I want one of her turkey and cranberry sandwiches she makes with the most perfect stuffing.

Cornflakes will have to do. Darragh follows me in and pours himself out a bowl. He's like a pig at a trough. Milk drips down his chin, and the noises are loud and disgusting.

"You're turning my fucking stomach," I tell him while shifting in my seat so I don't have to look at his slobbering face.

"What's wrong with you?" he asks with his mouth full of cereal so I don't answer.

"Ah, you got blue balls." Now I glance at him.

"Why is everything about sex with you?" I ask while shaking my head. I know he's prodding me to see if I will spill, but I won't.

"There are four things that are everything to me." Darragh holds up his spoon.

"One is sex." He grins, and I continue to eat my cereal, not really caring what the other three are, but he

91

wants to share. "The second is money, thirdly partying, and last family."

I snort. "In that order?"

He actually thinks about it. "Yes, but hold up. So the four P's Partying, Pounds, Pussy, and Papa."

Sometimes, I want to deck him. He starts rhyming it off again, trying to sing when Shane walks in.

"You're a jackass," I tell him as I place my bowl in the sink.

"I'm with Finn on this," Shane says, but he's grinning at Darragh. It's odd to see Shane smiling, and I don't ruin the moment with morbid thoughts.

"Okay, fine, what about the four F's?" I'm a glutton for punishment and actually wait to hear how he will rhyme this off.

"Family, Fun Times, the Fifties and fanny's." I'm laughing when I shouldn't, but it's so bad it's funny.

"Don't start singing that at the table today," Shane says, sobering up the room. He goes to the fridge with no idea of the change in atmosphere. He's like Liam in ways, they don't seem to understand human emotion or the impact their words have. I could only hope the meal was quick and quiet.

VICIOUS IRISH

***

Dad sat at the head of the table with Shane to his left and Liam to his right. I sat beside Liam and across from Darragh, who was playing with his peas. One bounces across the table, and we all focus on it. I gulp my wine. It wasn't always like this. Once this table had been filled with laughter, but we had lost too much.

Father raises his glass. "To family. *An Clann*." He says the English and the Irish of it, and we all repeat his words as we drink. I look at Darragh, his glass is empty, so he is sucking in air. He looks across at me and winks before his foot connects with my leg. I don't shout out like I want to as Dad isn't finished speaking.

"I have allowed Connor his vacations many times," he says this with a wave of his hand, but my heart races. "This one has been the longest and I'm ready for him to return home." I want to see Connor so bad, and I'm angry at him for leaving, but the thoughts of him being dragged back here isn't fair. He deserves to find his happiness, and I know he will never find it in this place.

"You know where he is?" I ask. The stillness around the table tells me I'm not the only one who has been impacted by my father's words.

"He has a job, a place to stay. A friend of mine is keeping an eye on him. But I want him home now." Father's words are said as he looks at each of us. When he looks at me, I speak up.

"I'll go," I say. I'm angry at Connor for leaving but to have him back would complete me. Especially after finding Siobhan. God, he would really like her. I know having him back would be selfish, but I'm not an angel.

"No." My father turns to Shane. "I want *you* to bring Connor home." Shane nods and raises his glass. We all follow suit. I look at Darragh, and he is no longer messing around. I hate that Shane is the one to get picked again. He always gets picked. He doesn't even get on with Connor, but Shane will bring him home. My heart might over rule my head, and I would tell Connor he didn't have to come. Maybe father saw that weakness in me. Should it matter who brought Connor home? The fact he was coming home was the important part.

"To Connor," he says, and I find myself smiling, I was about to get my brother back.

"To Connor." We all repeat except for father. He does raise his glass, but he never toasts to Connor.

VICIOUS IRISH #1

WILD IRISH SERIES

BY VI CARTER

VI CARTER

PROLOGUE

"Pass me the shovel." I gesture to Finn as I stare into the shallow grave. The smell of decay rises up to greet us. Recent rainfall has caused the grave to sink in further. Coming here tonight was the right thing to do. If we had left it any longer, the body would be exposed.

"I can't do this."

"You will do this." I glare at Finn to drive my words home, and he's shaking his head like he has options.

Sinking to his hunkers, he runs both hands down his face, like he can erase what he's seeing. "That's Siobhan's aunt." His eyes are glued to the grave. Regret at bringing him here is starting to slowly raise its head. Finn and Darragh, who were the youngest of us brothers, got it way too easy. They were born with silver spoons in their mouths. So right now, I just wanted to dirty Finn's hands a little bit. The idea was giving me far too much joy.

"I don't really care who it is. Now pass me the shovel."

Finn gets up and takes both shovels that lean against the boot of my Mercedes. His steps are careful across the bog. The land we purchased was deliberate. A bog was ideal for what we were doing right now. The lights from my car shine on the ground and stop just at the grave. The sun is nearly gone, and soon, the car will be our only source of light, so I want this done before that happens. Once the shovel is in my hand, I start to dig. Finn stands still, leaning against his shovel, watching me.

"Finn," I warn, and he starts to dig. It doesn't take us long before all the clay is off the body. Wild life has gotten to her. We had wrapped her in plastic, but her head hangs out, her neck twisted at an awkward angle.

Finn turns away and gags repeatedly. His early dinner splashes on the mud and on his shoes. "You'll take off your shoes before you get back into my car," I warn him. Holding my breath, I pull the body fully out of the grave. We need to dig deeper. We had buried her in a panic in a shallow grave.

"You're heartless." Finn wipes his mouth with the back of his hand.

"Who was the one who bashed her head in?" I question, and his eyes shift away from me.

"You had one job, Finn, to keep an eye on Darragh, but you couldn't do that could you?" His head snaps up, his eyes bulging.

"I'm not his fucking babysitter."

"That's exactly what you are," I remind him. "If you hadn't been lying with that girl, none of this would have happened."

"Shane, don't bring her into this." He's taking a step towards me. I'm not threatened by him. My shovel sinks into the wet ground easily, and I start digging, ending our pointless conversation.

We work in silence and once the grave is deep enough, I dump the body in. Finn looks away in horror, and I suppress a smile.

"Jesus. We should say a prayer."

Prayer? Like that will bring her back.

I leave Finn to say his prayers. The heavy plastic that I pull off the dead animal releases a smell and a swarm of flies. I turn my head to the left to avoid a mouthful of them.

"Finn." I call. His low words cease, and he tuts before he joins me. I have already tied ropes around the front of the cow's legs. It's an odd-colored cow. Black, white, and red, it's a mixed breed. Not that it matters. Picking one of the ropes up, I hand the other to Finn. He's gawking at me, and I exhale loudly.

"We use the cow to cover the body, so if anyone digs, they hit the cow first and don't bother digging any further," I tell him and start pulling. He doesn't say anything but pulls too.

It's heavier than I expected, but we manage to get the cow into the grave. We push it in on top of the body, and the impact is loud.

"Did you hear something break?" I ask Finn and his eyes narrow.

"Are you fucking joking?" He has no sense of humor.

We finish off covering the body with clay just as the sun sets. I close the boot once everything is cleaned up and stop Finn from climbing into my car. "Remove your shoes." I hadn't forgotten him retching up on them. He shakes his head but kicks them off. They join the rest of the stuff in the boot.

"I need my bed," Finn says while closing his eyes and leaning back against the headrest. The first pitter-patter of rain hits the windshield as I start the car.

Leaving the bog, I then drive home to Whitewood house.

CHAPTER ONE

SHANE

My father glances up from his desk as I close the double doors behind me. Dark circles under his eyes, along with his disheveled appearance, make me want tell him to go to bed. He has loosened his tie and opened the top button of his shirt. After his declaration that he knew where Connor was, I had to talk to him. I didn't like finding things outalong with the others. I had thought I was more privileged than them. He had asked me to get Connor, his request taking the sting out of it, but not enough for me to let it go. "How long have you known where Connor was?" I ask. His rising hand, along with the letter opener that he holds, cuts me off. A half-opened white envelope is the only thing on his desk.

"I don't." He shakes his head while he speaks, then puts down the letter opener. "I had eyes on him until last week."

The bookcase that fills the wall behind his desk is a display of colors of mostly browns, reds and greens. I always hated the smell and general appearance of the books. Right now, I feel the same about them as I always do. As I sit down, I try to make sense of what my father is saying. "So why only send me now? Why not a week ago when he went missing?" Irritation pours over my words, and I don't try to lessen it.

Connor is a valuable source to our family. He isn't exactly family, but we need him. He maintained a balance that we couldn't seem to find without him. We tried, but things never sat right until he was here.

"I thought maybe he was having an off day. But a day turned into a few. I've recently had word that he's crossed the border." Father rubs in-between his eyes, and I find myself picking up his letter opener and standing it up on the desk. This isn't good. Crossing into the north isn't allowed. It is declared by a different group. One we don't interfere with. They claim to be the real Republican Army. So, we keep far away.

"Why would he do that?" I ask while sitting back and taking the letter opener with me. It's not sharp; I stick it against my thumb and spin it.

"I'm not sure. But I want you to find out why, and I want you to bring him back." Father holds out his hand, and I tap the letter opener against my palm. I want him to answer another question before he dismisses me. "Did you ring Tom and have it confirmed?" His eyes narrow at my question, and his jaw clenches. He holds out his hand again, and I give him what he wants. Once he has it, he finishes off opening the letter that he had started.

"Of course I did. He's seen and heard nothing." My father won't meet my eye, and I question what he's holding back. I sit back in the chair and twist the silver band on my thumb in circles. "And you believe him?" I quiz.

I don't get an answer. Loud commotion in the hall has both of us standing up and leaving the study. Finn, Darragh, and our stepsister Una are in the hall. My eyes snap to Liam. He stands to the side, still wearing a full suit as he observes Darragh, who is drunk, and Finn, who is the only one trying to control the situation.

My attention is drawn back to Una. She has always had an ability to capture my attention. Her red fiery hair hangs dark and limp down her back. She looks like she just stepped out of the ocean. A pool of water is gathering around her, but she doesn't seem aware of it. Her cream top is see-through, and a bright pink bra is visible and full.

"Get me some towels," Finn barks at Darragh. Darragh doesn't move. He stands still and laughs at Una. He's pointing at her like he's five. I turn as I hear receding footsteps behind me to find father leaving.

"Finn, take care of this," he calls over his shoulder. Finn's head snaps up, and he looks ready to lose it.

I don't try to defuse the situation. Instead, I stand and observe to see what will happen. Finn doesn't ask me or Liam to help. Maybe he knows we won't. Once again, Una captures my attention as she pulls a plump lip in between her teeth and bites it. A laugh leaves her mouth, and she opens her eyes. They still manage to hold me in awe, one blue the other green.

I've never seen anyone like Una. It suits her. She is two very different people. She's unpredictable, and

I often think that's why I'm drawn to her. Right now, she holds out her arms and starts to twirl.

"Una, stop it." Finn tries to pull her hands down, but she keeps spinning, and Darragh joins her. That's when I decide I've seen enough. I cast a quick glance over to the spot where Liam stood, but it's empty.

As I enter the garage, I don't have to flick on the lights. They are already on. Liam waits for me by my car. "We need to take a drive." I don't question him but slide into my Audi as he gets into the passenger seat. The garage door opens as I back out.

"You look at Father differently recently." I glance at Liam. He isn't looking at me but out the window.

"What are you talking about?" I take a left out onto the road.

"Just an observation," he says, and when I peek at Liam, he's staring at me with brown eyes that are almost black. They're the same eyes I see in the mirror.

"Don't try to analyze me. Stick with analyzing Finn and Darragh," I tell him.

"Is this topic making you uncomfortable, brother?" Liam is enjoying himself. He likes to torture me in the smallest ways. The ways I don't like.

"Of course not, brother," I answer as my hands grip the steering wheel.

"Take a left at the next crossroads," Liam informs me, no teasing in his voice now.

"He's different," I say, and at once hate that I said it. Liam is watching me again.

"How so?" To anyone else, his voice doesn't rise and fall. It's almost a monotone. But listening to him for so long, I can hear that tilt in his words. It happens when he is truly curious.

"I'm not sure. I think he is hiding something." I take a left at the crossroads as he had instructed.

"What were you talking about in the study?"

I laugh. I can't help it. This level of curiosity, especially for Liam, is unusual.

"Indulge me." His lips lift slightly as he speaks. "Take a right at the next crossroads," he adds.

"If you told me where we were going, it would make this easier. Is it Kells?" I question.

"It doesn't matter. Now tell me what you were talking about."

I grip the steering wheel again at his demand. "It was about Connor. He doesn't really know where he is." This conversation is annoying me. I glance at Liam, and he sits back, not facing me any longer. He now stares out the window.

"To the land."

I stop at the crossroads and take a right back towards Nobber. "You've just taken us in a full circle," I say, but Liam has gone quiet. I turn up the music as I put my foot down and drive at a hundred and twenty kilometers an hour the rest of the way. We reach the land fifteen minutes later. I pull up along the lane and lower the music.

"She's been declared missing," Liam says looking out onto the land.

My stomach tightens, but I knew this would happen. "But nothing is pointing at us?" I question, and Liam gives me a quick glance before he starts fixing his cuffs, then his collar, fixing things that don't need to be fixed.

"No, but I have a bad feeling. I want to dig her up."

"Liam, it's been weeks," I remind him. An old moldy body after a few days wasn't something I wanted to dig up.

"We didn't go deep enough." We had buried her late at night, and he was right. We hadn't gone deep enough. It was something that had bothered me too.

"I went back a while later. I buried her deeper." Surprise is visible on Liam's face. It's small, but his eyebrows lift slightly. To anyone else, he would seem emotionless.

"I covered her with the carcass of a cow," I add.

"You did it all by yourself?" Now I'm smiling at his question. I pull out away from the land. "No, I had help." It wasn't the nicest thing I had ever done, getting Finn to help me move his girlfriend's aunt's body, but it had been fun.

"I got Finn to help me." I can see the wheels turning in Liam's head.

"You should have left him alone," he says, and I glance at him.

"Why? Because him being upset just might upset poor little Darragh?" I hate how soft Liam is when it comes to Darragh. I don't have a clue why. If I had a choice, I would have both Darragh and Finn out of the family business. They're a weakness and cause more problems than we need.

"No, Shane. You did it with emotion, and that is stupid."

"He's a little spoilt prick. He never has to do anything. He has it easy. I just wanted to get his hands a little dirty." I'm smiling again. I can't help it. It was satisfying to see him squirm and panic.

"His hands are dirty now," Liam says, and I hate how he sounds. It's like he's telling me it will come back and bite me in the ass. I don't care.

I drop Liam off at home. He says no more about Finn or the body, and I pull away from the house before anyone else comes out. This time, I blare the music and let it pound into my head. It's senseless music, the type you can get lost in. I lose myself for the next twenty minutes as I make my way to the last place Connor was seen.

I park in a gravel car park that holds two cars and make my way into the stone building. A few men are drinking while watching a show about darts. They study me as I enter, and I let them. My clothes speak of wealth and good taste. I know how I look. Everything is tailor-made. The barman is wiping the same spot he has been since I entered. I don't sit but stop at the bar.

"I'm looking for my brother," I say, and he snaps his head up at me and then at the picture I have of Connor. It's a few years old. But I couldn't imagine he changed too much in the last two years.

Recognition lights up in the barman's eyes. "Connor is your brother?" He sounds unsure, and I don't blame him.

"Half-brother. I'm the good-looking one." I flash a quick smile to add to my joke, and it puts him at ease. I ask my questions, and he tells me that Connor was a good tenant, and he always paid his rent on time.

"Would it be possible to see where he was staying?" I ask.

"Sure. Just give me a minute." I don't even have to wait the full minute before I'm taken upstairs, and he leads me into a small, poky, and unlivable space. I'm not sure what I thought I would find here. But a single bed with a double-doored wardrobe is all that greets me. I leave with no leads as to where Connor is.

***

It's getting late, so I call it a night. The house is quiet when I return home. A drink is what I need. The hallway is lit by the lights that hang over large paintings. Rugs under my feet make my footsteps silent. Dark wood gives the large hallway warmth it shouldn't hold for its sheer size. I enter the bar and find my father smoking a cigar, sitting on a Queen Ann with his eyes closed.

"Any luck?" he asks, not opening his eyes, and I am curious about how he knows it's me. I pour two whiskeys, and he opens his eyes when I place his glass on the table beside him, the one that holds a large crystal ashtray.

"No, none." I take a deep drink before putting the glass on the table beside the couch that I sit down on. Air brushes my skin as I roll up my sleeves. I had a tattoo done, the skin still fragile.

A large blank band that goes the full way around my arm joins the other eight. The tattoo had started at my elbow, and now it reaches my wrist. Nine bands one for each life I took. My father's eyes linger on my tattoo. It's something we never spoke of, but it is my way of remembering every life I ended. I never take a life easily. But sometimes, it's a matter of theirs or mine. Or my family's.

"Una is asleep now. I couldn't get a coherent word out of her." Father sounds tired again.

"Send her home." Even as I say it, I know it's a lie. I don't want her to leave. But this place has a way of twisting people, and she isn't someone I want to see hurt.

"I'll discuss that in the morning with her. But while she's here, I expect you to keep an eye on her." I nod into my glass, knowing I would be asked. He might give Finn responsibility, but really, it's me and Liam he trusts, and Liam makes most females uncomfortable.

"Of course," I tell him before emptying my glass.

We say good night as I leave the bar. He's still smoking his cigar, and puffs of smoke swirl above his head.

A part of me says to take the left once I reach the top of the stairs, but I take the right. I should turn back, but I don't. Instead, I stand outside the room that is Una's. She never declared it, but it's a room we all know as hers even if she doesn't. I open the door and step in.

She's lost in the four-poster bed. Her hair has dried out and fans around her head like a burning sun. The covers are to her neck and tucked in around her body. She's afraid of the dark. She thinks if her leg or arm isn't tucked under the quilt that something will grab her.

I smile now. That's what she told me when we were kids. But she always tucks the blanket tightly around her even as I watched her grow from a girl into a woman. I relax as I focus on her sleeping form. It's something I have always done, snuck into her room and watched her sleep. It helps me. I stay for a while until she stirs. She's never caught me in her room before. I leave now, not wanting to make this the first time.

CHAPTER TWO

UNA

I stretch out my arms and legs, and still, my legs don't dangle out of the bed like they would at home. A strangled scream is pulled from my mouth as I open my eyes. Darragh is sitting on the side of my bed, dressed and freshly washed. His blond hair is combed back. The red collared t-shirt is pressed and sits perfectly on his lean frame.

"My God, Darragh, you nearly gave me a heart attack." I sit up and clutch the quilt to my chest. His blue eyes disappear as he starts to laugh.

"What are you doing in my room?" I'm still angry, as my heart hasn't returned to its normal rhythm.

"Do you know you talk in your sleep?" Darragh tilts his head, his eyes fill with devilment.

I narrow my eyes at him and loosen my death grip on the quilt. "No, I don't," I reply and his smirk grows.

"How would you know? You were asleep."

An excellent question, just one I wasn't going to give him an answer to. "What are you doing in my room?" I ask again as I lie down. My headache returns with a vengeance. "How much did I drink last night?" I ask also as I cover my eyes with my arm. His laughter isn't doing my head any good.

"You jumped into the lake."

I sit up again as snippets come back, and I let out a groan. I had. I remember now. Partying down at the lake. Darragh had dared me. "We are so stupid," I tell him, and he grins now as he gets up off my bed.

"No, correction, you are stupid. I didn't jump in. I dared you to jump in, not thinking you would actually do it." He walks around the bed and sits on the other side now. "I had to send Fran in to get you."

I cover my burning face. I remember a boy with long blond hair pulling me from the lake. He pulled me on shore. I could have drowned if not for him.

"Why didn't you rescue me?" I ask now, observing him through my fingers.

"The jumper I was wearing was brand new. So…"

"Get out of my room." I'm pissed at Darragh again. Not about him not jumping into the lake to rescue me. Two drunken people in the lake wouldn't have been the best idea. Especially Darragh and me. But the fact he picks a jumper over me, yeah that stung.

"Are you staying with us?" Darragh asks, backing out of my room, but he doesn't sound offended at all at me asking him to leave the room.

"I'm not sure," I tell him honestly. I need to talk to Michael first.

"Well if you are, I have a party we can go to." He grins as he closes my door, not waiting for an answer. Darragh knows how to party hard. I'm not sure my head is up to it.

***

After a shower, I get dressed. I came with nothing, but had left some clothes here last summer. Jeans and a moss green jumper are the best that I can pull out of the bundle.

I find Michael in the kitchen. Something tells me he has been waiting for me.

"It's great to have you home." His arms are outstretched, and I can't stop the smile that spreads across my face as I walk into his arms. His warmth envelopes me as his arms circle around me.

Just like that, I'm a little girl again. Michael has always had the ability to make me forget the bad.

"But what's brought you here?" he asks before planting a kiss on my head. I want to stick out my bottom lip and ask him to skip this part, but I know we can't. Michael gets me a coffee as I push my drying curls out of my eyes and sit at the breakfast bar.

"I needed to get away," I answer as he pushes a coffee into my hands.

"You want me to have a chat." I smile and pat his hand.

"Nope, I already had words with her." I shrug as I take a drink of coffee.

Michael takes a drink of his own coffee before setting down the mug and fixing his tie, which is slightly crooked. "You can stay here as long as you want."

Relief bubbles through me. I never thought he would throw me out, but hearing him say I could stay relaxes me. He stands again and comes around to me. Brushing curls off my forehead, he gives me a kiss. "But there is a condition, my dear."

I raise both eyebrows as I wait for Michael to tell me. I can see a spark of mischief in his eyes.

"You will have to work. I will get Shane to give you a job." Michael releases me and puts on his suit jacket.

The thought of working with Shane does funny things to my stomach. I've always crushed on him. But he has always looked at me like I was repulsive. A part of me kind of got it. My hair and eyes didn't exactly make dating easy. I've been called every variation of red and not in a pleasant way. And my eyes get me a lot of attention. It's a mix. But I've been called a freak because they are different colors.

"It won't be hard, Una." Michael has taken my internal struggle as a problem with him getting me to work. I shake my head.

"No, that's fine. Sorry, I was miles away." I push a smile forward, and Michael nods.

"Okay, I'm off to work," he tells me as he takes his coffee down to his office.

After the conversation with Michael, my mind moves to my mother. She was angry the last time we spoke. I was studying accountancy, following in her footsteps, and I could do it. I found myself getting bored. I did it because she wanted me to do it. I had one final year, and I was qualified. I knew finishing made sense, but I had enough of silence and numbers. Her life wasn't for me.

I leave the kitchen with a granola bar. Mary would fix me breakfast if I wanted, but right now, I wanted the fresh air. I spent way too much time indoors, and I hated it. It was foggy this morning, but warm, so I didn't need a jacket. I could hear the horses in the stables as I walked along the pass. The boys had no idea just how lucky they were living here.

Stephen, one of the stable masters, comes into view. His navy boiler suit covers him as he shovels out the stables.

"Good morning, Stephen." I nearly give the man a heart attack and laugh.

He smiles. "Una, you're back."

I shrug. "Yeah, I think so." His brown peaky cap covers his balding head. He's been here as long as I can remember.

"How is she?" I ask as I make my way to the third stable.

"She's good. Her form lately has been off," he tells me as he leans the shovel against the stables and walks down to me. I stop outside my mare's door, and there is that sudden rush of sadness and happiness at seeing her. She moves back away from me, dancing slightly.

"I've had a hoof trimmer here. Her shoes are fine."
I'm nodding as I open the door. But she's unsteady
while moving deeper into her stable.

"How long has she been like this?" I ask as he
closes the gate after me.

"A few days."

"Would she be pregnant?" I hold out my hand, and
when my fingers meet her hair, she settles, allowing
me to rub her side.

When Stephen doesn't answer me, I glance at him,
and he's smiling. "You're the first who got to touch
her." At his words, I lean my face into her and
inhale the warm air that rises from her coat.

"We checked, but it could be too early to tell if
she's pregnant. But it's possible." I stay with her for
a while just rubbing her, and she lets me. I never
named her. Shane bought the horse for me on my
sixteenth birthday. I thought if I referred to her as
'her' or 'the horse' that I would never get attached. I
was wrong.

It's a while later that I leave. The cold and hunger
drive me back inside, and I smile when I see Mary
in the kitchen. She's taking cookies out of the oven.

I knock on the door, not wanting to frighten her. She's a weak heart already.

"Hi, Mary," I say. Her eyes widen, and her eyebrows rise. "Una. You are more beautiful each time I see you." She's always been too kind to me. Before she pulls me into a hug, she places the cookie tray on the counter. "Are you staying long?" she asks the same question that everyone has asked, and I'm not sure what I'm doing.

"For a few nights," I tell her as I sit down while focusing on the cookies. "They smell lovely," I say, and she bustles over to the coffee machine first where she fills me a mug. I sit at the breakfast bar and watch her move around the kitchen.

Mary moves fast, but she's a stout woman with short curly hair that's always wild. Her hair is kind of like mine. Unmanageable.

A tray with milk, coffee and sugar along with cookies is placed in front of me as Liam comes into the kitchen, and the atmosphere changes. Mary doesn't like him, and she doesn't hide it. Liam, to me, has always been different. But he doesn't scare me off.

"Cookie." I offer him. His eyes flicker to the cookie, and he actually takes it. Not what I was expecting, nor do I expect it when he sits down across from me.

He could be a model waiting to have a photo taken. He isn't exactly fully sitting on the stool; one foot rests on the floor. He unbuttons his suit jacket and rests one hand on his leg. He has no idea of how he appears as he eats the cookie. I want to laugh, but don't. Instead, I pour my coffee and thank Mary.as she leaves the room.

"How are you, Una?" He doesn't glance up at me as he speaks, his focus solely on the cookie that he still eats. His words are filled with boredom, like somehow he is being forced to make small talk.

"Great, and you Liam?" I ask. Some amusement has slipped into my words, and he peers up at me.

"I have no complaints at all, Una." His monotone has me hiding a smile behind my coffee mug. He gets up and bids me a good day. Nothing weird or odd about that at all.

I spend the next hour searching the house and grounds for Shane with no luck. I find Darragh and Finn fighting in Darragh's room. My mind is taking in the floor that is covered in clothes. Darragh's room is like a teenagers room, and he has banned Mary from cleaning it. It's something I must say to him once I stop Finn and Darragh from killing each other.

"Okay, okay calm down." I step in between them. It hasn't come to blows, but it doesn't seem like that's far off.

"Una, this is private."

Finn's sharp words at me sting, but I fold my arms across my chest. "And what? Let you kill each other?" I ask.

"Don't fucking speak to her like that." Darragh jumps to my defense, and I snap my gaze to him. His jaws are red, and his fists clenched. I'm not sure what has wound him up so much, but seeing Darragh angry was odd.

"It's a private conversation. That's all I said," Finn says back. He's calmer now.

"It's my fucking room. And Una stays."

"Do you know what…" Finn doesn't finish his sentence but storms out of the room. I watch him leave, questioning what has everyone fired up. I turn to Darragh to ask, but he throws himself on his unmade bed. "Don't ask," he says, and his serious tone has me leaving it alone.

"Your room is disgusting," I tell him, glancing around me. How does he live like this?

"Yeah it is," he agrees and starts to smile. "Want to go to a party."

***

The "party" that Darragh takes me to is in a small village. The pub has locked its doors, so you're free to party. Smoking is prohibited in all pubs, but right now, I walk through another cloud of smoke. The smoking isn't the worst that's happening here. Most people are high and jump around as a guy with a red long beard beats the shit out of a bodhran.

Darragh takes my hand and pulls me through the crowd. He looks alive as he smiles at me, and I find myself loosening up.

"Una, this is Brian." I'm introduced to a really good-looking guy. He's tall with wavy blond hair and sparkling blue eyes that you would fall into. He gives me a quick glance, but his attention is back on Darragh.

"You better have brought my money." I focus on the floor as Darragh smiles and promises his way out of not having the money for Brian. I steal glances at Brian. He's really good looking, but he knows it. All eyes are on me, and it's for the wrong reasons. Now I wish I had tied my hair up and put on some sunglasses. But the more rebellious side of me sticks out my tongue at them. It's fun, and when

Darragh swings around and places a pink pill on my outstretched tongue, I swallow it with a long drink from the bottle that I hold.

Time moves in a funny pattern. I'm dancing. All the colors, I can't catch them. The vehicle under us is moving. Blond hair and blue eyes fill my vision.

"Brian," I manage to say, and everyone laughs. I'm sitting in the pool house. Brian's there again, and his lips move against mine, his tongue forcing its way into my mouth. The weight of a small tablet registers with me as he passes it into my mouth, and I swallow.

The tiles under my feet are cold but shiny. They move like water. I touch them, and they bark at me.

"Una, leave the dog alone," someone shouts. The beast moves towards me, and I run towards the light. I know its safety. I'm in a glass house. Water fills my mouth, and I can't breathe. Someone pulls me back.

A girl laughs. "What are you doing in the shower?" Shower. A solid cold pane of glass presses against my fingers. I'm in the shower. She puts something into her mouth while offering me a small pink pill. I decline. I'm aware what's happening is happening, but it seems like it isn't.

She shrugs and puts the second pill in her mouth. I watch her slide slowly to the ground. I reach out to her, but my head collides with glass, and I find myself on the ground with her.

Laughter bubbles from my mouth. Large legs cross my vision. I see blond hair from the back. "Brian," I whisper, and he grins down at me. He's so tall; he's like one hundred feet high.

I try to reach out to him, but my hand is tiny. "My hand!" I panic, but he laughs, and I laugh too. Brian's mouth is huge, stretching and growing, and I blink a few times before the darkness consumes me. I try to fight it, but it's no good.

CHAPTER THREE

UNA

Three people lie beside me, their hands behind their heads. I blink and three becomes one. My stomach tightens with the pain that rips through it. I manage to crawl to the shower where I heave. Every glance I flicker towards the girl on the floor doesn't make her move. I want her to move; my brain is telling me she's too still, too pale. My hands tremble as I wipe wet hair from my forehead. I notice then that I'm soaking wet.

I'm looking around the bathroom trying to make sense of this. I need someone to tell me what happened. I use the tiles to hoist myself up; standing is a challenge that I somehow manage. I'm so cold. *How long have I been lying here?* My attention draws to the girl again, from this angle, I can see her face fully, and she's dead.

Her coloring isn't natural, nor is the stillness of her chest. I've never done CPR, but I know I can't stand here and do nothing. My hand trembles as I reach out to her, while kneeling down, covering my hand with my other hand as I close my eyes.

You can do this, Una.

Slowly, I open my eyes. I try again, but I can't touch her. She's dead. I know she's dead. I move back away from the body and glance around the room. Once again, no one is here. The floor is rising and falling as I rock back and forth. A single black marble tile becomes my sole focus as I try to calm myself, but it isn't working.

It's wet, and I reach out and touch it. The tips of my fingers turn red. I yank my hand back to my chest. My breaths are bursting from my lungs, and I can't stop blinking as I stare at the body.

"What happened?" Arms pull at me. The dead girl disappears, and Darragh's face fills my vision.

"She's dead." My words are a whisper.

"What happened to your head? Da is going to kill me." A burning pain ignites in my head as Darragh's fingers brush across my forehead. Automatically, my own hand joins his. My fingers are red when I glance at them.

Darragh moves out of my line of vision, and the dead girl is back.

"She's dead," I whimper, and this time, Darragh seems to hear me. He's returned with a towel, but doesn't put it to my head. Instead, he joins me in staring at the dead girl.

"She's dead?" he questions.

"Yes." I can't process this. What was going to happen to me? Would I go to prison? Was it me who had killed her? Was it the drugs? Who would be held responsible? Okay, Michael was going to kill us for bringing this into his home. My mother? My mind is growing more frantic.

"She's dead." Darragh's shout snaps me out of my own inner turmoil. He paces the floor. A vein bulges in his neck as he roars. "Fuck. We are so fucked."

Tears burn my eyes at his words. "Do something," I tell him as I start to rock again.

"This isn't my mess." His calm accusation knocks me out of my state.

"Darragh, this is your party. There is a dead girl in your bathroom." Now I'm the one shouting.

"Everything okay?" someone asks through the door. Darragh is staring at the door, and I'm staring at Darragh. We can't let anyone else see this. I get up and make sure the door is locked.

"Yeah, be out in a minute," I say and wait for a few seconds. Darragh is now fixated on the body.

"Darragh, give me your phone." I don't have a clue where mine is, so I hold out my hand.

"What do you want my phone for?" Confusion fills his voice. It must be the shock.

"To ring the Gardaí and an ambulance. We need to report this." He turns his back on me, but he is shaking his head.

"Darragh, we need to report this." I shiver again at the thoughts of what will happen to me. But leaving her lying on a cold tiled floor seemed wrong.

"Darragh," I shout his name and get his attention.

"Yeah, I'll ring. You get rid of everyone." He seems together, and I find myself nodding. He comes to me, and I want to roar, crying in his arms, but he moves my hair. "We need to cover the cut so no one asks questions," he says before stepping away. His coldness is something I have never seen before, but I tell myself it's the shock. A dead body wasn't something either of us had seen before.

There are three people left in the pool house, and they are easy to shift. No one seems to search for the dead girl, and I feel relief but guilt that no one remembers her. I search the room for a bag or jacket something to give the guards so they can identify her, but there is nothing in the room. When I return to the bathroom, I find Darragh sitting beside her, having a fag.

"How long will they be?" I ask, and he gapes at me with that confused stare again. "You go on to bed. I'll sort this."

I laugh. "Go to bed?" My chest is tight, and I'm struggling to breathe. I don't need him to go into shock on me right now. I need him to be strong until the Gardaí get here.

"Fuck sake, Una." He's up quicker than I expect. Throwing the half-smoked cigarette into the sink, he marches towards me and yanks me by the arm.

"What are you doing?" I ask trying to get free, but Darragh is stronger than he looks.

"Go to bed," he says before leading me out of the pool house. I'm left standing outside, freezing and confused. Darragh glances back at me over his shoulder. He looks focused and angry, but he doesn't appear to be in any kind of shock

SHANE

I check my phone. It's four in the morning. I'm not sure what woke me. I lie back down as I hear another loud noise coming from down the hall.

Climbing out of bed, I pull on jeans and grab the bat from behind my door. The hall is dark, and I keep it that way moving along the wall slowly. My bare feet help keep me soundless. I start to realize it isn't an intruder as light shines under the door from the fourth bedroom down from mine. Also, an intruder wouldn't be as noisy. Another bang sounds before a female voice curses.

What is Una doing? I lower the bat but still keep it in my hands as I open the door. She's wet again. This girl has a thing for water. She's searching for something in the wardrobe. In the process, she's knocking boxes and clothes onto the ground.

"What are you doing?" I ask.

She spins around, her wet long hair flicking water with the speed of her movements. The wildness in her eyes has my stomach tightening. I'm beside her, searching her face. Her gaze lowers now, and she's shaking her head.

"Una, what's wrong?" I ask the crown of her head, and when she peeks up at me, her eyes are watery, and she stares at me unblinking. A tremble has entered her body, and my heart starts to pound. "Una, what's wrong?" I want to grab her and shake her, but touching her has never been a luxury I have allowed myself. Right now, I seem unable to move.

"I can't find dry clothes." She blinks, and tears fall.

I loosen my grip on the bat. "Because this isn't your room," I tell her, taking a step out of the wardrobe, but she doesn't follow. She moves around the wardrobe like it's her first time seeing it. She's shaking as she slowly skims her fingers across a pile of blankets. There's blood on her hands. I take her wrist as I step back into the wardrobe, and she flinches at the contact, and her eyes widen. I have dealt with blood before, but her blood is doing something entirely different to me.

I'm searching her face, her arms, but I can't see anything.

"It's my head. I don't... I don't know..."

I find it quickly. It's a deep gash. "We need to get you to the hospital."

She's shaking her head. "I didn't know."

I don't have a clue what she's babbling about. Right now, having her standing here bleeding and cold wasn't doing any good for my heart. "It's fine. Let's get you sorted first." I smile when she nods. Finally, I can take care of her.

When I release her wrist, her eyes widen, and she shakes her head again. "We need to go to the pool house." She moves past me, and I'm trying to catch up with her.

"Una, why?" I'm whisper/shouting, not wanting to wake up anyone else.

"Shit." It's not until I'm out in the courtyard that I remember I have no shoes and no shirt on. The cold air has me moving faster after Una. All I want to do is get her head looked at and out of those wet clothes.

The pool house is a mess. The embers of a party dying slowly.

"Una." I call her again as she makes her way to the bathroom. Her blue lips and pale skin have me itching to get her to a doctor, and whatever she wanted to show me, I would check out so we could go. I curse Darragh, because I knew this was his doing. He is a heavy hitter when it comes to partying, and I question now if Una is on something. I am going to kill him.

Una steps inside the bathroom, and I follow her. What I find isn't what I was expecting. I wasn't sure what I was expecting, but Darragh is sitting beside a girl. A girl whose lips are blue, her body lies limply on the floor, and this is the last thing I expected to find.

Darragh's eyes snap up to mine as I step into the bathroom. I try to control my anger as I take in the mess before me.

"She's dead." Una's crying beside me, but all I take in is Darragh. What a fuck-up.

"Get the fuck up," I tell him, and he jumps up quickly. I check the girl for a pulse and don't find one at first, but there's a flicker of life there.

"What has she taken?" I ask Darragh, and he shrugs.

"You are so fucking useless." He lowers his head. Una is still shaking, her eyes shooting everywhere. She is in shock.

"Una. I need you to focus, sweetheart." Her eyes snap to me, and she blinks, allowing more tears to fall.

"She isn't dead. But what has she taken?" She moves quickly, and she's beside me, her bare arm brushes mine, and I hold my breath at the contact.

"She isn't?" She's smiling, her fingers moving up my arm, and I'm staring into her eyes, not sure how to sort through everything. Right now, I need her to stop touching me. Her eyes search the floor now as if she can see the past play out before her. "She took pills." Her head snaps up, and she's almost excited with this information.

Darragh takes out a pack of fags, getting ready to light one up. "Darragh, take Una back the house and get her dry clothes. Then take her to my car where I will meet you. We need to get both to the hospital. You think you can manage that?" I speak between clenched teeth.

"Yeah, yeah of course." He answers like a fucking victim. He makes me sick. Turning to Una as she clings to my arm, I force a smile.

"Go with Darragh. Everything will be okay." She's nodding now, but it's like she's boneless. The adrenaline is leaving her body. I snap my head to Darragh, and he helps Una stand. I wait until they have left the room before I hoist the girl up off the ground. I'm trying to wake her and shaking her and even slapping her across the face doesn't have any impact. She's getting cold, and I check again. *Had I imagined the flicker of a heartbeat?* It's still there.

I bend her over before opening her mouth and sticking my fingers down her throat. Nothing happens at first, but she starts gagging before sick pours over my hand and out onto the floor. I hold her up as liquid continues to pour from her; I repeat sticking my fingers down her throat until there is nothing left for her to bring up.

When she pushes my arms away, I lift her up onto the counter and get her a glass of water; she brings back up the first sip but manages to keep the second mouthful down.

I leave the girl there as I return to the house and get dressed.

She's still in the same place when I return. I carry her to the garage. Una sits in the front of the car, her eyes are wide, and I can see the quick rise and fall of her chest as she stares at the girl. She's in dry clothes, and that relaxes me until my gaze settles on Darragh sitting in the back of my car. I open the door.

"Get out," I tell him, and he does as I place the girl in the back. Once I have the door closed, I turn to Darragh and grab him by the neck.

"You're such a fucking waste. Go and tell Liam the mess you made while I take these two to the hospital." I let him go, pushing him away from me, and he rubs his neck. His anger I can see, and I almost want him to put his hands on me so I can hurt him. But he turns away and goes back into the house.

Una wrings her hands as I start to drive to Navan. It's the closest hospital to us.

"How's your head?" I ask, and she shoots me a side-glance. She pulls her lip between her teeth and chews on it.

I need to focus on the road and not Una.

"It's sore now. I didn't really notice it earlier."

I nod. "It was the adrenaline that was keeping it at bay. We are nearly there, so you'll be seen too soon."

She isn't sitting as straight now. "Una, don't fall asleep." I flicker a glance at her, and she rubs her eyes.

"I'm so sleepy all of a sudden." Her words are slurred.

"Yeah, it's the cut on your head. You've lost a lot of blood. It's important that you don't sleep okay."

"Okay." Her one word, I don't like.

"Stephen told me you saw the horse I got you," I say, and straight away, I regret it. It's not her reaction. She sits a bit straighter, but it's how it makes me feel. It was the first time I tried to show her I cared.

She had been so excited that day, and getting her the horse was the best decision I had ever made. But that day as she had sat proudly on top of the horse, Dad had squeezed my shoulder. His words had my stomach tightening, "You're a good brother to her." The way I looked at her was not how a brother looked at a sister. I had shrugged his arm off. "She's not my sister." My angry words where heard by all, even Una, as I stormed off.

"Yeah, she's the best." Her words are still slurred, but she's happy, and she's talking. "I'm not sure if I ever thanked you." She reaches for my arm, but her hand flops down half way across. I glance at her, and she is smiling at me with lids half closed.

"You're welcome, Una," I tell her before focusing on the road. I remember the day I saw the horse. She was wild. The handler wasn't able to control her, and all I saw was Una. I knew they would be a perfect match, and I was right. "We're nearly there," I tell her, and she shifts pulling herself up more. The sign for Navan has me lifting my foot off the pedal. But I still move quickly through the empty town. It takes five more minutes before I pull up outside the Accident & Emergancy Deparment.

I open Una's door and help her out. The fresh air has her eyes opening a bit wider. I close the door and lock the car leaving the other girl in the back. She's asleep, and my number one priority is Una. For now, she has forgotten about the girl. She allows me to lead her into A & E, where a few people wait. I smile at the receptionist. She doesn't return the smile as I give Una's details.

"Fill in this form and take a seat." She slides the form out to me.

"I'd like to be seen to now," I tell her glaring over her shoulder in search of a doctor.

"And so would the man behind you with only three fingers. We're moving as fast as we can." I don't look at the man in question. This place makes my skin crawl. I hate being so close to other sick people. I direct Una to a seat and kneel down in front of her.

"I'm going to step out for a moment, but I'll be back," I tell her.

She's far more alert now. Her eyes focus on my face, and my stomach tightens. My thumb brushes her thigh, and she jerks, I quickly get up and go outside.

I carry in the girl, and the receptionist raises an eyebrow. I give her another smile, and yet again, she doesn't return it. "I found her on the sidewalk. I think she's taken something," I tell the receptionist.

"Her name?" she asks with fingers hovering over the keyboard.

The girl is heavy, and I move her to the closest seat and sit her up, but she slumps over. The receptionist continues to observe me.

"I don't know," I answer and return to Una. I've done my part. Now I need to figure out what the hell we are going to do with Darragh.

CHAPTER FOUR

UNA

My head hurts. I get four stitches and strict orders to stay awake for the next twelve hours as a precaution. I'm waiting to be discharged, and Shane is sitting in a plastic chair while he scrolls through his phone. I still can't believe all he has done for me tonight. When he peers up at me, my pulse spikes. I want to ask him why he is being kind to me. But the doctor returns.

"Okay. You're all set to go." He hands me a prescription. "If the pain persists, take one every four hours." I'm nodding as Shane rises and tucks his phone in his pocket.

He reaches out his hand to the doctor. "Thank you," he tells him, and the doctor takes his hand. The silver band on his thumb reflects the light grabbing my attention. My eyes roam up his arm where a small band of black is visible but disappears under the sleeve of his jumper. When my eyes meet his, my heart leaps in my chest.

"Ready to go?" he asks, and I give a quick smile and get down off the bed. "I'll take that." Shane reaches out his hand for the prescription, and I give it to him.

He's always careful not to touch me. But earlier, I could have sworn his thumb stroked my thigh. Maybe I imagined it. My head wasn't exactly in a good place.

Back in the car is the first time my mind wanders to the girl. "The girl, is she okay?" Shane starts the car backing out of the hospital. The sun is up. It's nine in the morning, and I'm sleepy now but exhausted from everything.

"Yeah, they pumped her stomach, but she's going to be fine." Shane focuses on the road as he drives and I steal glances of him. This is the longest I have ever been in his company, and my opinion of him has changed. I always fancied him, but never got close to him. He wasn't an easy person to get close to.

We don't go home. Instead, Shane pulls up at Whitewood lake. There is a fog sitting on the lake. I don't move as Shane climbs out of the car and goes to the boot. I unbuckle my seat belt as he opens the door.

"I thought the fresh air might help keep you awake." I step out of the car, and he places a large jacket around my shoulders.

Now all I smell is Shane, his cologne along with the scent of leather and trees. It's a weird combination, but it was uniquely Shane. My stomach trembles as he leans around me and closes the door.

Shane walks with his hands behind his back, but there is a bounce in his step. He doesn't seem like someone who has been up half the night. I can only imagine my appearance from the night, instead of focusing on that, I give all my attention to Shane.

"Do you know that Whitewood Lake has its very own monster?" I love the lilt that enters Shane's words. It makes me glance at him and expect to see a small grin, and I do. I find myself smiling at him.

"I've been around these parts for a long time, and I've never heard anything about a monster," I say. His grin expands into a smile, and my heart skips a beat. But I don't lose eye contact. His beauty entrances me.

"In 1981, it was spotted and sounded similar to the Loch Ness monster."

"May be a relative," I answer, and Shane gives a small laugh that has my stomach erupting in butterflies.

We are silent for a moment, and I find myself staring into the water, questioning if things like monsters really are under the murky surface. Shane walks on the inside; he's closer to the rippling waves. He seems at peace, his face relaxed, and there is a constant smile visible. My mind goes back to what happened, and most of all Darragh.

"Can I ask you something?" We stop near two large trees, and I'm nervous all of a sudden now that Shane is facing me. His brown eyes are like orbs of chocolate; they could really pull a girl in. I was so sleep-deprived that I couldn't focus for a second.

"Of course." Shane folds his arms across his broad chest as he stares out at the water. A chest I had seen bare a few hours ago. To see him standing in only a pair of jeans in the closet had nearly undone me. He's waiting patiently, and I pull my mind from the gutter.

"When I thought the girl was dead, Darragh was supposed to ring the Gardaí, but he didn't." I chew my bottom lip pondering if I had said the right thing. Shane was his brother after all, and I don't know what I was trying to say.

"Maybe he was in shock," Shane tells the lake.

"Yeah, maybe," I respond, but I don't believe that. I don't know what I believe. But he wasn't in shock. It doesn't really matter now, I suppose, since it turned out all right. I pull Shane's jacket tighter around me, trying to smell it without making it noticeable. Shane takes my movements as if I'm cold.

But I don't argue as we get back into the car. I don't remove the jacket, and Shane doesn't ask for it. His phone rings, and he struggles to get it out of his pocket.

"Need a hand?" I ask, and his no is resounding and quick. I sit back a sting of embarrassment on my cheeks has me snapping my head away. He manages to get the phone out and answers it. I want to tell him driving and talking on a phone is illegal. But I do it all the time.

"I can't talk right now." It's Liam on the other end of the phone. "Yeah, we'll talk when I get home." More of Liam's voice, but I can't understand what's being said. But Shane laughs, and it's not a sweet laugh. "Like I said, we'll talk later." He hangs up without saying goodbye, and the car moves faster under us.

"Everything okay?" I ask after a moment, and he slows down slightly.

"Yeah, it's Liam being Liam." We pull into the drive, and I feel disappointed that this time with Shane will end. I sound like a deprived girl. I don't speak as we make our way up the drive.

I expect Shane to pull into the garage, but he doesn't. Instead, he drives out back and through the courtyard, and we pull up outside the stables. I glance at him, but his fingers drum on the steering wheel as he faces forward. He doesn't speak as he climbs out, and once again, he opens my door for me.

"I thought you might like to check in on your horse." He's holding open my door, but he isn't looking at me, and now I question what Liam had said to him. He seems far away. As I get out, he's still holding the door, my face flush with his chest.

"Shane," I whisper, and my stomach twists as he looks down at me. My heart starts to pound as he stares at me.

"Good morning, Mr. O'Reagan." Shane gapes at Stephen like he materialized from thin air. Shane steps out of my way and gives me a quick nod. He greets Stephen stiffly, and this is the Shane I have become accustomed to, the one who treats the staff like tools and not people.

"Morning, Stephen. How is she today?" I ask as I make my way down to the stables. Stephen walks beside me.

"She's a lot better. Still can't touch her, but I'm confident you can." He's grinning at me as he veers off to do his jobs. I stop at my horse's stable, and Shane stands a few feet away. He doesn't join me. I'm not sure what he's doing, but I open the door and step into the stall. She moves back as I slowly approach, but settles as I place my hand on her before leaning into her coat. My face heats up against her skin.

"She was kicking and bucking the day I saw her. She was uncontrollable and the handlers couldn't break her." I lean out as Shane steps into the stable with his hands behind his back. He doesn't make any attempt to rub her or come closer as he tells me about the horse.

"She had reared back, and her mane caught the sun and I don't know..." Now he's frowning. "I thought of you."

My heart flutters at his words.

"She was unpredictable." He looks at me for the first time. "Untamable."

My pulse spikes, with how he looks at me, and it might be the lack of sleep, but I feel like I've stepped into a twilight zone with Shane. It's like that feeling when you're lying under the stars knowing the world is asleep. It's magical, but it has to end.

"I remember that day also Shane. When you told everyone how I wasn't your sister." It was childish of me, but it had hurt that day. He had said it with such disgust that it has stayed with me through the years. I never looked at him as a brother, but it was the disgust in his voice that had shattered me. I remember thinking I couldn't blame him with how odd I was, and odd isn't always good.

The moment I flicker my gaze at Shane, I regret my words. His jaw is clenched his shoulders tense. At least I know he remembers. I didn't really expect that.

"Sorry, that was childish. It was a long time ago."

He shakes his head. "No, I hurt you."

My throat burns as he speaks, because he really had hurt me. "It's fine." I rhyme off as I continue to run my hands along my horse. When Shane's hand rubs close to mine, I freeze along with the animal under us.

"I'm sorry." His words are low and precise. Like he's trying out a new language. I glance at him, causing our shoulders to brush, and this time, it looks like he's the one who freezes. He takes a step away from the horse and me. "You need to eat." The declaration is like a light bulb going off over his head, and I can't help the smile that grows on my face.

"I do?" I question, and he smiles, sending butterflies scattering to the corners of my stomach.

"Yes, you do," he says before leaving.

I shake my head while I give my horse a final rub. I glance around me making sure Shane is gone and that Stephen can't see before I bury my face in Shane's coat and inhale.

A giggle erupts from me. I was acting crazy. It was the bang to the head that was causing me to act odd I decide as I lock the stables and make my way to the house.

The kitchen is warm, and Mary smiles at me the moment I enter. "Una, I'm making your favorite." The smell of pancakes has me drooling. I didn't expect to see Shane sitting at the table. It's set for two people. He's on his phone, fingers moving rapidly across the screen. He has such a serious expression on his face.

"Orders from Master Shane," Mary adds and that grabs my attention and Shane's.

"Master Shane?" I question not wanting to mention the fact that he knew pancakes where my favorite.

"Sit down, Una." The demand is sharp and comes from Shane.

I don't like it. I shed his jacket and place it on the chair, but I don't sit.

He flashes a glance towards Mary as she prepares pancakes and coffee before they snap back to me. "Please." He says it through gritted teeth, but I take it and sit down. I'm sitting across from Shane, and the setting is almost intimate except for the bustle of Mary. Shane focuses on his phone, and I take in the circles under his eyes.

"You should go to bed," I tell him.

"I'm fine." He doesn't glance up from his phone as he answers me. Mary places a coffee in front of me, but pauses as she hovers over me. "What happened to your head, sweetheart?" I had almost forgotten about it.

"Oh..." I start to explain, but Shane cuts me off.

He stands up and takes the paper from his pocket handing it to Mary. It's my prescription. "I'll finish up here. You go and get the prescription."

Mary glances at me and hesitates, and it's like I can see the wheels turning in her head as she looks from me to Shane. The way she glances from me to Shane makes it appear like she thinks Shane did this to my head.

"I fell," I tell her, and she moves slightly back, her eyes widen before narrowing in disbelief.

"Why are you still here?" Shane's words are quiet, but they would move a stone. She leaves quickly, and Shane is up making pancakes. I've lost my appetite.

This is how I remember him with the staff, an actual asshole. I don't speak even as he puts a plate of steaming pancakes in front of me. They aren't as perfectly circular as I have become use to, but he buttered and sugared them just as I like. A jug of maple syrup is on the table and I don't hold back coating them in the sticky substance.

"I really shouldn't eat your pancakes since you were so rude to Mary," I say as Shane sits down.

He's rolled up his sleeves his tattoo on display. It's an odd one, large thick black bands circle his arm. I often wondered what it meant but never asked. "No you should starve yourself, and that way I will be kinder to Mary." He takes a forkful of the pancakes, and I'm transfixed on his mouth as he chews. He doesn't show any remorse as he pauses and raises an eyebrow. "Eat, Una," he tells me once his mouth is empty, and I gaze at him as he refills his mouth.

Before I lose all self-control, I start to eat the best pancakes in the world. "Okay, these are delicious," I tell him, and his lips tug up into a smile. Shane has finished his, and he sits watching me eat mine. I can't stop smiling in-between mouthfuls. "Why are you watching me?" I ask, but I don't mind that he is.

"Why are you smiling?" he fires back.

"Because you're watching me."

He smiles now, and I shake my head. He's gorgeous. "I've been thinking about your job."

I don't like the change in the topic, but I try to hold the smile. I want to talk about why he is watching me eat not some stupid job. I sugar and milk my coffee. "Let's hear it," I say, and he sits back a slow grin forming across his face.

"I need a bookkeeper." He waves his hand in my direction, like he made me the 'bookkeeper' appear.

I'm shaking my head, and he sits back, his recent confidence leaving. "What you have done for me tonight is more than anyone has ever done for me," I answer honestly. When he leans in, his eyes crinkle at the corners, but I hold my hand up knowing I need to finish.

"Like seriously, I can't thank you enough. But working with numbers, I can't. I mean…" I'm now cleaning a spot on the table that isn't dirty. I swallow, surprised by the level of emotion that is coming with my words. "I'm not her… I don't want to be her. I'm not my mother, Shane."

His eyes light up with understanding now. "You don't want to be an accountant," he asks, and I nod my head, trying to keep the tears back. "So what do you want to do?" Shane takes a drink of his own coffee, and his brown eyes have softened.

"That's it? You're not going to try to convince me that I'm throwing my whole future away." I'm not sure if that's what I wanted to hear. But it's what I was used to hearing. So having someone accept what I was saying was a shock.

"When dad asked me to get you a job, I don't recall him telling me to make you miserable." His small smile has my heart beating faster.

"I know what I want to do." My heart is racing. The idea that I could do what I truly love is rushing the blood through my body. "I want to work with Stephen. Help out with the horses." It was Shane buying me the horse that made this love for horses grow.

It was because of him, in a way, that I no longer wanted to be an accountant. That I wanted to be free. Be me. In a way, I should be thanking him for more than tonight.

"Okay, we can organize that."

I'm beaming with joy. "Seriously?" I ask, and Shane's eyes are soft as he smiles at me. It sends butterflies erupting in my stomach.

"Yes. It's so nice to see you happy."

I'm a little speechless right now. I'm ready to burst with so many emotions. I take a drink of coffee. Glancing at Shane over my coffee, my pulse spikes as our eyes clash. "Thank you." It's nearly a whisper, but it's the most heartfelt thank you I have ever given to anyone.

"You're welcome," Shane says with a slight nod. We sit and sip coffee while staring at each other. It's perfect until Liam walks in, and I know our time together is up.

CHAPTER FIVE

SHANE

There's the smallest smudge of blood near her hairline, I notice it when she tilts her head. Otherwise, her face is flawless. Her skin has a shine to it. It's like the beauty inside her is trying to shine through. I love watching her mouth when she smiles. It's as fascinating as her different coloured eyes.

I take another sip of coffee and continue to take her in. She's sleepy, her lids dropping every few seconds, but we both sit up as Liam enters the kitchen. He's rang a few times, and we need to talk.

"How are you feeling, Una?" His words are precise as he speaks to her, and I want him to stop talking to her. I'm not entirely sure why. Maybe because he makes her uncomfortable. Maybe because he normally doesn't interact, so why with Una?

"I've had the best nurse take care of me," she tells him as she smiles across at me, but there is a sadness in her eyes that I don't understand.

"I see. We need to speak." Now his attention is on me, and that sits better on my shoulders. I get up and ring Finn.

"Una's in the kitchen, and I can't stay with her. I need you to watch over her for the next few hours." Una tries to object, but I keep my back to her. Finn agrees. I don't glance back at Una as I follow Liam out the door.

We go to my bedroom. I'm exhausted, and this day hasn't ended yet. I sit on my bed and start pulling off my top. Liam stands along the wall. He never sits. He never appears comfortable.

Now I question what my brother's relationships with women must be like. I've never really thought about it before. I never cared. But spending the day with Una makes me question if he has ever felt like that. I put on a clean t-shirt and sit back down on my bed.

"Did you talk to Darragh?" I ask pulling off my boots and socks.

"Yes, and Darragh is the least of your worries." Liam's controlled words make me want to lose control. I snort.

"Darragh is a huge problem, Liam. You will have to see it sooner rather than later. He's going to get one of us killed. One of us," I state pointing at myself.

"You can't punish him for something that hasn't happened."

I grit my teeth. "You can't ignore the signs that something will happen. And it *will,* Liam. Give him time."

"I'll have a word with, Finn." I'm shaking my head even as Liam says it. Finn has always been Darragh's babysitter, but he wasn't going to solve this. Finn wasn't himself since Connor disappeared. To me, the solution to this was to find Connor.

"A new supplier has moved into the area. He's trying to take over three of our areas. Dad wants it stopped and cleaned up straight away." I rest my elbows on my knees. This wasn't good.

"A name?" I ask, but Liam is already shaking his head.

"Nothing. But Dad's informant said Dublin will be the first hit." I snort again while glaring up at the ceiling.

"Dad's famous informant. I don't suppose he told you who it was?" I ask, already knowing the answer. But Liam is already moving to the door. This conversation to him is over.

"You need to sleep." I don't wait until he's gone before I climb into bed. I dream of Whitewood Lake and monsters.

I wake up and immediately check my phone. It's six in the evening. I've slept for roughly four or five hours. I can't even remember what time I went to bed at. My mind is still circling back to the monster in the lake with a mix of my conversation with Liam.

I'm out of bed, making my way down the hall. Once I push open the door, something twists in my stomach when I take in all her red curly hair fanned out around her head like a burning halo.

Her cheeks are pink, and I can relax at the rise and fall of her chest. She's wearing a white top, the straps only strings, allowing me to see a lot of milky skin. I should wake her up and make sure she's okay. A concussion was a very high risk with someone in her case. I gently and carefully shake her arm that is covered by the blanket.

"Una." I say her name gently as I shake her. But she doesn't stir. While standing back, I stare at her. Nothing, I try again shaking her with more force. "Una, wake up." It's a little too loud, and she sits up quickly, nearly colliding into me. But I'm quick and jump back. I don't get the smiling girl I had in the kitchen. Una's eyes are narrowed as she glares at me, her chest rising and falling quickly.

"What is with this family? You guys like waking me up."

"Who else wakes you up?" I fire back dryly, not liking that idea at all.

She shakes her head. "What do you want Shane?" She's almost barking, and I drop the whole subject of someone waking her up. But I will ask her another time when she's not ready to kill me.

"Go back to sleep, Una," I tell her, and her eyes grow in size. I want to smile. She's beautiful in the morning, but I know better.

"Go back to sleep, Una! What did you wake me up for?" She's shouting, and I can't help but smile as I make my way to the door

"To make sure you were alive," I say as a shoe hits the wall an inch from me.

"Can a dead person throw shoes?" She's red in the cheeks with temper.

"They say red heads have foul tempers. Now I have proof that it's true," I say as I make it out the door in one piece as something else hits the wall. I assume the other shoe.

I shower and change before getting into my car and making my way to a meeting in Dublin with one of our main customers.

It takes me forty minutes to reach The Marker hotel where I set up the meeting. I park in the underground parking before making my way up to the veranda where I have reserved a table. As the doors open, I'm greeted by a member of staff. "Mr. O' Reagan." I nod in greeting as I'm taken outside to my seat.

Overhead heaters keep the area warm, but the night's not cold. The large couch is comfortable, and I sit down, peering out over the city. Lights sparkle from the hundreds of windows, and it makes me think Una would like it here. I've never appreciated the view, but I would love to see it from her eyes.

"The usual, Mr. O'Reagan? Should I bring it now, or wait for your guest to arrive?" The waiter stands next to the table, one hand behind his back.

"You can bring it now and double the usual," I tell him, and he leaves as Gary arrives. Gary is a bull in a suit. That's what comes to mind when I take in his huge frame. The grey suit he wears could tear at the wrong movement. The white collar is open; he couldn't close it even if he wanted to. His neck was as thick as three men's.

He takes off his sunglasses as he sits down and puts them on the table. It's dark outside, so the sunglasses aren't necessary.

"Got to say, I was surprised when I heard you wanted to meet me. I'm not in trouble am I?" Gary is smiling as he speaks. Meeting me isn't necessary very often, unless prices go up or we've run into a problem.

The waiter arrives back and places a brandy in front of us. "You're not in trouble. Relax," I tell him, and he rubs his hands together while sitting back with his drink.

Gary reminded me of a blown up doll, but no matter his appearance, he wasn't stupid. He didn't supply nearly all of Dublin with drugs by being stupid.

"I wanted to check on business," I say and take a drink, relaxing back into the orange couch. Gary hasn't the same level of comfort that I have. The wicker chair is larger than most, but it wouldn't have the same space or comfort as the couch.

"Yeah, it's good." His eyes slightly narrow. "It's about the new supplier."

I clap for a moment. "Right to it. I like that, Gary. So what can you tell me?" I take a drink. He shifts in his seat before leaning forward. The joking Gary is gone now, and I'm eye to eye with the businessman.

"Look, his product is clean. I don't know where he's making it or how. But it's cheap, and right now, it's huge in London."

"What's his name?" I ask, and Gary leans back opening out his arms.

"Come on, Shane. You know I can't do that. You're not losing me as a customer. Just this guy has a new product."

A product that I am sure we could replicate. "Do you have a sample?"

"On me? No man. Gardaí everywhere."

I don't fully believe Gary. I don't trust any of my customers. A man who can take a life isn't an easy man to figure out, and Gary has taken a lot of lives.

"I need a name Gary?" He tilts his head at my request, as if to say he doesn't know.

"Have you ever met my brother, Liam?" I ask, and he sits back again.

"Bernard," he finally coughs up.

***

"I didn't do anything." Neill has his hands in the air. He's four-foot-nothing, an easy target to people, but I'm not here to hurt him. After leaving Gary with the name of this new supplier, I decided to drop in on an old 'family' friend.

"Is that how you answer your door?" I ask, and he quickly drops his arms and lets me in. I double-check that my Audi is locked. It's a council estate, and black wood from a recent burning still sits in the center of the play area outside Neill's house.

The sitting room holds battered couches. Neill scoots around me and turns off the television, but I catch what he was watching. When I return my gaze to him, he shrugs.

"I might be small in height, but I'm big in other ways," he tells me as he sits down on the couch.

I'm not here to talk about his dick. So I don't. I sit down in the armchair across from him. "Any new fighters or people moving through your circle recently?" I ask. Connor was his number one fighter, and he made a lot of money off my brother.

His feet dangle. They don't reach the floor as he sits back in the couch. His white tracksuit is cheap and a copy of a popular brand.

"A few new ones. None like Connor." He's smiling with genuine affection for Connor. Connor wouldn't exactly be the friendly type. I often saw him as a mix of us all. At times, he reminded me of Liam, but he could be a mess like Darragh. Only Darragh was women and drugs where Connor was fighting and drink.

"Have you heard the name Bernard going around?" The moment I ask, I can see that he has heard of him. His eyebrows lift at the same time.

"Yeah, I have. He's been supplying some new drug. Some of his men where giving out samples at one of my fights. But I ran them off."

"You personally?" I know he didn't, but I couldn't let this conversation go by without him understanding that I could crush him.

"No, my bouncers. Shane, I respect you and your family. You have my word that I'm not holding back." So he knew what I was doing.

"Good." I stand now, not wanting to spend any more time here than necessary. "If you hear anything, I expect you to call me," I tell Neill as he shuffles off the couch.

"There is one more thing." I wait until he is standing.

"He had a northern Ireland accent." That was the last thing I wanted to hear.

"You're positive?" I ask, and he nods. This wasn't good at all.

***

I arrive home close to eleven. The house is quiet, but that doesn't mean that everyone is asleep. I find myself upstairs knocking on Una's door. When I don't get an answer, I enter, but the room is in darkness. The bed is made, and Una isn't here.

I find her in the library, sitting barefoot on a Queen Ann chair. She's twirling a curl around her finger while holding an old paperback in her other hand. I can't read the title but can tell she's enjoying it. I'm about to leave, when she peeks up from behind the book. Surprise filters through her eyes.

"Don't' throw the book at me," I tell her, and she sticks her tongue out at me, making me smile. Her tongue is really pink, and I'm glad when she puts it back in her pretty mouth. It's tantalizing and distracting.

"I think I will have to start locking my door." Her tone is playful, but I freeze. Does she know that I watch her sleep? I'm not sure what she sees on my face, but she laughs.

"I'm joking. It's just; I'm not a morning person. I had Darragh the other morning, and you this morning." I relax and enter the room now. So the other person was Darragh. He had no respect.

"I apologize about Darragh," I tell her as I sit down.

"And who will apologize for you, Shane?" Once again, her tone is playful, but I sense she knows that I watch her.

"I have nothing to apologize for," I tell her, and her smile slips at my serious words. I don't like sitting here and being questioned, but I don't want to leave her either. Standing, I focus on her, and each step I take closer to her causes a strain on her shoulders.

"I'm going to check your head," I tell her, and she bends her head for me. It takes a few seconds to find the cut with all her hair. The stitches are neatly done. And honestly, there isn't really a reason for me to check it. I rub her hair between my thumb and forefinger. It's extremely soft.

"What are you doing?" Suspicion coats her words.

"I told you, I'm checking your head so hold still," I tell her, she hadn't moved, but she shifts now under my hands. She doesn't like being told what to do.

"It feels like you're touching my hair." I grin now.

"I am touching your hair; I have to move it to see the cut."

"It's taking a pretty long time." She huffs, and I can't stop the smile.

"There is a lot of hair to move."

"I'd move a dead body quicker." Her dry comment has me laughing. I don't think she has any idea how ironic it is that she would say that.

"What's so funny?" I quickly step away from Una as Darragh comes into the library. His smile slips as I stare at him.

"What do you want?"

"I just want to talk to my sister," he says, jutting out his chin. I want to scream at him that she's not his fucking sister. If she was, then she would be my sister, and that was too messed up.

"I want a word," I tell him, leaving the library I don't turn to see if he follows. I know he will.

He has the sense to close the library door as he leaves. I stop two doors down from it, not able to contain myself.

"She's off limits from now on." Darragh opens his mouth to speak. But I click my fingers in warning. "I don't care what Liam said. I don't care what you feel or think. She is off limits."

He's shaking his head. "Why do you even care?" he asks but takes a step back while he speaks.

"Because father has left her in my hands, and I'm not a fuck up like you." I can see I've hurt him. Darragh takes another step back.

"Don't forget, Shane, you're not Liam in his eyes either." I hide all emotion at his words, but it stings.

It's always been there. I know Liam is the next in line to take father's place, not me.

But when I was younger, it never bothered me to support my brother. I knew he was more vicious than me. He was more controlled when he needed to be, and he could lose control when he needed to as well. My emotions played too heavily into my actions.

Darragh hasn't taken two more steps when the door opens, and Una steps out. I can tell from her red cheeks that she's all fired up. Darragh doesn't even stop when she speaks.

"How dare you? I can talk to whoever I want. You or your father can't make decisions like that for me." I glance at Darragh's receding back. His words about Liam still stinging me.

"I'm speaking to you, Shane." I snap my gaze to Una, and right now, I can't do this.

"Go back in and read your book," I tell her, expecting her to do as I say, but her dry laugh reminds me she isn't like other people.

"If I had the book, I'd throw it at you right now." Her words are said with hands on her hips. "That was a horrible thing to say to Darragh."

Now I'm starting to question her anger. "Which part?" I offer through clenched teeth.

"You're a piece of work." She shakes her head and storms back into the library. But I can't let it go. It's starting to sound like she has feelings for Darragh. I'm right behind her.

"Why are you getting so mad over Darragh?" I question, and she swings around.

"What are you trying to imply?" Hands have returned to her hips now, but I can see the strain in her face as I keep stepping closer to her.

"You're hell-bent on defending Darragh. Now that I think about it, you spend a lot of time together." Her face blazes at my accusation, but she takes a step closer to me and pokes me in the chest.

"He's my brother." She pokes me a second time. "He treats me with more kindness than you could ever muster up, Shane." She pokes me again while saying my name. I move closer, stopping her from poking me. Her hand smashes against my chest.

"He is *not* your brother. I'm not your brother." The moment I say it, I regret it. The hurt that crosses her features has me leaving before I explain to her why I said that.

VI CARTER

CHAPTER SIX

UNA

His broad back fills my vision, and I want to pull all the books from the shelves. I'm angry with myself more than him. I allowed myself to feel for him, when all along, I was a job. His father told him to take care of me. That's the whole reason he went above and beyond to help me.

Tears burn my eyes at how stupid I've been. It was like I had spent my whole childhood and into my twenties craving attention from someone I saw as untouchable. Then he gives me a few hours, and I'm falling at his feet like he's some kind of God. The burn that travels up my neck has me covering my cheeks.

It's the burn of shame. I've been such a fool. He must be laughing at me. I don't allow the tears to fall. I'm stronger than this. I leave the library, and with each step, I want to defy him. No one has any right to tell me what to do or who I can hang out with. I go to the bar knowing that's where I will find Darragh. He's smiling when he sees me.

"I knew you couldn't resist the dark side." He pours me out a shot of vodka, and I stamp to the bar.

"I'm so fucking angry right now," I tell him and take the shot. It burns my throat, but it does nothing to quench the fire that's burning in my veins.

"Wow," Darragh yelps while he slaps the bar. "I knew red heads where fiery." He refills the shot glasses, and we both take them at the same time. "Let it out," he tells me, refilling the shot glass again.

"I don't think I could ever let out all the anger I'm feeling right now." Darragh refills his shot glass and downs it.

"He's a dick. Don't let him get to you." Darragh comes around from behind the bar and puts his arm around me. "Fuck him, Una. It's Shane. Just like it's Liam. They aren't like us. We are free," he tells me with a smile before pouring himself out another shot and placing the one I hadn't drunk in mine. "To freedom," he says holding up his glass, but I can't drink to that.

"We aren't free, Darragh," I say quietly, because it's true. I'm caught up in what my mother wants me to be. And Darragh is being pushed into a box he refuses to stay in, yet no one is listening to us.

"I don't think I like it when you're acting like Debbie downer." Darragh drinks his shot, takes mine out of my hand and drinks it. And just like that, because I'm not partying, I'm not wanted.

My temper flares, and I swing around in the chair grabbing the bottle of Vodka. When I hold it up, Darragh smiles placing the two shot glasses on the bar. I fill them, but don't let him take his. "You answer a question, and then you take a drink," I tell him.

"And what, I ask you a question and then you drink?" He's smirking.

"Yeah." I agree, and he rubs his hands together.

I go first. "Why don't you stand up to Shane?"

"What the fuck kind of question is that?" Darragh is as volatile as me. I smile to ease the tension.

"Do you want a drink or not?" I say, and that does it. He settles.

"Because I am only here as long as he allows it," he answers, and I don't even get that, but he knocks back the shot, and I remember now he gets to ask me a question.

"Do you have a boyfriend?" His question surprises me.

"No." I drink my shot. "What do you mean you're only here as long as he allows it?"

Darragh refills both shot glasses. "He doesn't like me, and if he had his way, I would be gone." He drinks his shot.

"You don't really believe that?" I question, and he grins.

"That's a second question, and it's my turn."

I reel in my irritation.

"When was the last time you slept with someone?"

"You get to ask me anything, and that's what you ask me?"

Darragh grins. "That's my question."

I roll my eyes. "About three months," I answer honestly, and he hoots while slapping the bar.

"Three months." He roars like I said three years. I knock the shot back.

"What do Shane's tattoos mean?" I ask. The moment it's out of mouth, I can see the wheels turning in Darragh's head.

"This is starting to sound like it's all about Shane." My heart starts to pound, and I force a laugh while refilling the shot glasses.

"It doesn't matter then. It was a stupid question." I take a shot and Darragh rises.

"He's a prick, Una." The way he says it has me nodding at him. His fists are clenched.

"I know," I answer weakly.

"You're such a fucking liar." He storms from the room, and I feel terrible.

I shouldn't have started this stupid game. It was selfish of me. I take a swig from the bottle and chase after Darragh. My feet aren't as steady as I expect, but I catch myself before I stumble.

"Darragh." It doesn't seem to matter how many times I call him. He won't stop. It's not until he goes into the pool house and sits down that I can see his face.

"I'm sorry," I tell him knowing quizzing him about Shane wasn't right. "I was curious…"

"Liar." He's shouting again, and I'm questioning if following Darragh was the right thing to do. I want to tell him to calm down, but something is stopping me.

"It's always get close to Darragh to get close to Shane or Liam. Keep Darragh quiet. People can hear him. Hide him away, so no one can see him. I'm fucking sick of it." I'm frozen as he takes his anger out on a wooden chair smashing it to pieces.

Violence isn't something I've ever been around. Darragh's anger has me rooted to the spot. "I see how you look at him. You always have since we were small. You looked at him like he was a fucking God." He's too close for comfort, and I step away from Darragh. He throws his head back and really laughs.

"Go on, sweetheart, run back to your prince. You have no idea of who he is."

I want to shout at him to tell me, but speaking doesn't seem like the best idea. He's staring at me, and it's like someone snaps their fingers, and he's Darragh again.

"Jesus, Una, I'm sorry." I'm shaking my head, trying to tell him it's fine.

"You're as white as a ghost. I've really fucking scared you." My heart is still pounding, but my muscles relax slightly as Darragh steps away from me and sits on the couch.

"It's obviously something you need to talk about," I say from the same spot. Darragh is sitting down and pours white powder onto the small coffee table. He uses a card and cuts the cocaine up.

"Nah, it is what it is." Clearly not. I think, but don't voice this as he rolls up a fifty and uses it to snort the powder up his nose. As he sits back, he inhales deeply before lying back into the couch.

"Want to go to a party?" He's up now, rubbing his nose. "Have some," he says pointing at the two white lines that are still on the table.

"No I'm fine," I tell him, and he shrugs before snorting up the other two lines. Watching him, I see how far he's gone. Does his family see how damaged he is?

"Your nose is bleeding, Darragh," I tell him. My heart is heavy for him, but he grins and goes to the bathroom. While he's gone, I start to tidy up the smashed chair. He was going to get himself in trouble with that temper. God forbid hurt someone or himself.

"Do you want me to get Finn for you?" I know they are close, and I don't want to be around Darragh, but leaving him alone isn't a good idea either.

"He's off duty tonight. Don't worry, Una. You can go. You don't have to stay." He lights up a fag, and there is so much wrong with the sentence that I wouldn't know where to start.

I don't move, and I can see the irritation in his shoulders. "What are you still doing here?" As he blows smoke into the air, he focuses on the floor to the left of my foot. I tell myself this is Darragh. I had nothing to fear. We all lose the cool now and again.

"Where's the party?" I ask, and he's grinning, and now, so am I.

"Let's party," he tells me, throwing the fag into the pool. We leave, and I don't allow myself to think. I get into his car with him.

VICIOUS IRISH

***

I'm not sure how we make it safely, but we do. I'm still pumped from the speed the car was going and from the near misses. I wasn't an adrenaline junkie, but the vodka and rush has me alive as I get out of the car along with Darragh.

The party that we are going to is a rave, and it's being held in an exhibition center in Navan. Its beat can be heard from where we parked, which is like the size of three soccer fields away. From the moment we step out of the vehicle, the party has started. There's people everywhere. Laughing, drinking, making out, getting sick, and even having sex. Yeah, there seem to be no boundaries.

"Darragh." Brian moves towards us, saying Darragh's name in a deep voice. They embrace and when Brian notices me, he winks.

"Red. You came back for seconds," he says, moving towards me. He reeks of cologne and alcohol, but those blue eyes are a vortex.

"I didn't realize I had firsts, blondie," I tell him, and he grins handing me a bottle of something. I take it, and it burns. Whiskey, I think. When I cough, the two girls behind him giggle. They both wear bikini tops and short denim skirts. I am over dressed in jeans and a jumper. But I'm not here to get laid.

Blondie hasn't taken his eyes off me, and I start to question what exactly happened between us.

"What was the stuff you gave me the other night?" I ask, and he throws his arm around my neck as we walk towards the rave. I glance back to see Darragh with an arm around each girl.

"You want some more red?" I glare sideways at Brian and shrug his arm off me. He's hot and all, but something about him isn't right.

"No, I'll pass, and stop calling me red," I tell him, and he laughs at me like I'm a little child having a cute tantrum. "Find me later when you mellow out." He walks on into a crowd and greets some guy with a shaved head. I give his back the fingers.

"Come on, play nice." Darragh is beside me with a blond under each arm. Both smile in unison at me. I give Darragh a fake smile. "This is me playing nice," I tell him, and he laughs.

We get split up the moment we enter the rave. The heat has started a coat of sweat over my body. My skin is itchy and tight as I push through and make my way to the bar. Drink is slopped everywhere, and my top soaks up some from the counter.

"A large Vodka," I roar at the barman. He has one of those really big ear piercings that must be painful.

"Mixer?" he shouts back, and I shake my head. He pushes a pint of pure vodka towards me, and I pay a twenty for it. I don't mind. I stand at the bar and drink the whole lot while holding my nose the whole time. When it's gone, I'm not out of it yet enough to join everyone around me as they move to the music.

Whatever pumps through their bodies has them in their own little world. I want to be in mine. The heat has the air hot, and I pull off my jumper. My pink bra blends in with all the multitude of colored bras that flash around me. Wrapping my jumper around my waist, I move through the crowd. Warm flesh pushes against mine, most wet with sweat, and there is something freeing about it. Closing my eyes, I let the beat take over, and the vodka fully enters my blood stream.

When I open my eyes, Brian is there, and I smile as he wraps his strong arms around me. His mouth goes to my neck, and I wrap my arms around his neck, pulling him closer.

"I was searching for you," he whispers in my ear, and my smile widens.

"Yeah?" My one word slurs, dragging out the end of the word. I try to make myself more alert. But I'm cocooned in heat and bodies, and now Brian. I don't want the world to come back into focus. When his tongue finds its way into my mouth, I don't stop him, not even when the sizzle of something on my tongue reminds me of the last time I kissed him. I swallow the tablet, and when Brian moves away, and I allow the music and the drugs to take me.

Lights burn my eyes, and I move away. "Get up, Una." Brian is there. Why does my face sting? Grass is under my hands. The music pounds behind me. I must be outside. Lights are still shining, burning me.

"Knock off the headlights." Brian is shouting now, and the light vanishes.

My body bounces up and down. "Put her top on." I'm sure that's Darragh's voice. The vehicle moves under me. I can smell smoke, trying to sit up has me falling over, and someone laughs. I join in their laughter.

The car stops, and a door slams. "Hurry the fuck up." It's Darragh's voice again.

"Brian, put her top on. How many more times do I have to fucking say it." I'm dragged roughly off the floor of the car, and my stomach hurls.

"Open the door quick." I'm pushed out onto gravel as my stomach empties all over my hands.

"I'm so fucking dead." I'm not sure who's speaking now. And darkness moves in along the edges of my vision.

CHAPTER SEVEN

SHANE

It's one in the morning when I leave dad and Liam. I've informed them of everything I found out about the new supplier. Dad wants me to take a step back from it until we find out exactly who this person is. Anyone crossing over the border isn't someone we want to get tangled up in.

I can hear what he is saying, but to me, this is a different time, and we should attack first, not sit back and wait to be attacked first. This is our turf, and I wasn't letting it go. I didn't care about the cost. But we had more problems. It seemed to be coming from all sides. Liam was over all the brothels in the area, and there was a huge demand for virgins. Something we couldn't seem to meet. It wasn't my problem, and I was pretty confident that Liam was capable of handling it.

I find myself outside Una's door again, and a part of me knows I should stop this. I had hurt her so much today, and maybe that's all I would ever do to her. I rest my head against her door as I try to talk myself into going to bed. She's asleep now, and if I keep sneaking into her room, I will get caught. No matter the thoughts that go through my head, I find myself opening the bedroom door. I'm not sure how I feel when I see her bed made. She isn't here. Maybe she returned to reading her book. I needed to give her some space. I return to my own room and climb into bed.

I wake up and check my phone. It's four in the morning. I will kill Darragh. I climb out of bed and peer out the window. My room overlooks the courtyard. I see Darragh's car parked out back. Another one has arrived, the noise and rattles of a hole in the exhaust bangs away until they park. The people in the car climb out, and I get back into bed. Once they are all in the pool house, the noise disappears.

I'm out of bed again as my stomach tightens, and I find myself at Una's door, pushing it open. I curse. Her bed is empty. I return to my room and get on a t-shirt, jeans, and this time, I put on shoes and socks and make my way to the pool house. The closer I get, the clearer the noise of music and laughter is.

I open the door and am surprised to see Brian here with Darragh. Both of them cheer when they see me, like they've been awaiting my arrival. My eyes skim the two half-naked girls as I search for Una. Fear tightens like a fist in my stomach.

"Where is she?" I'm in front of Darragh, and it's taking everything not to kill him right now.

"Shane?" The bathroom door has opened, and Una is standing in the doorway. She tilts her head and furrows her brows in complete confusion at seeing me. My heart pounds in my chest as I take her in.

"I told you to put her top back on." My head snaps to Darragh, and with narrowed eyes I give him his last warning. If I don't leave now, I will kill him.

Everyone is silent.

"Put your clothes on," I tell Una quietly and stop
staring at her chest. It takes a lot of my will power.
Her eyes are dilating rapidly, and whatever she took
is still in her system. I'm not sure if she's heard me.
Her mouth moves like she's trying to form a word,
and I cross the room and pick her up. She gives a
little squeal as I carry her out of the pool house. The
air is cold on her bare skin, skin that I am trying not
to stare at.

But Una is lying back in my arms, her head thrown
back, and there is a smile on her face. But I don't
feel like smiling. I don't know what's happening to
her. She never was like this. She was outgoing, wild
in a way, but not going out and doing drugs. I won't
allow myself to think about why she is half dressed.
I can't.

"Brian." I tighten my grip on her as she calls his
name, and instead of thinking about her calling
another man, I keep moving forward. My sole focus
is on each step I take as I climb the stairs.

Una stirs, pulling herself closer to my chest as she
tightens her arms around my neck. I wish I could
take the steps two at a time. With her breath on my
neck and the soft flesh against any available skin I
have on display is driving me mad. I make it to the
landing when she speaks again after inhaling
deeply. "Shane." My pulse speeds up as she says

my name, and I shush her. Her chest vibrates with laughter.

"Still telling me what to do." She leans out so she can stare at me, and I'm surprised at how alert she is. Small marks are on her cheek, like she was scraped. I want to run my fingers along the area and remove the marks from her skin. I'm close to my room now, and I carry her into it.

"You won't listen, Una," I say back, and she smiles at me, her eyes staring at my lips.

"You're gorgeous, Shane."

I stop walking and stare at her, and for a moment, she's sober and knows what she is saying, and that's how she really sees me. But reality kicks in, and I snap my gaze away from her smiling face and carry her into my bathroom. She has her own in her room, but I haven't a clue where anything is.

I slowly lower her down onto the closed toilet, and she becomes intrigued with her surroundings. "Will you stay here for a second?" I ask her, and her eyes rest on me. She nods but doesn't speak. I quickly grab a t-shirt, and she is still sitting on the toilet when I come back in. She doesn't object as I carefully put it on her.

Her eyes never leave my face, and no one can make me unsettled as Una does. A smile grows on her face now as she reaches out and embraces my face. I'm frozen. "I've crushed on you for so long." The confession is said with a small laugh, and I want to hear this, but the drugs are making her talk crazy.

"Let me check your face," I say to her, leaning away from her hand so I can get some disinfectant wipes. She doesn't move. Her eyes flutter closed as I return.

I dab the area, and her eyes shoot open. "I'm sorry," I tell her as she bites her lip.

"You were untouchable to me. So out of my league." Once again, I focus on cleaning her face. She is distracting, and it's taking all my willpower not to listen to her words. She laughs softly again, and when I flicker my gaze to hers, her eyes are glistening.

"You'll just keep hurting me, and I'll keep letting you." I don't have a clue what she is talking about. But her eyes are filling up, and I'm not sure what to do.

"You need to wash your arms, Una," I tell her, and she nods. She seems more together, and I leave the bathroom and sit on my bed. I don't leave the bedroom in case she needs me.

Taking out my phone, I ring Finn. It's close to five in the morning, but he answers. "You need to get home and sort Darragh out," I tell him, expecting him to do as I say. What I don't expect is for Finn to say no. Now wasn't the time for him to grow a pair of balls.

"How would you like for me to reunite Siobhan with her Aunt?" I'm standing now because I don't need his back-talk. "I don't care about her. I'll make it so fucking slow. Now get your ass over here and sort Darragh out, and I want Brian off my property too." I hang up and sit back down. I need to calm down before I go down and sort it out myself.

The bathroom door opens, and my head snaps up. Una is standing there, one arm behind the door. She looks so good in my green t-shirt. That's all she's wearing now. She has removed the rest of her clothes. I swallow as my eyes drink in the sight of her. She's in my room, how many times had I fantasied about her. She takes a step towards me, and I grip the blanket under my hands. She isn't thinking straight, but I can't find the words to stop her as she advances towards me.

She reaches me, and I reach out settling my hands on her hips, stopping her from moving any closer. "Una, you don't want to do this," I tell her quietly. Her skin burns under my hands, and I'm losing the will power to stop this as she easily moves forward.

I release her as she straddles me. I keep my eyes closed at the contact and breathe her in.

"Una." I say her name as I grip the quilts. This is wrong, but her body this close to mine feels so right. When her hands grip my shoulders, I allow my eyes to reach hers.

"I want this Shane," she tells me.

My heart pounds, and I release the quilt and flip her around until she is under me. Her eyes are wide, her chest is moving quickly, and I'm waiting for her to say no. I'm searching her face for a sign that I need to stop this, but she reaches up and caresses my face, her body pushing against mine, and I can't stop the moan that escapes my lips.

Her hands direct my face closer to hers, and I can't stop staring at her. I can't stop this. I'm falling too deep, and I don't think I can climb back out. Her breath brushes against my lips, and everything in my body jerks. She will undo me, and I want her to, but not like this. When my forehead touches hers, I try to calm my pounding heart.

"Una," I say her name, and it's what gives me the strength to pull back. I remove her hands from my face, and already, I can see the damage my actions are causing.

I'm shaking my head searching for the right words. Her eyes grow wider, and her nostrils flare, and she's wriggling under me. "Let me up now." Her voice is rising, and I don't release her. She's too angry, and when she's angry, she seems to do stupid things.

"Let me up now, Shane. I'm going back to the party. Brian will give me what I want." I push her hands above her head, my anger at her words barely containable. The air is being sucked out of the room at her words. I'm searching her face, but she's grinning at me like this is one big fucking joke.

"What do you want?" I'm shouting at her now and her grin slips, but I can't figure her out. She wriggles, and I push my body harder against hers.

"You will answer me," I demand, and her eyes flare to life, and I know with Una I've pushed too hard. Now she will push back.

"Not this," she tells me, and I'm off her in a second, imagining what she must think of me.

"I'm sorry," I tell her. And I want to pull down my t-shirt so it covers her legs, but I don't dare move as she sits up on my bed.

She wraps her arms around her waist as if she has a pain in her stomach, and I take a step closer to her.

Her head whips up at my movement, and she raises a hand. "I'm going to bed. Don't you dare follow me." She rises, holds her head high and walks out of my room. I count to ten before I follow her. I check to make sure she does go into her bedroom. She slams the door. She has some temper. I don't know what to do. I can't stand in the hall all day and night and guard her. It's been a long time since I felt this close to snapping. I leave my room and make my way to the gym that's located in the basement. I need some sort of release, and violence will have to do.

CHAPTER EIGHT

UNA

I wake with a sore head, my cheek stings as I brush it off the pillow while turning. As I slowly sit up, I try to remember how I got to bed last night. My bedclothes send alarm bells ringing in my head. It's not that they are nonexistent. Instead, I'm in a man's t-shirt. I quickly snap my gaze to the left side of the bed, but no one is there. While hanging out over the bed, I scan the floor for anything to suggest what happened last night, but there are no clues.

Dancing at a rave. I remember that. Brian, now I groan. As I slowly begin to remember the rave, the car drive home. It's all foggy like a dream, but I know it happened. A squeal leaves me as I start to also remember Shane. "Nooooo," I cover my mouth trying to push last night's words back down my throat.

The burn of humiliation has me burying my head in my quilt. "Noooo," I growl into the quilt. I told him that I liked him. I said he was a God. I tried to seduce him. Right now I want my brain to short circuit. He turned me down. Oh God. This was humiliating. I could never face him again. I try to calm myself by taking deep breaths.

It's okay. I tell myself. He will avoid me like the plague. He won't want to be around a desperado. Oh God, I told him I wanted to sleep with him. I bury my head deeper in my blanket. The burn on my face isn't lessening. It's spreading to my whole body. I want to die. I think dying from humiliation is possible.

"Good morning." I freeze, holding my breath, and I hope I'm still remembering. I'm praying that Shane isn't the one saying good morning to me. I can't cope. I slowly raise my head and yelp when I raise my gaze up and he's standing in my bedroom. Shane is fresh and clean and gorgeous in tanned trousers and a black fleece jumper. I'm on fire with embarrassment.

"Can't you knock?" I shout while pointing at my door. I want him to disappear. I can't deal with this.

"I did, several times," he answers drily. My hands grip the end of the t-shirt that I'm twisting in knots under the quilt. Then I remember it's Shane's top, and I release it quickly as a new burn erupts across my face that travels all the way up to the tips of my ears.

"Fine, what do you want?" I want this to be quick. Like pulling off a bandage. I imagine an apology is in order for throwing myself at him, I hope not, but if it ends this torture, I am willing to consider it.

"You have work in thirty minutes. You've been slacking off since you arrived here. So you either meet me in the kitchen in fifteen, or you can pack your belongings and go home."

I'm stunned momentarily. What the hell is his game? He can't kick me out, and then I see he wants me to run home with my tail in between my legs. He might not like me, but I swallow the humiliation that burns through me. I keep eye contact as I throw the covers back and am glad when his jaw clenches. A reaction.

"I'll be down in fifteen," I tell him as I stroll past him. I'm not sure how the hell my legs are carrying me as I go into my wardrobe. It's there I tell myself to breathe as I gather fresh clothes with trembling hands. When I return, Shane is gone, and I let out a shaky breath.

***

As I enter the kitchen, I'm repeating a mantra in my head that Shane isn't there. But everything is working against me. He's there on his phone. My attention snaps to Mary who smiles at me, but it fades as her eyes roam my face. "What happened now, Una?" Shane clears his throat, and I keep my back to him.

"Me being drunk and stupid last night. I fell on the gravel." Mary inspects me closer, and I want to tell her to leave it, but she's always been a mammy to us when we are here. Well to some of us.

"You cleaned it out?" Shane clears his throat again, and I'm tempted to offer him a glass of water.

"Yes," is all I say before sitting down the furthest away from Shane as I can. I don't glance up to see if he is watching me. But I sense his eyes on me. His hands had been gentle cleaning my face last night. If I keep this up, I will be permanently red. I remind myself that I am stronger than this. So he turned me down. I needed to get over it already.

"Two fried eggs and one piece of bacon?" Mary asks once I'm seated.

"Yes, that's perfect, thanks Mary." She turns back to the pan, and I focus on the fixture and fittings of the kitchen.

It has every mod con a kitchen can have. An island that six people can sit at dominates the large space. A breakfast bar runs half the length of the kitchen separating the cooking area from the dining area, where I sit now. I'm a bit over-enthusiastic when

Finn arrives in, but sitting in silence with Shane is painful.

"Good morning, Finnbar. I haven't seen much of you," I say, and he grabs a banana and starts peeling it as he makes his way over to the table and sits beside me.

"Yeah, I've been busy." Shane clears his throat again, and Finn and I are on the same page as we both ignore him.

"What happened to your face?" He takes a huge bite of the banana as he speaks.

"What happened your face?" I throw back. Lord, it was a scratch.

He holds his hands up. "Hung-over are we?"

"Sorry, yeah, a bit. But don't tell anyone," I say with a grin, and he smirks.

"Where's your other half?" Now Finn isn't smiling.

"In bed sleeping off the mother of all hangovers."

"Are you not going to greet me, brother?" Shane asks as Mary places my breakfast in front of me. Everyone's attention falls on to Shane, and the tension in the room seems to grow. Mary shuffles back to the stove, and I start to eat. I'm not hungry, but I don't know what else to do.

"Why should I? You threatened Siobhan." Siobhan was Finn's new girlfriend, and from the sounds of it, their relationship was serious. But to hear that Shane threatened her has me raising an eyebrow at him. His jaw is clenched, and he flickers a glance at Finn and away from my questioning stare.

"Don't be so petty. It was a few words."

A vein is flickering like a heartbeat in Finn's neck. "No, it wasn't. You know what you said, and I'm not having it." Mary puts a fry in front of Finn, and he quickly thanks her.

"What are you going to do?" Shane is leaning forward, and there is something in his stance that tells me this is far more serious than it appears to be.

Finn has a death grip on his knife and fork. They appear as deadly weapons now. His nostrils flare as he stares down at Shane, and he looks like he wants to hurt him. But Shane's eyes are shining with violence. It's like he's excited at the idea of hurting Finn.

I want to defuse the situation, so I do the one thing I can think of. I knock my coffee over with a little more force than intended. I wanted to send the coffee pouring over the side, but the mug goes too, smashing into pieces on the floor. All eyes are on me now.

"Sorry, my hand slipped," I say getting up. Shane is staring at me, and I'm not sure if he's mad or what he is thinking.

"I'll get it. Una finish your breakfast." Mary is there with a cloth, but I start picking up pieces of the mug.

"Una, leave it alone before you cut yourself." Shane's words are barked at me, and I am close to losing it with him. I take the cloth off Mary. "Please, Mary, I'll clean it up." She gives me a nod before leaving me.

"Mary, clean it up." Shane stops her in her tracks, and I grind my teeth. He was controlling. I gather up the rest of the mug and stand.

"Mary, it's done. Seriously, it's fine." She's waiting for Shane's word, and he nods at her she goes back to the kitchen. I'm shaking my head in disgust at him, and I really want to throw the broken mug at him, but I can't. Michael picks that moment to enter the kitchen, and he smiles when he sees us all.

"Ah, I was wondering where everyone was." He stops me as I make my way to the bin and kisses the top of my head. When he sees the broken mug in my hand, he leans out. "Be careful you don't cut yourself."

"That's what I said," Shane chimes in from the corner like I'm some fragile little flower.

"I won't. It's a mug. Not a sword." Michael doesn't appreciate my smart mouth, but lets me pass as he sits down.

I'm ready to return to the table and eat my breakfast when Shane stands up all cheery. "Are you ready to start work, Una?" he asks me like we are best pals. I narrow my focus at my breakfast, and Shane flashes a glance at his watch. "If you need more time?"

I wave his comment away. I'm hungry, but I'll be dammed if I ask for more time. "No. I'm good to go."

"I'm very proud of you." Michael's words cause a swell to rise in my chest and deflate, leaving a sense of tightness behind. My father always told me he was proud of me. Weather I made a daisy chain or passed exams, he was there raising me up. Swallowing the lump, I tighten my lips before nodding.

"Thanks," I tell him and quickly leave the warmth of the kitchen. My mother never told me she was proud of me. If I really think about it, I was always a disappointment. I never stuck to anything, and she hated it.

She enrolled me in Irish dancing that lasted a week, drama class lasted a day. Football, ended up being the longest, lasting three months, but she pulled me from the team saying it was too boyish. Piano I hated, the violin, someone shoot me. I had tried many things, but I hated them all. The first time I fell in love with something was on my sixteenth birthday when Shane bought me the horse. The happy memory dissolves as Shane walks ahead of me in wellies.

"What are you doing?" I try to catch up with him. Panic is making me stand in his path.

"I'm going to work?" He walks around me, and I'm standing there stumped but soon catch up with him. Working with Shane today isn't a good idea. "I'm fine with Stephen, Shane. I seriously don't need you babysitting me."

"You needed me last night." His smart-ass words have me storming ahead of him.

"No I didn't. You needed me to need you last night. That's why you arrived like some avenging angel." I'm talking through my ass, but I haven't a clue what to do. When I look back at Shane, his jaw is clenched like I've really hit a nerve, and I think, *good*.

I check the area, but can't see Stephen. I start to call him but get no answer.

"I told him he could have the day off," Shane informs me. When I flicker a gaze at him, he's leaning against the wall staring at me as I run around like a headless chicken.

"So what, you're working with me today?" Now he smirks, and it isn't a nice one.

"No you're working. I'm overseeing." I could walk away as this was just a game to him, but I had my pride, and I wasn't afraid of work. I get my gloves on and start at the first stable. Wheeling up the barrow, I then leave it outside the stable as I shovel it out. Once I have that done, I fill it with fresh straw and remove any strands of loose straw from the drinking sink in the corner.

Shane does as he promises. He watches me, or oversees things, as he put it. I remove my jacket as I get to the fifth stall and start again.

"What is your job?" I ask him. May as well have someone to talk to. The farm brings in most of their income, but when I really think about it, I never see any of the boys around the farm working.

"The family business." Shane's answer captures my attention, and I stop working and rest on the shovel. I push hair out of my face. I had tied it up, but some curls have managed to burst free and find their way into my eyes.

"Which is the what? The farm? I never see you do any work." Shane is staring at me now. It's unsettling, but I hold my ground firmly.

"We have other businesses," he answers, and I can see this will be like trying to get blood from a stone. I return to work.

"It wouldn't be exactly above-board." Now I narrow my eyes at Shane. His look of innocence causes a smile of surprise to spread rapidly across my face.

"An upstanding citizen like you, Shane? Never." I joke, and his lips tug up, sending my stomach erupting with butterflies. Butterflies that I want to crush under my wellies. They have no business being here anymore. That ship has sailed.

"I don't think you would approve, Una, if you knew." He lowers his lashes as he speaks, but his smile is gone, and I'm taking a step closer to him. Now I want to know.

"Maybe I will," I tell him seriously, and his lashes rise. He's studying me carefully, making an assessment to find out how serious I am.

"Let's just say it isn't legal." His answer has me rolling my eyes.

"That's just like saying it isn't above-board. It means the same thing. So, what, all of you work in the unsavory business section?" I do unsavory with air quotes, and Shane smiles at me.

"You could say that," he answers.

"I could say a lot of things," I mumble under my breath and return to work, but from his soft laugh, he has heard me.

"We need to talk about last night." That is the last thing I want to talk about.

"No, we don't," I tell him. I glance up as the straw crunches behind me.

"We do," he says way too close to me, and I need to save face. I take a deep breath and turn around. My pulse spikes at his closeness.

"I had too much drink on me. I have needs, and you where there." Heat rushes across my face, but I hold eye contact.

"That's all it was?" he questions, and I can hear the control in his words. I'm searching his face. My heart is ready to leave my chest.

"I don't know why you came down there and got me. I can't make sense of it." I turn the whole thing on him, hoping to deflect from my embarrassing behavior.

"You had no idea where you were. You were half naked, Una. Hanging out with a bunch of low-lifes." He stuffs his hands in his fleece pockets roughly like if he doesn't, he might strangle me.

"I'm sorry you don't approve of who I hang out with. But let me remind you that one of those low-lifes is your brother, and Brian is nice." Okay, that last part was a lie, but I could see it was winding him up.

"Brian is nice? He's a scumbag. You should be thanking me for coming down there and getting you."

I laugh with anger. "Or what, Shane? God forbid I enjoyed myself."

"With Brian? You were mumbling his name." I want to wipe the smirk off his face.

"I was mumbling lots of stupid things." I'm breathing heavy, and I don't want this conversation anymore. I go to leave, but Shane stands in my way. His hands are now lost at his side. When I raise my lashes and gaze up at him, I can see he is working a muscle in his jaw. He's no longer smiling.

"Did you mean anything you said?" His brows are furrowed, and there is something vulnerable in how he is looking at me. My heart kicks up a notch, and I'm confused now. I'm not sure if I want to hurt him, or be honest. But being honest seems to lead to one road, and that's hurt.

"I was just looking for some fun." He lowers his lashes and gives a quick nod before he peers back up. His brown eyes appear almost black as he stares at me.

"It's lunch time," he tells me, and I stare after him as he walks back towards the house. Something is sitting on my chest, and I can't breathe. Drops land on my cheek. I'm crying. I stay in the stall and cry. I'm not sure why, exactly. It wasn't like he cared. *So why did he look so hurt?* But God damn it, he hurt me.

CHAPTER NINE

UNA

I'm not a girl who cries over boys. This isn't me. But deep down, I know this is more than a crush. This has been years in the making. I didn't think it would end like this. Tears keep falling without my permission, and I wipe them away angrily. I leave the stables and make my way to the ones that the livestock are being held in. There, I find my horse. She's not as jumpy, and she lets me rub her straight away.

"Una." I inwardly scream leave me alone. But it's Finn, and Finn is sweet. I pop my head out of the stall. "I'm here," I tell him with a smile. His eyebrows dip. "Are you okay?"

Ah shit. He can see I've been crying. "Yeah, I got some dung in my eye," I tell him with a wave of my hand. But the O'Reagans are always hands on, and Finn is holding my face. He's taller than me; all the boys are, so he's looking into my eye.

"Don't blink," he tells me while stretching my eye slightly, and I can't stop blinking.

"I don't see anything," he says but still hasn't released me.

"Must be gone," I tell him, and he steps back.

I rub my eye to add to my story. "Yeah, it's a bit sore, but I think I'm good."

He smiles now. "I thought, for a second, Shane had upset you. He has a habit of doing that."

"I see that. He sure upset you," I say closing the stall. "When am I going to get to meet Siobhan?" I add before looking at him. I don't want to talk about Shane and me. Our names being uttered in the same sentence does something funny to my heart.

"Soon, I hope. We will organize something."

I smile genuinely now. "I'd really like that."

"I've been sent out to get you for dinner."

"I'm not hungry."

Finn shrugs apologetically. "Dad's orders." Well, I couldn't say no to Michael.

When we arrive in the house, I wash up before going to the main dining room where everyone is sitting. A seat is vacant in between Shane and Liam the seat is pulled out for me already. I sit down with dread as I face Darragh who winks at me. Michael nods in approval, and Mary starts to bring in steaming plates of dinner.

"How's your eye?" Finn asks, and I want to kick him for directing all attention on me.

"What happened?" Shane the caveman is sitting forward, looking ready to start a war.

"My eye is fine, Finn. Thanks so much for asking." He gives me an apologetic smile at my sarcastic tone.

"I leave you for ten minutes, and something happens?" I turn to Shane, because I can't believe his attitude.

"Yes, you're right, Shane. Where would I be without my knight in shining armor? I suppose you would have deflected the lump of dung and stopped it from hitting my eye." Darragh snorts, and Liam shifts beside me. I turn to him, and I could swear Liam's eyebrow rose slightly, but I could be wrong. Shane on the other hand, was angry. His face was tight, and he gives me a quick nod.

"There's no need for such hostility," Michael says, and I remember my manners and that I'm in someone else's home, and fighting with his son wasn't nice. Michael isn't looking at me. He looks at everyone as he speaks. But his words are for me. I am being hostile.

"I'm sorry, Michael. I'm tired and cranky," I say against every fiber in my body, and Michael seems pleased. Mary has set a plate in front of everyone, and when I stare forward, Darragh is still smiling and mouths "Woman's things" to me. I give him a glare of pure disgust.

Michael says a short prayer to God over the food before we start eating. I'm starving, and the roast dinner is divine. I pour more gravy over my spuds, and when I glance up, Michael is smiling. "Nothing as nice as seeing a girl *really* eat."

I smile at him, not sure if that was really a compliment. I dig back in to my food when he returns to his. Shane's arm keeps brushing off mine, and I flicker a quick glance at him. His face is serious, but his movements seem intentional.

"Your mother rang," Michael kicks off, and I freeze. My fork held in mid- air. My eyes shoot to Darragh, then to Finn, as they glance at me and then at Michael. I put the fork in my mouth and chew the food that has turned to lead.

"She's worried about you," Michael continues. Now I'm questioning if this is what the dinner was about. And she was no more worried about me. She was worried about what the neighbors would think when

I wasn't around. Or what my work must be saying since I never arrived in. Or what college was saying. That's what she cared about, not me.

I pour more gravy over my food. "Anyone want some?" I offer. Darragh and Finn are shaking their heads, trying not to make eye contact with me. Like I might freak out any second. I offer some to Liam, and he meets my eye. "Please. Just on the carrots." Odd. But okay. I pour until he tells me to stop. I don't want to turn to Shane and Michael, but I have to.

"Gravy?" I ask Shane, and his eyes have softened for the first time since he left me in the stables. I don't need his pity. He nods his head, and I pour nearly half the jug over Shane's food.

Michael is peering up at me, and I hate it. I don't offer him gravy. I hate that he brought her up. He was married to her. He divorced her because he knew how she was.

No one speaks to me again as I finish my dinner. But a nice flow of conversation takes over the table. It's about cars, but it's really soothing to hear the boys getting on. Even Liam chimes in, and I try not to stare at him when he laughs. It's not a huge laugh, but it's not a sound I've heard before.

Shane eats his dinner that's soaked in gravy. It must be stomach turning, but he never complains, and I start to shift in my sit at every forkful that enters his mouth. I'm angry because he turned me down. He didn't deserve my anger. I try to cheer up as the dessert arrives. It's pavlova and strawberries with cream, and this meal is looking like my favorite food. The lump in my throat is back.

"I bought a bike over the summer," I offer up, trying to join in the conversation.

"With like pedals?" Finn says, and I laugh at him. Darragh snorts too, and Shane shakes a little beside me.

"You are so funny. No, with an engine." Now the room grows serious, and I don't need a lecture about safety.

"I have a helmet," I add, and laughter erupts around the table.

"I bet it's a moped," Darragh offers up, and he laughs harder.

"No, it's a scooter," Finn teases.

When I glance up at Michael, he's really smiling. I join the laughter. I love seeing him happy.

"Is it running?" The serious question comes from Liam, and I turn to him.

"No, I was saving up to restore it. But I will get it running," I tell him, and he gives me a nod of what looks like approval. "What make is it?" Liam was being quite the conversationalist. I was surprised.

Mary arrives in with teas and coffees, and I thank her before answering. "It's a Honda. Really sweet. It needs a few parts, a bit of a paint job, and it should be good to go."

"Shane's really good with engines." Darragh gives up this information, and when I glance at Shane from under my lashes, my stomach tightens.

"If you want, I can check it out." My pulse spikes at how he's looking at me.

"Yeah. That would be great," I tell him. This could be a peace offering on both ends.

"I might get a bike too. We can ride together." I laugh now at Darragh.

"You'd be dead in a day," Finn tells him. "How many cars have you gone through?" Finn adds.

"A few." Darragh shrugs now. Like it's no big deal.

"Try six. I know, because I pay for them."
Michael's words have my mouth dropping open.

"Six!" I'm staring at Darragh now. "You are so spoilt," I tell him.

"You bought Finn a house. No one's shouting about that." Darragh is firing back at his dad.

There is an odd silence around the table. But my mind is finding this conversation crazy. He bought Finn a house. What dad does that?

"I bought you one, too," Michael says before taking a fork full of dessert.

I follow suit taking a bite of dessert. Darragh's face turns slightly red. Now I question why they live here, if they both have houses. And if they do, there is no doubt that Liam and Shane have their own homes. But this house was enchanting. I would live here, too.

"You are all spoilt," I say before shoveling a fork full of the most delicious pavlova ever in my mouth.

"I'm glad someone said it." I grin at Michael, and we finish our desserts. I don't want to leave. Michael chats about his first car, and I love listening to old times. Liam excuses himself and then Finn. Darragh isn't far after leaving me with Shane and Michael.

"Do you still have the car?" I ask, wanting to see it. It sounded like something from the movies.

"I do. I'll show it to you some day."

I'm smiling. I have a love for old things. I don't know exactly why, but I do. Shane hasn't said much beside me, and I glance at him to find him watching me with a soft smile on his handsome face. "I wasn't aware you had a love for old cars."

"Yeah, I've always loved Cadillacs and Pontiacs, cars like that."

"You're so like your mother." The softness in Michael's voice surprises me. But I don't like the comparison. I also don't want to spoil the evening.

"She liked cars?" I ask, and Michael laughs.

"No, she wouldn't be able to tell one car from the other. No, her passion for life. When she talked about something she loved, she would light up, and so do you."

The compliment has me blushing.

"She's a good woman."

I can now see where this is going. "Is that why you divorced, because she is such a good woman?" I can't help the scratchy tone to my voice.

Michael lowers his spoon, and already, I want to apologize, but he speaks. "No, your mother and I weren't compatible. That doesn't make her a bad woman, Una." Michael daps his face with a cloth napkin before excusing himself.

"Sometimes, I don't know what's wrong with me," I say to the almost empty table. I'm waiting for Shane to leave, but he doesn't.

"I think you're hurting." I glance at him sideways, and he is staring me.

"I think so, too." I whisper the truth, and a lump forms in my throat.

"Do you want to talk about it?" There is a gentleness in his tone that nearly undoes me.

"No, yes." I laugh. "I'm not sure."

CHAPTER TEN

SHANE

I wait, not speaking, allowing her to make up her own mind. I want her to tell me. I want to know every part of Una, but I won't rush her. She's staring down at her coffee cup, and I take in the beauty of her face. Her lashes lift, and I'm looking into her eyes. My stomach squeezes.

"My looks come from my dad," she says with a sadness tugging at her voice and eyes. She pulls a curl and lets it bounce back. I'm picturing a male version of Una, and I try to imagine her with him.

"He got it, you know. He got how it felt to look different." Now she angles her hand at her eyes.

"He must have been very handsome," I say, and she smiles sweetly. Her head dips, and she rests her face on her hand. She smiles. "I think he was," she tells me. The sadness is still there, but she's smiling.

She glances away and licks her lips, and her brows pull down. She's so close to crying. "I miss him," she tells the floral wallpaper. I want to reach for her, comfort her, but I wait until she looks at me again.

"What happened?" I asked. I knew her dad had died when she was young, but I never knew how.

"It was a freak accident. A tree had fallen, blocking the road. My dad being my dad, tried to clear it." One free tear falls, but she doesn't stop talking as I follow a tear as it drops off her chin and onto the table. "Another fell and killed him."

"I'm sorry," I whisper the words, knowing right now to her they are meaningless, but she takes my hand in hers. "It's a long time ago, and I know you lost too. With your mum." I'm nodding, but all the blood has rushed to my hand where she touches me, and I allow myself to touch her back. I rotate my hand until our fingers line up, and I entwine them. Una sits back, slightly startled, but she doesn't pull away.

"Yeah, that should have never happened," I tell our entwined fingers. My mother was far too young to die.

"Did they ever find out?" I glance up at Una now, my focus on her lush lips. She licks them, and my attention is taken with her pink tongue.

When it disappears back into her mouth, I speak. "No. But we will." I stare at her. "I will," I add. My mother had been murdered in a drive-by shooting. She was in the wrong place at the wrong time. But even so, I still wanted to find whoever did it and kill them myself.

Una's focus is on our twined fingers, and when I glance down, I find myself smiling. "My mother bought me that ring. She said when she saw it, it was very Shane." My smile widens as I gaze up to see Una smiling at me. "I've never taken it off. I never would." Una's head lowers, and my body stills as her lips graze the band on my thumb. Her lips make contact my flesh, and I wait for her to sit back up.

"I wish I had met her," she says, but my mind is reeling from the kiss to my thumb.

"She would have loved you." I'm searching her face, knowing I speak the truth.

"Sorry, I was just… I thought you were on your own." Darragh has entered the room, but he pauses and goes to leave and then turns back around. I release Una's hand, and she stands quickly like we've been caught doing something wrong.

"I better get back to work," she says, not meeting my eye. She squeezes Darragh's shoulder as she leaves. It's a simple touch, but I don't like her touching anyone else.

"You have my attention now," I tell Darragh. He hesitates at the door. "You're wasting my time, Darragh. Come in," I tell him. Even looking at him makes me want to hurt him.

"It's okay," he tells me, turning back towards the door.

"Close the door and sit down now." I push the mug and plate away from me as Darragh closes the door. I don't need any temptations. I even move my chair away from the table and pull up one of my legs onto the other to create some kind of barrier.

"I'm having a…" I cut him off. "Don't sit there," I tell him as he goes to sit down on Una's chair.

"Where would you like me to sit?" He shakes his head as he speaks, and I point at the chair opposite me. He sits down with a huff.

"You kill people, and you don't seem to care," he says, anger lacing every word.

"Is that a question?" I ask, because I'm not sure what he is doing here.

"No." he grits his teeth and shifts on the chair. "I can't sleep."

I release my leg. "Go to a doctor." I'm done with this conversation.

"I can't sleep, because I keep seeing her face." He swallows, and his brows pull down.

"Whose face? What have you done?" I sit forward questioning what kind of mess I will have to clean up now.

"Siobhan's aunt. I keep seeing her face. It doesn't seem to matter how much drink I consume. She's still there. Her head is all smashed in. Blood bubbles from her mouth."

The sad part is, I understand how he feels. I have to live with nine lives I took or helped take. At night, they come for me. Darragh rubs his neck. It's now I notice the strain on his face, the bloodshot eyes from lack of sleep. He's thinner than before. I hadn't noticed until now.

"You need to find your peace with her."

His head snaps up. "How?" The way he asks is like I have some secret ingredients that will make all this go away. But it's not that simple. I think about what I do to survive. If it becomes a question of me or them, it's an easy one to pick.

"Think about why you killed her. You need to remind yourself that she attacked." I wanted to say it was a life or death situation, but with Darragh, I didn't think it was. I was pretty sure he lost control.

"She didn't attack me." The confession pours from him quickly. "I wanted to know how it felt. I wanted to be like you and Liam. I wanted…"

I stand up, closing my eyes and cutting him off. I can't believe what I'm hearing. "You wanted to know how taking someone's life felt." Oh God, this was much worse than I could have imagined. I had always known that it hadn't been self-defense, and that was disturbing enough. But to think he did it so he knew how it felt.

"Yes and I wanted to be accepted by Dad." He's shouting, and I can't stop the laughter that bubbles from my mouth.

"How did it feel, baby brother? Hmmm did you enjoy taking her life?" I ask when the laughter dies down.

"Fuck off," he tells me getting up to leave.

"You're a coward. I'm ashamed to call you my brother." My words have him pausing, but he rips the door open and storms from the room. I should stay and let him go, but I can't.

"You couldn't even finish her, Darragh." He pauses now. The rise and fall of his shoulders is heavy. "Once again, me and Liam had to clean up your mess. You couldn't even kill an old woman." I was jagging him. I wanted him to face what he had done. He turns with clenched fists.

"Shut up. I'm glad I'm not a killer like you. How many lives have you taken?" He starts walking back to me. "Who tattoos themselves every time they take a life?" he continues when he's reached me we are toe to toe.

"You wear your kills like a fucking badge." He's screaming now.

"Darragh." It's Liam. Darragh deflates straight away. He doesn't step away from me. He's huffing and puffing.

"Darragh." Liam's raised voice has Darragh stepping away. "Leave." Liam's one word has him racing down the hall. Liam takes a few steps towards me. "What has he done?"

"He killed that woman just to kill her." Even as I speak, the words, I'm struggling to accept that he really did that. Taking a life was down to a final decision. It was either you or them. That's how I always say it. There were no half measures, and in our line of business, people died. But each one had a reason. To have none, I couldn't imagine it.

"You have to leave this alone, Shane." I snap my gaze up to Liam, and I don't expect him to start shouting, but his easy words have me shaking my head.

"What do you do when he kills someone else, and then the bodies are stacking up?"

"He won't." Liam sounds sure.

"He killed, Liam, just to know how it felt." When Liam looks at me, there is something in him that I don't recognize, and now I ponder if that is what he and Darragh have in common. Did Liam recognize the darkness in Darragh that I see in Liam? I could never tell what it was, but what if it was this?

"Have you ever killed for no reason?" I ask, not backing away from this. I need to know who I'm sleeping under the same roof with.

"No. But I've been curious."

"I've been curious when I heard older men talk about it. I wondered what it would be like. I didn't go out and actually do it. I'm curious about a lot of things, Liam. It doesn't mean I act on them." I can't believe he would try to dismiss this.

"It is our fault that he's like this."

"I feel like you've put two and two together and got 50," I tell Liam, not accepting what I'm hearing.

"We have always pushed him away, and this is our price." I glance down the hall that Darragh had disappeared down.

"We treat Finn worse, and he hasn't killed anyone for the fun of it."

"We don't know that." Liam blinks now as Mary makes her way down the hall.

"Leave it with me. Let me deal with it," he asks as we stand shoulder to shoulder facing each other. I always place my trust in Liam, but I wasn't sure I could let this one lie. I nod at Liam, and he nods back before leaving.

The smell of fresh air is nice. I still can't shake off what Darragh has done. Flaming red hair comes into view. I needed to check on Una. I hated it more now that she hung out with Darragh. What if he got an impulse again, only this time it was Una he hurt? Something sits on my chest, and I breathe in through my nose and out through my mouth.

"Hi." Una is waving at me, while she leans on a pitchfork, and her voice settles me, the weight lifting off my chest.

"Hi," I say and walk toward her while stuffing my hands in my pockets. It gets them out of the cold, but it's also something to do as Una smirks while she studies me. I was aware of myself.

"Just wanted to check on you," I say when I reach her, and her smirk turns into a full smile.

"Make sure I'm doing my work?" she teases.

"No. I wanted to make sure you where okay after our conversation." Her smile slips, but her eyes still hold it.

"That's really sweet of you."

I give a short laugh. "Sweet. I don't think anyone has ever called me sweet before."

Una is trying to suppress a smile, but she fails. We are smiling at each other when my phone rings.

"Just give me a second," I say as I pull it out of my pocket and see Neill's name on the screen.

"Go ahead," I tell him as I take a few steps away from Una, not wanting her to hear the conversation.

"At a fight last night, one of the guys dropped dead. I knew he was off his head. But I thought it was cocaine or something. It's that new stuff from Bernard." I was starting to question where this was going. "And I managed to get some for you," Neill says proudly, and he should be.

"I'll be around soon to pick it up," I tell him before hanging up. Una is still observing me and wears a smile on her face.

"My mind is still reeling with you calling me sweet," I say because I want her to continue to smile. This time she laughs.

"I regret saying it already. I think your ego is big enough Shane."

"Tá tú go hálainn," I say in Irish because I'm too much of a chicken to say it in English. But I realize my mistake when Una turns red and repeats my words to me in English.

"You think I'm beautiful?" Why does she sound like she doesn't believe me?

"Now I think our egos are the same," I tell her and something crosses her face. She doesn't focus on me now as she speaks. "You said that for my ego." I can hear the hurt in her words, and I question why everything I say comes across as an insult.

I take a step toward her, and she tilts her head up. Her eyes shift left and then to the right. I keep my focus on Una. "I said that because I do think you are very beautiful." She smiles but covers her mouth with a gloved hand.

My heart pounds as I remove the shovel from her hands and place it against the wall. Una's hands fall to her side, but I take up the right one and remove her work glove. Raising her hand to my mouth, her eyes are wide and her mouth has formed a small O as I place a kiss to the inside of her wrist.

Her pulse beats quickly against my lips, and it satisfies me that I have evoked that emotion in her. I want to linger longer, kissing her flesh is sending waves through my body. But I tell myself not yet. I stand up straight and put her glove back on. She's still focused at me with pure awe on her face, and I want to kiss her lips, I find myself leaning in, and she swallows hard before wetting her lips.

A horse neighs a few stalls down, and Una clears her throat.

"I have to go. I might see you later," I tell her, and she nods. She doesn't smile but stands watching me leave. I glance back at her, and she's still staring at me, and now I smile.

***

I wish I didn't have to go. I ring Neill back as I make my way to my car. He answers on the second ring.

"I need a job done. Are you up for it?" I ask him and smile when he repeatedly says yes. I remember now why I liked him.

"I need that stuff sent up to Dublin. I've a friend Rachel who works in the Dublin lab. She'll expect you in one hour. Can you do that?" I ask.

"Yeah, of course, man. No problem. Consider it done." Neill's answer is quick. But I wouldn't consider anything done until it was done.

"I'll text you the address," I tell him and hang up. I need to see what's in this new drug, and if we can replicate it, hopefully cheaper than what Bernard is selling it for.

Once I text him, I get into my car and visit some old friends to see if they have heard anything about Bernard or Connor. But all avenues turn out to be dead ends. No one seems to know anything. To me, that is worse than someone knowing something. It means they are being careful. Careful people are dangerous people in my eyes. They have something to hide.

***

I return home to a dark house. It's two in the morning when I get inside and make my way to Una's room. She's asleep, and I can't stop the smile when I see she's wearing my t-shirt. I don't stay long tonight. Instead, I go to my room and take a quick shower before getting into bed.

I get up around nine and get dressed. Pushing open Una's door, I'm surprised to see her bed made, and her window is open. Mary comes out of the bathroom, surprise lights up her face.

"Shane." She says my name like she expects an explanation.

"Mary," I say back, and she quickly looks away.

"Are you looking for Una?" Her question is said as she polishes the windowsills.

"Why, is this Una's room?"

She narrows her eyes at me over her shoulder. "Yes."

"Since you are keeping records of Una's whereabouts, where is she?" I can see the further annoyance in her eyes, but she shields them, letting her lids close. When she opens her eyes again, she's better composed.

"She's at work, Master Shane." I'm done talking to her; I leave and make my way down stairs. The smell of freshly baked scones in the kitchen makes me pause, but I don't linger. Instead, I grab my wellies and jacket and go in search of Una.

I don't have to search very hard. She's in the yard with Stephen. I dare him to look at me funny. Today, he decides to ignore me, and that suits me fine.

"I got quite the shock when your room was empty this morning," I tell her, and she looks up from brushing one of the horses. It's cold this morning, and the tip of her nose is red. Our breaths come out in small white puffs, but Una is alive now. The outdoors really suits her.

"You know I'm thinking of getting a lock put on my door," she tells me, but her words are soft.

I lean across the stall door. "Why? You already have a perfectly working lock on your door," I tell her.

"Yeah, but it's funny there isn't a key? I can't find it anywhere." That's because I took it. But I don't tell her that.

"That is funny," I say, and she smirks.

"So why are you looking for me this morning?" She rubs the horse while she speaks. I'm not even sure she knows what she is doing.

"I was thinking after dinner, we could take a look at that bike of yours?"

She stops rubbing the horse. "Yeah. Yeah that would be so great." She's smiling, and I love that I put it on her face.

"It's a date," I say, and a laugh falls from her lips as she quirks an eyebrow.

"A date?" she questions.

"You know what I mean. I'll mark it in my diary," I tell her with a serious tone.

"Nope, that's not what you said. You said a date." She's unsure if I'm joking or not.

"Oh…" She lets out a heavy breath. "I'd need you to help me get it." She sounds miserable, and I'm not sure why.

"It's at my parents' house," she volunteers, and now I get it.

"I'll be there with you." I hope my words comfort her, and she focuses on the horse and then ground before looking back at me. She's chewing her lip, and I don't push but wait for her answer.

CHAPTER ELEVEN

UNA

I agreed to let Shane come with me. I've braided my hair to the side. My eyes rise in the mirror, and I hate what I see. Pulling out the restricting neckline of the black polo jumper doesn't help. I appear professional, presentable, as my mother would put it.

I'm wearing black trousers and a pair of small-heeled boots. I'm ready to walk into an office. Grabbing my black long coat, I go downstairs to find Shane in the kitchen. The moment I enter, he raises both eyebrows.

"You look..." he starts, but I roll my eyes.

"Stuck up. Stiff." I could think of a few more names.

"Older," Shane offers.

"Oh," I say as he stands up and stuffs his phone in his pocket. After getting into his car, I put on my seatbelt and try not to touch everything. I open the glove compartment and have a look in. Shane glances at me but doesn't say anything. Instead, he backs out of the garage as I continue to have a nosy.

He has chewing gum, tissues, and a pack of wipes in his glove compartment. The middle pocket holds two phones. I glance at him, and he's focused on driving out into the courtyard. There is nothing really in his car. But it's a few months old.

I wait as he gets out and has Stephen help him attach an Ivor Williams trailer to the back of the Audi. Placing my hand on my, leg, I stop it from jangling. When Shane gets back in, I don't look at him but stare out the window.

"You should know you're not walking into a friendly environment," I quickly tell him. Already thinking of how wrong this could go. Shane shifts gears.

"I'm used to hostile environments."

I know he is, but still. "My mother can have a wicked tongue," I say, looking at him.

He glances at me with a smirk. "I remember."

I laugh at that. Of course he remembers. How could he forget my mother? "I don't know why she disliked you so much," I say more to myself.

"Most women dislike me." He sounds sure.

"I don't," I say honestly. His gaze flickers to mine, and I hold his stare until he looks back at the road.

"I knew you fancied me," he says, and I laugh, like proper laugh, and it's nice.

"You don't fancy me?" he questions my laughter while trying to appear wounded, but he isn't, and I know this is my chance.

"I told you before that I did." His eyes dart from the road to me.

"I wasn't sure if that was the drink."

"It was all me," I tell him. My heart is pounding.

He nods his head. "That's good to know," he says, and I smile at the window.

My smile is short-lived as we arrive at my house. My mother's red car is parked in the driveway, and all my hopes of her not being home are dashed. Shane hasn't even knocked off the engine when she's out the door, and I can see it in her eyes that she's livid.

My mother is still attractive in her late fifties. High cheekbones and full lips are still her best features. Her hazel eyes also show her emotions easily, and I know I'm in a lot of trouble.

"Stay in the car," I quickly tell Shane as I jump out. My mother stares at Shane before her head snaps to me.

"How could you? Do you know how worried I was?" She folds her arms over her white shirt.

"I needed to get away," I tell her. My voice is small.

Her hands rise in the air, and she shakes her head while jutting out her chin. "Una does what Una wants, be damned everyone else."

"No. I'm sick of doing what everyone wants," I say.

My mother glares at Shane again before turning back to me. "Get in the house." She's pointing at the front door, before she folds her arms again, and I deflate. Sadness has me stepping closer to her, I don't want to fight, but I want her to see me as I am. I want my mother to see *me*, not an extension of her.

"I'm not staying," I whisper with a pleading in my voice that she ignores. She moves around me and is banging on Shane's window.

He's staring at her. Her banging isn't necessary.

"Mum, what are you doing?" I'm beside her. "Get in the house, Una," she says again as Shane rolls down the window.

"I don't' know what she told you, but you can go on home now. My daughter is staying here with me." My cheeks and neck burn, and anger replaces my sadness as Shane addresses my mother in a tight tone.

"It's up to Una what she wants to do, Niamh. She's a woman now." My mother moves back from the window like he slapped her. Her eyes widen with some realization, and she lets out a bitter laugh.

"A woman? Is that what you have been filling my daughter's head with?"

I was a woman, but I can read between the lines and understand what my mother was implying. Mortified took on a whole new meaning for me. Before either Shane or me can respond, my mother swings around towards me. "I pray that you haven't been near Liam. Tell me you haven't?" Why does she look stricken?

"Mum, what are you talking about? God, you sound crazy." My anger snaps, and Mum takes a step back.

"I can't stop you, Una. But that family isn't right."
She's pointing at Shane, but he doesn't as much as
flinch.

"They are good to me," I tell her pleading again not
wanting us to part on such bad terms. "You
belonged to it once. You raised me with them. I
don't understand," I tell her, and I have no
understanding why my words deflate her.

"You've come to get your stuff." She sounds
resigned to that fact, but when I tell her I'm here for
my bike, hope blossoms in her eyes. "I need some
space," I tell her, but she shakes her head in disgust.

Folding her arms again she shrugs. "I'm here when
you come to your senses." She doesn't look at me as
she walks back into the house.

***

I undo my hair, letting the curls free; they bounce
around my face and shoulders like they rejoice in
their freedom. Shane had loaded my bike into the
trailer. I am not sure where we are going now, and
honestly, I didn't care. My mother's coldness was
cutting me deeper than I expected.

I glance at Shane, but he grips the steering wheel,
his face tight. Yeah, he's pissed. Maybe even at me
for having him sit there as my mother scolded him

like he was a child. I want to apologize, but I don't. I sit back and stare out the window at all the passing trees.

When Shane pulls up at the biggest store in Monalty, I'm tempted to tell him to leave it. But he has taken time out of his day to help me. I unbuckle my belt.

Shane's hand covering mine stills me, and I gaze up at him. "Are you okay?"

I'm looking into soft brown eyes. Flecks of gold seem to move, and I swallow. Was I okay? I wasn't sure.

"I will be."

I'm still staring into his eyes, and my body moves closer towards his. The heat of his hand on mine is sending warmth up my arm.

It's Shane who breaks away, his eyes snapping forward.

"You better get started," he says, trying to sound happy, but the strain in his voice is the opposite of happy. I'm still looking at him, confused at his change again. I was beginning to think that Shane O' Reagan, hadn't his mind for a minute or was playing games with me.

Either way, it wouldn't end well for me. I climb out and close the door with more force than necessary. I don't turn to check if he follows. Instead, I walk right into the store. The bell behind me rings, and I know Shane is in. He's beside me in a second.

"You want to tell me what's wrong?" he whispers close to my ear, his shoulder brushing mine.

I'm not doing this here. "Why would anything be wrong?" I ask him sweetly.

"Can I help you with anything?" A tall man, he must be over seven feet tall, approaches us. His voice is droll, and his nametag reads John.

"Yes," I say the same time Shane barks no. John departs like a sensible human being, but I'm pissed that he listened to Shane and not me.

"There is clearly something wrong," Shane offers through gritted teeth, and I smile sweetly again while blinking several times.

"You are mistaken." I walk off again with no idea where I am going, and Shane clicks his fingers while calling John over. It's disgusting.

He rhymes off everything I need, and John makes a joke that a new bike would make more sense.

"Una, can I purchase you a new bike?" Shane asks, but he isn't looking at me.

"Of course not," I bite back.

"See," he says to John as if to say I'm awkward.

"I'll get my parts another time," I tell John and leave the store. I can't do this right now with Shane. I'm at the car when I realize it's locked. Glaring back at the store changes nothing. I can't see in, but the Audi unlocks with a click. I climb in and wait for Shane. He comes out, and John is behind him with a trolley of all the parts. I'm shaking my head as Shane gets in.

"I told you I would get them another time." I was never going to get them all at once.

"We are here now," he says while buckling his belt.

I want to scream. "Why don't you listen to me?" When I narrow my eyes at Shane, I'm surprised to see him smiling. "You are very sexy when you're mad."

My mouth opens and closes like a bloody gold fish. I have no words. Secretly, I'm smiling, but I stare out the window and don't show it to him.

***

When we arrive home, Shane drops me off at the front door. I don't argue. I want to get out of these clothes. Entering the house, I pause on the third step. The sound of laughter and a strange voice has me walking towards the kitchen where I find Finn and a girl who is fabulous-looking.

She's big brown eyes, long hair, and her complexion is something any girl would envy. Mary is smiling, her cheeks red. Darragh winks as I enter. He even looks happy. There is a nervousness with Finn as I walk in, but he seems to relax when he sees I'm alone.

"Una, this is Siobhan," Finn says.

I take Siobhan's outstretched petite hand. Her skin's so freaking soft.

"Hi, I've heard tons about you," I say, and she smiles.

"All good I hope," she says still smiling. Her teeth are sparkling white, and when she looks back at Finn who smiles at her, I can see they love each other. "Of course all good," Finn says, with a hand over his heart. She slaps him playfully.

"It was all good," I say sitting down. Darragh is having a bottle of Miller, but he isn't drunk or anything. He's only started.

We chat a while. When I learn that she's a caregiver in Cavan hospital I have a million questions. Like what's the worst injury she has ever seen, what's it like to see a baby born? Has any patient ever hit on her and any hot doctors? This gets a laugh out of Mary and Siobhan, but not out of Finn.

Darragh stays a while. He doesn't say much, and at times, I think I see guilt or sadness in his eyes. He leaves, but I stay. I like Siobhan. She's easy to chat to. Of course, she asks me about myself, and I tell her I dropped out of college and right now I'm not sure what to do.

Shane arrives in the kitchen, and I think that both Finn and me stiffen together, for two completely different reasons. I tell myself to relax, and when I peek up, Shane is staring at me, not hiding the fact that he's staring at me. I drop his gaze, and he comes and sits beside me so close that his thigh is brushing mine.

"Did you meet Siobhan?" I say, glancing at him. Our shoulders brush at the movement, and all of a sudden, I need space.

"No," he tells me, and I narrow my eyes. She is sitting three feet away, surely watching this. When he looks away from me to Siobhan, he's the perfect gentleman and takes her hand in his.

"Pleasure to meet you. Finn has spoken very highly of you," he says, and Finn's mouth opens slightly. I don't like the fact he's still holding her hand.

"Siobhan's a nurse," I say, and everyone turns to me. Shane releases Siobhan's hand.

"I'm a carer," Siobhan corrects me, and I roll my eyes playfully.

"Potato patato. You practically do the same," I say, and she grins.

"That is true. Just don't tell the nurses." We all relax fully, and Shane soon excuses himself. I am tempted to follow him but don't. The conversation flows easily, and when Finn keeps throwing glances at the door, I question if he is waiting for his dad to meet Siobhan.

I excuse myself quickly, saying I'm going to the bathroom, but instead, I make my way to Michael's study. I hope he's there. It would make Finn's day to have everyone meet Siobhan. I can see the nervousness in him, but he is proud of her and delighted with how well it went with Darragh and Shane.

I reach the study and Michael and Shane's voices have me pausing. Ugh, I don't want to walk in with him there, but getting Michael is more important to me. I freeze this time as the conversation that is taking place behind the door is on my mind is finding hard to process.

"I've Rachel looking into duplicating the drug."

"We can't have someone else coming in supplying what we can't," Michael reinforces, and Shane agrees.

"There is a new shipment arriving in the docks on Tuesday. I have Gary picking it up." There is movement, and I'm not sure what's happening.

"It better be cleaner stuff than the last," Michael says sternly.

"It's seventy percent cocaine. After it's mixed, it will be thirty percent, but that's still high."

I'm moving away from the door, and I'm struggling to breathe. They are drug dealers. Big drug dealers. As I pass through the hall, all the paintings, furniture even the rugs are too rich for a farmer. I wasn't aware of this before, but now everything was in my face.

I can't go back into that kitchen. I'm making my way for the front door. I need air.

I find my way to the stables as the first drop of rain falls. The sky is low now, grey like my mind. It's a jumping jumble of too much. I'm overwhelmed with what I heard. I question did I hear it, could it have been code words? But I know what I heard. My heart picks up speed when I think of this family with their secrets.

My mother's warning comes to me now, and I ponder if she knew. She couldn't have. She would never have let me leave, but she must have seen the wealth and knew it didn't come from farming. I move into the stable that holds my horse and out of the rain that's coming down in sheets.

Shane is a drug dealer. It's hard to picture, but not. Michael is a drug lord. I'm laughing now, hysteria taking over. Darragh and Finn couldn't. They are nice. Liam? I think and rub my forehead. My head hurts, and I know I need to get away, now, before I start to really freak out.

When I climb on my horse bare-back, she doesn't protest. Neither does she protest as I direct her out of the stable. I duck my head under the door, and once outside, rain pelts down on top of us. I move her through the yard slowly.

I want to race now, but I wait until we are in the open fields. It's not until then that I open her up. Holding her mane, I allow it all to go and focus on riding her. It's freeing, and I'm shaking but smiling a few minutes later. The rain has soaked me, but that doesn't bother me. The lighting that crosses the sky is what I don't like. I'm in the middle of the field, wet, on horseback. There's an old outbuilding near here, I remember from when I was young. I gallop there quickly as the storm grows closer.

I can't bring the horse into the outbuilding, but she seems to stay close to the stone structure. I'm lucky the roof is still on it, but the two small windows and door are gone. I'm really cold now and pace the small space, waiting for the storm to pass. But time seems to tick by slowly, and the storm grows more frantic.

My horse races away at the roar of thunder. I don't chase after her; instead, I stay and wait. The roar of an engine doesn't give me the relief that it should have. I was being rescued. Dry clothes, maybe hot food. My stomach rumbles now. But the idea of seeing them has my heart pounding.

I'm peering out the door and can see the land cruiser tear up the ground as Shane drives like a lunatic towards me. He jumps out and runs straight towards me. I question what he is going to do.

CHAPTER TWELVE

SHANE

"What is with you and water?" I ask her while taking off my jacket. She's soaking through, and a shiver has taken over her small frame. There is a strangeness in her eyes that I don't like. As I take a step towards her, she takes one back and holds out a shaky hand.

I recognize the fear. She swallows while frowning at the ground before looking back up at me.

"You told me that what you do is illegal," she says, and I nod.

"Una, you're soaking. We can talk in the jeep." I take a step towards her again. Her hand collides with my chest, and she shakes her head.

"No, I'm going nowhere with you." I have no clue what's gotten into her, but she's upset, and I want to take it away.

"I heard you and Michael speaking," she tells me. Her hand flutters away from my chest and falls limply to her side, yet she still stands tall, holding my stare.

"About what?" I ask, knowing what father and I have just spoken of. I can't hold her eye now, because I don't want to see that look in it. The one of disgust and fear I see now.

"You know what," she shouts, her hand slamming into my chest. My eyes snap to her face. My chest tightens, not from the impact of her hand, but the way she looks at me now. Like I'm a despicable human being.

"Say something," she shouts, hitting me with both hands. I shift back slightly from the impact.

"What do you want me to say?" I growl. "You want me to paint you a pretty picture. You want me to tell you that you heard wrong."

She curls her hands into a fist and hits my chest again, and I let her, hoping that the disgust will seep out of her with each hit she places on my chest.

"No, God damn it, Shane. I want you to be honest." She wheels away from me, her back rising and falling quickly.

"Yes, what you heard is true. We make our money by doing illegal…things." She spins around, a fire in her eyes, and she laughs, but it's full of anger.

"You can't even say it," she spits out.

"We supply drugs to most of the North East of the country. We earn our money from brothels. We hurt people. We launder money. We are criminals." The more I say, the paler she becomes. But for me, there is something satisfying about telling someone the truth for once in my life.

Her chest is rising and falling quickly now, but she stands taller. "Okay. Okay." That's all she says before she walks past me. I turn and watch her climb into the passenger side of the jeep. I have no clue what that means, but I follow her and get into the vehicle.

Her shivers are worse now. I don't know if it's a mixture of the cold and shock. I turn up the heat. "Take off your top," I tell her while I pull my own jumper off and fix my t-shirt. When I glance at her, she's staring at me.

"Don't make me take it off, Una," I growl at her, and she stares at me for a moment before she pulls her top off over her head. I don't stare at her but focus my gaze out the window as the rain continues to beat down on us.

The storm is overhead now. The lightning is coming quicker. Once she has her top off, I hand her my jumper. She pulls it on, and my shoulders relax a bit more. My eyes move to her trousers, and she shakes her head, but still she sits up and pulls them down. I drink in her long, creamy legs.

"Stop staring at me," she barks, and I snap my attention forward. I flicker a glance at her as she removes her boots before pulling off her trousers. I don't want to drive back to the house, not with so much hanging between us.

"Did my mother know?" she asks once she has her trousers off and is sitting back up.

"No, of course not," I answer her. Her lips twist in a snarl.

"So what, you have a secret life?"

To me, it wasn't a secret. It was all I ever knew. I can't meet her eyes right now, not when they hold so much hate.

"What about Finn, Darragh?" Her voice takes on a shriek the panic rising. I turn to her as she pulls her legs up to her chest. I'm not even sure she's aware of what she is doing. But all my eyes see is her skin, and I pull my focus to her face.

"Yes, it's a family business."

Her mouth opens slightly, and silence fills the jeep for a moment.

"I'm sorry," I tell her, because I am. I'm sorry that she got to see this side to us. It's a relief for me, but a burden for her.

"Sorry that you didn't tell me or that you got caught," I blink at her.

"Both," I tell her honestly.

Her hands are still shaking as she wraps them around her legs. "Jesus, Shane. This is crazy. I just… I know it's true, yet I don't," she says, and I don't answer.

When I glance at her, I hate the fear I see there. When I reach for her hand, she pulls back, and it's like a slap in the face. I turn to her fully.

"I would never hurt you, Una," I tell her. She searches my face. For the truth in my words? I'm not sure.

But I reach for her again slower this time, and when I take her hand, she doesn't pull away, and it's like a balm to a burn. The tips of my fingers line up with hers, and I slowly take her hand fully in mine. Once I have twined our fingers, I gaze at her. Her eyes appear huge in her pale face.

"You know that, right? I would never hurt you."
She swallows, and then she nods.

"I know," she admits, and it's a baby step, but it's good.

"I don't want to lose you," I tell our entwined fingers now. When I glance up at her from under my lashes, I can see the rise and fall of her chest. I want her to tell me what she is thinking, but she stares at me. A tear falls from her one blue eye.

"You won't."

I smile even though I can still see the uncertainty in her face. She doesn't return it. "Can I take you back to the house to get you dry clothes?" I ask her softly, and she swipes away another falling tear but nods. When she takes her hand from mine, I miss her warmth. I drive slowly back across the fields while ringing Stephen.

"Una's horse got loose. I'm sure I've seen her in the field that runs along the river where the old stone house is," I tell him, and he says he will get her once the storm passes. I glance at Una once I have the call made, but she still has her knees up to her chest, and her far-away gaze is focused out the window.

***

Una's in the shower, and I'm sitting on her bed with no idea of what to do. She will have questions, and I'm prepared to answer some of them. I look out again into the hall for the hundredth time, making sure no one is nearby before I close her door over again. This time when I sit down, she comes out of the bathroom.

She's wearing a grey coloured cotton dress, with emerald green sleeves and a band of emerald green color around the waist. She's beautiful. She pads across the room barefoot while towel-drying her long hair. Her eyes seemed to bounce around me. Like I'm not here, and I can't sit still. I stand and move toward her. She pauses drying her hair and peers up as I take the towel from her hands and drop it on the floor.

I take both her hands and direct her towards the bed where I make her sit, and I sit beside her. She looks like someone who just woke up, like she's not entirely sure what's going on.

"Are you okay?" I ask, releasing her hands. She immediately folds them cross her chest, and I try not to focus on the V of the dress where her plump flesh is rising and falling quickly.

"I don't know. I'm just…" She doesn't finish, and when she settles her gaze on me, I glance away. She's hurt. Her lips have tugged down into a frown, and it looks like she might start crying.

"I just…" She can't seem to find words, and she stands up now, moving away from the bed. When she turns around to face me, my stomach tightens at the intensity of her stare.

"I don't want to get hurt." Her words are whispered, and before I can respond, she does a bizarre thing. Una kneels in front of me and takes one of my hands in hers.

"I know you would never physically hurt me." She's speaking to my chest now. I'm holding my breath as I stare at the crown of her head. "But it's emotionally I'm worried about." Now she peers up at me, her eyes wide and softer now.

"I will never hurt you in any manner," I tell her while embracing her face. She leans into my hands, and the motion makes me feel powerful.

We stay like that for a few moments before she slowly stands and sits down beside me. Once again, we are silent, but it's a different kind of silence now.

"Do you sell the drugs yourself?" she asks but straight away retracts it. "Don't tell me. I don't think I want to know." She's standing again. Her emotions raging. Something crosses her face, and tilts her head. "Does Brian work for you?"

I don't want to lie to her, but she must know the more she knowledge she has, the worse this will all be. "Why do you ask?"

"Don't answer my question with a question," she fires back.

"Yes. Now why do you ask?"

She nods at my answer and wrings her hands before she loosens them and shrugs. "Do you try to get people addicted, and you charge them or what way does it work."

I don't like the light she shines on this. "You're a million miles off. I don't nor have I ever touched or sold a drug. I supply. There is a difference." She snorts, and I clench my fists.

"You want to explain to me what this has to do with Brian?" I ask her. Had she seen him push drugs on someone to get them hooked? It didn't make sense.

"Just, it's nothing." She shrugs again, and I'm standing as her eyes shoot around the room, refusing to stop on me.

I stand in front of her, and she has no choice but to look at me. "It's nothing, Shane," she tells me with too much false bravado.

"I'll decide that," I tell her.

"It's just when I was with him."

"With him in what way?" I cut her off with a growl.

She throws her hands in the air. "I can't talk to you," she tells me, and I reel in my frustration.

"I'm sorry," I say softly.

She eyes me. I'm ready to lose my cool, but thankfully, she speaks.

"Twice, while we were kissing." I clench my fists but stay still. "He slipped a tablet into my mouth. I was pretty drunk, but I was out of it after that. So whatever he was giving me, was really strong."

I'm struggling to breathe. A tightness has banded itself around me. Her voice is still there. I hear her words, but it's like she's further away. She takes my silence as permission to go on. "It was weird. He gave me the creeps, but I don't know. I don't think I'm the only girl he did that to."

"Did he touch you?" I manage to ask, and my voice has her standing a little straighter like she was

confessing this to the room, and now she remembers
I'm standing in it.

"No. No..." Her no's trail off, and her brows draw
closer as she bores holes in the floor with her gaze.
She takes a slight step back.

My hands clench and unclench as I see the growing
doubt on her face. There is a pounding in my ears,
and my pulse elevates as I walk away from Una.

"Where are you going?" She's grabbed my arm, the
panic in her voice rising.

"I'm going to kill him," I tell her and try to walk
away, but she doesn't let me go. She's in front of
me, her eyes wild as her fingers run across my
clenched jaw.

"No, he didn't touch me."

It doesn't matter. He drugged her, and that, for me,
was enough. The desire in me far outweighs
anything now.

I remove her hand from my face and take a step, but
she's blocking me. I try to calm the rage in me, just
for a moment, promising myself that it's only for a
moment.

Taking her face in my hands I want to remove the
worry and strain that tightens her eyes.

"Shane, please leave it alone." Her pleas are said through a trembling lip, and I know if she cries, I won't be able to leave.

Quickly, I pick her up. The action elicits a squeal from her. Dumping her on the bed, I leave her room with an order not to follow me slung over my shoulder.

If she does follow, I don't hear her. All I can hear is the pounding of blood in my ears, and the want for violence courses through my veins.

CHAPTER THIRTEEN

SHANE

Smyth's pub has a few lads hanging out the front all smoking and huddled together. I'm sitting across from it, ignoring my ringing phone. I don't check to see who's calling. I won't allow myself to picture Una upset. I unload the gun regretfully and stick it in the waistband of my trousers before climbing out of my car.

I enter through the lounge where I hope I'll find Patrick. He takes a quick glance up as I enter and goes to return to his conversation with three other men at a small round table, but he does a double take. His brows rise in surprise.

"It's closing time," I tell him, and he rubs his hands down the front of his yellow t-shirt, but he doesn't hesitate as he makes his way behind the bar. As I leave the lounge area and step into the bar, he rings the bell, alerting the younger and louder crowd that closing time is upon them. The ringing bell has groans and curses coming from the crowd, but the loudest of them all is Brian.

"Nah Patrick, this ship is still sailing," he tells him. Patrick turns a bit paler as he looks to me. Brian slowly follows his gaze, and it takes everything in me not to attack him. I wait as the bar slowly empties. Patrick rings the bell more urgently, and soon, it's Brian and one of his friends. I don't as much as glance at or acknowledge them as I walk towards him.

"Shane, what's up man?" he asks, trying to sound calm, but I delight in the hiccup of fear I hear. I shove him into the booth and slide in beside him, trapping him. It's then that I give his friend a moment of my attention. A tall thin boy, with freckles. His eyes shine with too much drink.

"I'll talk to you later," Brian tells him.

"Sit down," I tell the boy, and his eyes bounce from Brian to Patrick then back to me before sitting down. I nod at Patrick now, and he leaves, taking his dismissal. The pub is silent, and when Brian goes to speak, I snap. My fingers grip his neck, and I smash his face into the table, causing all the glasses to rattle, one falls off and smashes on the ground. His friend makes a move to leave, but I snap my gaze to him, and he stays still.

"Jesus Christ, Shane," Brian cries out, and I slam his face into the table again, knocking over a pint on his friend who learns fast and sits still. His nose pumps blood all down his white shirt as I yank him back up. His blood feeds my rage.

"What's wrong?" He's crying. His hands move to his broken and smashed nose.

"You drugged Una," I say.

"Who?" His response is unsatisfactory. I slam his face into the table once. Then I decide he doesn't need all his teeth. I put a lot of force behind it this time.

There is a lot of blood now. His blond hair is growing damp.

"You drugged Una," I repeat, and his cries come out in whines.

"Shane, I'll do anything," he starts, and I move to smash his face again, but he starts pleading, pushing against my hand. I release his sweaty neck.

"Get me a cloth," I tell his friend whose skin has turned an ugly grey. When he stands, I see his trousers are stained with all the drink that spilt, but he gets me a cloth. I use it to clean my hands. Brian continues to cry and plead beside me. But I don't feel satisfied. I take the gun out of the band of my trousers, and he slams his back into the wall.

"Ah no, Shane. Jesus, please." His hands are trembling and raised.

"Una was with Darragh a few nights, and you where there as well. Did you feed her drugs while she was drunk?" I ask while pointing the gun at his head. I know Una told the truth. I need to hear him say it.

"Yes, and I'm so so sorry." I slam the gun into his jaw, and my reward is his teeth on the table.

"Did you touch her?" I ask.

The no he gives me is hard to understand, but I make it out. I push the gun against his forehead and ask again.

"No, I swear. I'm begging you, please…"

"Shut up," I roar while I push the gun harder into his head. His eyes are closed tightly like a fucking coward.

"Open your eyes."

He does straight away.

"Did you touch her?" I ask again, and he cries a pathetic no. He's telling the truth, and that gives me some relief. But I want more from him. I use my fists, and the gun to pound his face. He tries to cover it with his arms, but I still make an impact. When blood spits back at my face and neck, I stop.

The minute I do, he slumps onto the table. I'm not sure if he's passed out or not. I stare at his friend for a second, breathing heavy before getting up and leaving the pub.

I'm driving home with red hands, covered in so much fucking blood. I take a quick glance in the review mirror and now I question whether or not Brian is dead or alive, but something is pushing me back to the house. Una.

I need her now more than ever. I need to touch her and tell the rage that she's fine and that she's mine. I'm not satisfied with just beating Brian. I wanted to pull the trigger.

When I enter the garage, I don't get out of the car immediately. The harsh lights wake me up, and seeing myself in the mirror has me trying to wipe some blood from my face. All I was doing was smearing it, so I stop. I need a shower.

I don't meet anyone as I make my way to my room. It's something I will have to deal with later, but right now, I want to wash the blood from my body. I

step into my room and pause as Una's head snaps
up. She's been sitting on the end of my bed, her
eyes downcast, but now her head snaps up, her eyes
shooting all over my face as she stands. She's
shaking her head, and her chin and lip tremble as
she races across the floor.

She's wearing the same dress from earlier, her hair
is now dry, and her beauty is all I see. I close my
eyes as her hands flutter to my face. She moves my
head to the left and right.

"Where are you hurt?" There's a touch of hysteria
in her voice, and when her hands run down my
arms, I know I should tell her it's not me, but I'm a
bastard for enjoying this moment.

"Shane." She's pulling at my top, and I open my
eyes. The tremble in her lip now has intensified. So
I speak up.

"It's not my blood," I tell her as tears slip from her
wide eyes. Her eyes slowly move down to my
hands, and she covers her mouth with her hand. It
trembles, and I take her by the shoulders. She's
shaking her head while looking at me.

"I'm fine," I reassure her. She searches my face and
then steps into me, her arms hugging me tightly.
She's not asking whose blood this is all over me.
She seems content to know it's not mine. But I want
her right now like I've never wanted anything

before. Her smell is everywhere, and the thoughts of anyone hurting her, of Brian putting his hands on her, drives a new need.

"I want you," I tell her, and she slowly releases me and leans out. She doesn't say anything but stares at me, and when I pick her up and carry her to the bed, she doesn't protest. One arm hooks under her cream legs, the other at the back of her head. I can't take my eyes off her. I know I need to claim her, brand her, make her mine. Adrenaline still pumps through my body, and focusing on anything tender is hard.

"I need you," I tell her as I lay her down, the rise and fall of her chest is the only movement from her. I kneel on the bed and wait for her to protest, but she doesn't. I move to her, and when I reach her, I position my body on top of hers.

She nods now, but her eyes are wide with fear and awe. I don't look away from her as I open my belt and pull down my jeans and boxers; I keep eye contact as I reach under her dress and move her underwear aside. I sit myself at her opening, and when she doesn't object, I enter her.

My hands move to her hair where I bury them. I thrust inside her again, and Una is perfect around me. She moans now, quietly, her hands clutching the quilt. She's everything I imagined she would be and more. I grip her hair tighter as I fasten my pace. Una releases the quilts, her hands reaching for my shoulders, pulling me closer to her, but we can't get closer.

I lay my head against hers and inhale her moans. Each thrust I take makes her become more and more mine. The ecstasy that crosses her face has me quickening my pace until I fill her. We are both breathless, and we haven't looked away from each other. A tear slides from her green eye along the side of her face.

CHAPTER FOURTEEN

UNA

My body is trembling from the rush of release and also because Shane is still in me. His hands are still buried in my hair—his hands that are covered in blood. There is a savagery in his eyes that is dying down now as he continues to breathe deeply.

My own breaths are still fast as I continue to take his perfect face in. The blood that flecks his face makes him appear wild. I should be afraid, but a sort of excitement at seeing him feral courses through me. I slide my thumb across his lips, and it's then that he closes his eyes.

I can't look away from him. I can't believe this is Shane. My mind is overwhelmed with what happened. When he opens his eyes, I move my hands away from him. Butterflies erupt in my stomach with the intensity of his stare.

"Are you okay?" he asks. His eyes are flickering over the tears that are leaking from my eyes.

I don't know why I'm crying. There's so much. Too much. I nod and swallow. Shane slowly extracts himself from me, and the loss is immediate. He goes to the bathroom, and I don't move. But for the first time, I can breathe. The noise of the tap running reaches my ears, and when Shane reappears still covered in blood, I inhale a quick breath.

He doesn't speak, and his stare has rendered me speechless as he slowly parts my legs and lifts up my dress. The lights are on, there are no barriers, it's like I'm baring my soul to him. The warm cloth he presses in-between my legs and cleans me with is enough to almost break me.

The gentle strokes, the awe in his eyes now. The thoughtfulness of the gesture. I stay still, and when he has finished, he asks me again am I okay.

"Yes," is all I manage. He's standing at the foot of the bed.

"Will you stay with me tonight?" The question has my heart pounding, and I still can't manage words so I nod, and it's enough for him. He goes back into the bathroom, and this time the shower is turned on.

I pull my legs closed; my hand flutters to my chest, telling my heart to settle down. As I lie there, I question so much, like why I still can't find it in me to ask him whose blood it is. I have a good idea it's Brian, but it's not the asking. It's that I don't care as long as it wasn't his. What kind of person does that make me?

My thoughts are cut off and shut down as Shane comes out of the bathroom wearing only a towel. I suck in a deep breath. His sculpted chest and wide shoulders are enough to make me want to reach for him, but I show some self-control.

I don't know what you would call what we just did, but I have never felt more intimate with someone, and yet now as I stare at his plump lips, I question what it must be like to kiss him. My stomach flutters now. His lip tugs up slightly into a half smile, showing some teeth, and I'm like a drowning sailor. I need to pull myself together; I sit up, pulling my knees to my chest.

"Are you okay?" This is the third time he has asked me this, I'm not sure what he sees, but I want to put his mind to rest.

"I am. I'm just... I'm just." Emotions lodge themselves in my throat. "I'm fine," I finish on. When Shane drops the towel, I turn into a twelve-year-old schoolgirl, and I actually cover my eyes. A small quick laugh leaves my lips. It's Shane's soft laughter that has me opening my eyes.

"Una, you're blushing," he teases as he pulls on black jogging pants and moves towards the bed.

I'm on fire, so blushing is a nice way to put it.

"It was just unexpected," I tell him as he climbs onto the bed. My emotions jump again, a giddiness taking over.

"You can't just do that," I add before I laugh, and Shane captures my face, my laughter dying in my throat.

"Thank you for tonight," he tells me, and my stomach hollows out at the words thank you. You say thank you to someone who buys you a drink, or someone who holds a fucking door open for you. You don't say thank you when someone lets you see a part of their soul. My breath catches in my throat and I try to tell myself to calm down. His lip lifts up.

"You look angry, so I must be saying this all wrong," he says, and my heart slows, my temper calming. I don't speak but allow him to.

He smiles and kisses me on the nose. I savor the pressure of his lips on me and think again what it would be like to have them on my lips.

"You were all I could think about. Tonight, your face consumed me. So I'm saying thank you for being mine tonight."

"You're welcome." I want to kiss him, but as I move in towards him, his lips move and I get a kiss on the forehead.

What the fuck.

You kiss your grandmother on the forehead or I don't know, old people, even someone dying. I close my eyes. I was over reacting. I needed to calm myself. Shane doesn't seem to be aware of the turmoil that barrels through me as he pulls me down in the bed and spoons me. He pulls the blankets up over us, and I'm still not fully accepting that I'm in his bed, in his arms. But there is a blissfulness that fills me again, and I snuggle closer to him.

He claps his hands, and the lights go out. I start to laugh. "That is the laziest thing I have ever seen. And why don't I have that in my room?" I can't see him in the dark. I clap, and the lights come back on.

His smile is wide. "I can get it installed in your room," he tells me and claps, plunging us into darkness, and like the child that I am, I clap again.

"Will I have to tie your hands together?" The question is asked with a serious face, but there is laughter in his tone.

I clap before he can, and the room goes dark. He pulls me closer against his body, and I let the temptation die away and focus on the sensation of his body against mine. It doesn't take me long to fall asleep.

***

I wake to someone turning on the lights. "What time is it?" Shane is asking as he sits up.

"What have you done?" I don't sit up at the sound of Liam's voice. It's like it rattles in his throat. It's an odd sound.

"What time is it?" Shane asks again and reaches for the black clock that sits on his bedside table. "It's four in the morning, Liam," he barks and climbs out of bed. I pretend to be a sleep. I'm not ready to face into this.

"Do you know the mess you have made?" Liam speaks again; he is barely controlling his voice. Not seeing his face, I can picture a snarl.

"We can talk somewhere else." Shane lowers his voice, but the threat in his words is clear.

"You did this for her?" He sounds almost disgusted, and it's odd to hear so much in his voice. I move under the blanket before sitting up. Liam's eyes snap to me, and I regret coming up.

"Father is beyond words," Liam tells Shane now, his voice more controlled now that he sees I'm awake. Shane ignores him and pulls on a top before coming back to the bed.

"You need to sleep. I'll be back later." His voice is soft, and I'm not sure how he manages to keep it that way as he speaks to me. Liam is boring holes into his back, and I want to warn him, but he smiles at me. "Go to sleep," he tells me again before turning to Liam.

"I'm not talking here," Shane growls, the contrast between the softness seconds ago to the anger now tells me so much. He cares about me. A lot. When they leave the room, I debate with myself whether to go and search for them, but I don't, knowing that would be stupid.

Yet I toss and turn, clapping the lights on and off. I'm curious; will it break if I keep this up? I do keep it up for a while as my mind keeps conjuring up images easily of Shane covered in blood again. What if Liam hurts him? I fling the covers back but don't get out. Liam would never hurt Shane. I clap turning the lights off, knowing I need to stay put. But what if they lose their cool?

Clap! Lights are on.

What if Shane hurts Liam? *Clap. Lights off.* For some reason that doesn't bother me in the slightest.

VICIOUS IRISH

I lie down and count sheep. At some stage, I manage to fall asleep.

The moment I stir, all I smell is Shane. The night comes rushing back, Shane covered in blood, Shane inside me. I open my eyes and glance over at his side. It's cold. He never returned. I sit up and gnaw on my lip. I should have searched for him, yet I knew that would make this worse. Maybe he did come back, and I didn't hear him.

I get out of Shane's bed and slip into my room to shower and change. I don't have a clue what to do. Going to work with the horses seems the safest bet right now.

Making my way to the kitchen is odd now that I'm aware of how everything in this house is paid for. It all seems strange. My skin stretches with anxiety across my face. Entering the kitchen, my pulse jumps, and I pause briefly. Liam is sitting at the table, with a paper in front of him. He doesn't glance up, and I question if slipping from the room would be a good idea.

"Good morning, Una," he says, and his controlled voice and suit give me a cold impression now. Before, I thought Liam was odd but cute. Now I don't know. A small shiver snakes its way through me. Now, I see someone dangerous.

"Liam," I say, getting a coffee. Mary isn't here, and that's typical. I put toast in the toaster and stand waiting for it to pop, hoping that Liam will be gone by the time I sit down.

No luck.

"We need to talk." I'm ready to butter my toast when he starts.

"Fire away," I tell him with as much cheeriness as I can manage.

"What Shane did was reckless and stupid." Now I take note of him. "You know he did it in your honor." His foreign way of speaking seems sinister now. "You implied that you had been drugged and raped."

I can't breathe at his words, is that what Shane thought, but had I said that? No. But yet when he had asked me if Brian had touched me, I couldn't answer him, because I wasn't one hundred percent sure.

"Words can be very powerful, Una, even more so, when they aren't true." I'm sitting silently, not sure what to say to Liam. My throat burns at what he is saying.

"You think I would have lied?" My lip trembles, and I bite it.

Liam shows no emotion as he speaks, and that hurts more. "Did you?"

The chair legs scrape along the floor is the only noise that fills the kitchen as I get up. I'm disgusted with Liam. He knows me better than that. I lean in, supporting myself with knuckles clenched on the table. "You can go to hell," I tell him.

His eyes burn into my back as I leave the warm kitchen and make my way out in the farmyard. I swallow the lump in my throat and try to focus on walking, but my mind won't allow me to.

Fire burns inside me at the idea that Liam thinks I would make something up. I don't know what happened with Brian. I don't think he raped me, but I never said he did. That fact keeps rotating around in my head.

"Morning, Una." Stephen is carrying two buckets of nuts. He places them on the back of a quad. "I'm going to feed the cows. I'll be back shortly," he tells me, and for Stephen, I force a smile as he gets on the quad and kicks it into gear. I give a wave as he drives off towards the cattle sheds that are close to the bottom of the landline.

I find my horse in its stable. She is relaxed more and more around me. "Hi girl," I tell her as I rub her down. Tears burn my eyes, and I stare up at the beams on the ceiling to try to settle myself down.

"It's not bats is it?" My heart trips over itself at the sound of Shane's voice. I don't turn immediately as I try to settle the weakness in my knees.

His smile is all dimples and teeth. My stomach squeezes, and I inhale a deep breath. "I hope not," I say on an exhale that carries a short laugh. My gaze takes him in, and every part of me tightens. His dark denim jeans fit him snugly, and the green wool jumper he is wearing today gives his brown eyes a softness.

I love him.

When I look at him, I fill up with love. I think I've loved him since I was sixteen. The summer he gave me the horse, the summer I secretly stalked him. I take a step toward his smiling face it slowly grows serious.

My throat is still burning. I'm an emotional wreck, but I have this need to give him something back.

"I've decided on a name for my horse," I tell him, and he closes the distance between us. His focus is on my hands as he takes them in his before they flick back up to me, causing my pulse to pound.

I want to tell him about Liam. I want to tell him I love him. I want to tell him I think I always have loved him. I need to explain how afraid I am right now, afraid of the rug being pulled from under me. But I say none of that.

"Summer, I'm going to call her Summer," I say slowly, my own focus going to his perfect moist lips before flickering back to those brown eyes that smile at me, the corners crinkling.

"It's beautiful. I'm glad you finally named her," he tells me as he raises my hands to his lips. Butterflies dance and swirl in my stomach as his lips press against my flesh, and it burns everywhere. What would it be like to have those lips on mine?

"You noticed I hadn't?" I ask with a breathiness in my voice that has Shane staring down at me.

"I notice everything about you," he tells me, and my knees weaken further.

I search his face. I'm not sure what for, but his words are overwhelming me. I hope he never gets used to me. I hope he never stops looking at me the way he is now.

"Why did you not come back last night?" I ask instead of saying anything else. Shane releases my hands, and the loss is instant. I observe him now as he stuffs he hands in his jeans pockets.

"I'm sorry I had something to take care of. But I'm here now." His words kind of sound like an apology.

"Yeah, you're here now," I repeat back as a smile crosses my face.

His lips twitch, and he lets out a breath on the word, "So…"

"Do you want to work on your bike today?" he finishes.

The idea of spending more time with Shane is perfect, and I agree.

"I've some other work to take care of but after dinner," he tells me taking a step backwards out of the stable with his hands still shoved in his pockets.

"It's a date," I tell him, and both his eyebrows rise, making me laugh.

"A date?" he questions playfully, and I shrug at his words.

"Only if you want it to be a date?" I'm still smiling at him now, and when he laughs with his head tilted to the side, it takes everything in me not to run to him and crash my lips against his.

"It's a date, Una álainn." My heart squeezes now. Beautiful Una. Hearing it from his lips has my heart pounding. The Irish language makes it more. So much more.

CHAPTER FIFTEEN

UNA

I work in a blissful daze after Shane leaves. I want to tell my own heart to slow down, that it is moving too fast on this, but I can't.

Dinnertime arrives, and I enter the wet room, peeling off my coat and boots. The cream wool jumper is three sizes too big for me, but it's warm. I enter the kitchen to find Michael at the table. The moment I come in, he smiles. It's odd now. I see him, I do. But knowing the truth makes it hard to hold his stare.

"Una, you don't belong on a farm," Mary says with a smile as she moves past me holding two steaming plates of food. The smell of roast has my stomach gurgling. After skipping breakfast, I'm not surprised. I pad in my wooly socks to the table and try not to act nervous with Michael.

"Why not?" I ask Mary as she winks at me.

"You're too pretty. You belong on the front of a romance novel." Now I laugh.

"I don't know what romance novels you're reading Mary. But this"—I point at myself—"isn't it." I tell her before taking in the plate of dinner. Marofat peas, carrots, stuffing, and roast spuds along with the roast makes this a mouthwatering dinner.

Mary scoffs before getting two more plates.

"Mary is right. You should think of modeling," Darragh says as he arrives into the kitchen with Finn behind him. Finn sits across from me and Darragh beside his dad. Now I'm facing all three. When Mary doesn't come with more plates, I'm relieved that Liam isn't joining us, but disappointed that Shane isn't here. There is such a weirdness to be around them now.

I give Darragh a tight smile at his compliment, and he narrows his eyes at me.

"Are you enjoying the work?" this comes from Michael, and I finally meet his eye.

Now he reminds me of the Godfather. My toes curl in my socks as I push them against the floor, while reminding myself that this was Michael. The reminder doesn't exactly help. "Yes, thank you, for the job." Oh lord, now I sound formal.

Darragh continues to assess me, and now even Finn seems confused at my tone.

"Good to hear it," Michael says with a tight smile. Wrinkles appear around his eyes, eyes that now appear sharp almost predatory.

I focus on my food, shoveling it into my mouth. Darragh's laughter has me pausing.

"Calm down, Una. No one is going to take it from you. Maybe you want to join the cattle outside." His words are said with laughter.

Heat rises in my cheeks at his words, and my whole face burns. I'm staring at a laughing Darragh, thinking he's part of this criminal world. He always appears un-criminalized and now I'm struggling to meet his eye.

"Are you okay?" Finn asks, and baby blue eyes focused on me.

Michael is studying me too, and it's all too much. I quickly excuse myself from the table and race up the stairs and back to my room; I make it the toilet before I empty the small amount of food that I had eaten into the bowl. Tears stream down my face as my body rejects the idea of what Shane has confirmed.

I can't find the strength to get up. I sit against the wall as I try to tell myself that this will pass. It's a bigger shock than I thought.

"Una." I would roll my eyes at the intrusion from Darragh, but right now, I don't want to see him. Privacy is really nonexistent in this house as Darragh pushes open my bathroom door with his foot. The permanent grin is on his face now as he raises both eyebrows.

"I'm not much for a chin wag, but I think you need to talk," he tells me, sitting down on the tile floor with his back against the wall. My focus goes to the gold band he wears on his pinky finger, a red ruby in the center. It's new and isn't cheap.

"Nice ring," I tell him, and he gives it a quick appreciative glance before flicking his hand like a rapper would.

"Yeah, it's alright," he says with a nod of his head.

"Looks expensive." I pull my knees closer to my chest. The black jodhpurs are allowing the cold of the tiles to pass through them easily.

"A few quid. So are you going to tell me what's wrong?" He nods his head again.

I'm not sure if it's for him or me.

"What's a few quid?" My throat is burning now. Sitting here with him, the sense of betrayal is almost stifling. How many times have we partied together, and yet he has never told me about his family's true nature? Now I'm giving him every opportunity to tell me.

"Do you want the ring?" he asks while taking it off. I stand, and he frowns at my actions.

"No keep your stupid ring." While retrieving mouthwash from the press, I rinse the taste of sick from it.

"Are you pregnant?" The easy way Darragh asks has me glaring at him in the bathroom mirror. He's standing now, his grin gone, and when he is serious, he looks so much like Finn. Both are extremely good-looking, and the saying that looks can be deceiving springs to mind.

I need to get a grip. Refilling my mouth with more wash I gurgle it before spitting out the mouthwash into the sink as I turn around to Darragh.

"No." I answer holding onto the sink with my hands as I try to calm my racing heart.

"On the rag?" he questions now while folding his arms over his chest.

"I know what you are," I whisper shout at him, and he drops his hands. A smile starts to grow on his face.

"Ah is that this movie, where the ugly guy is a vampire?"

I'm staring at Darragh, thinking he must be fucking with me. He can't be that stupid, but the smile on his face has me storming from the bathroom and into my bedroom where he follows.

"How much was the ring? How did you pay for it Darragh?"

It's a split second, but I can slowly see the realization of what I'm asking sink in. He's across the room in a second closing my bedroom door, and now I remember the angry Darragh. The one who had smashed the chair.

I'm backing away from him and towards my bed. I don't stop until my legs hit the frame.

"Say whatever you need to say." I swallow as I search his face.

He isn't angry, but there is a strain visible around his eyes and a tightness in his jaw.

"Una, I'm the safest person for you to talk to," he says to my silence, and I nod.

"I know you're a criminal," I say quietly, afraid of what my words will erupt.

He snorts but doesn't laugh. "Criminal is a nice way of saying it. But how do you know? Was it Brian? Is that why Shane beat the shit out of him?"

That's a lot of questions, questions I don't want to answer. So I answer the ones I don't mind answering.

"So you are one too?" I find myself saying as I sit down on the bed. I knew he was, but seeing the answer clearly on his face makes me question my judgment on so much. How the hell had I not noticed? First and foremost the wealth, yet no one actually worked.

Darragh sits beside me. "Yeah and no." His answer sounds sad, and I glance at him. I can't see his eyes. He's focused on his ring.

"I'm not like Shane or Liam." He speaks to his fingers. "I'm me." He shrugs. "But yeah, I do what they do." We fall into silence.

"So are you going to tell me who told you?" he asks, and I opt for the easy way out.

"No one told me. I figured it out."

Now Darragh eyes fill with doubt, and one brow rises in question.

"The wealth, no one works," I say, and his doubt melts away before he bumps shoulders with me. "This has got to be our little secret. You can't tell the others." I don't meet Darragh's eyes as I agree, but he isn't satisfied.

"Una, I'm serious. They aren't like me. Don't ever say it."

"Why? What would they do?" Shane would never hurt me, but the seriousness on Darragh's face has me curious about what they would do. Running his hand through his short hair he stands.

"I don't know."

"Would they hurt me?" I ask on a whim.

"Yes." His answer actually surprises me. I don't know what he sees on my face, but he's beside me again. "No, no I didn't mean that. Look, you can't tell anyone okay."

I can sense his panic, and I'm nodding again.

"I promise," I tell him, and he lets out a shaky breath. "I better get back to work." I stand back up, and Darragh nods several times while rubbing the back of his head.

"Right. Glad we had this chat. Good chat." He's rambling as he leaves my room, and I find myself smiling even as dark as this situation is.

I'm smiling, and that tells me I'm going to be fine.

After Darragh leaves, I brush my teeth and make my way back downstairs. I'm on the first step when Shane is there stealing my rational thoughts away.

"I was looking for you." He's eyes search behind me like he's waiting for someone else to materialize. His brows are drawn together, his fingers tightening around the banister. "Finn said you left the table in a rush." I move down the steps quickly until I'm on the one above his. This puts us the same height, my eyes flicker to his lips before I reach up and touch his drawn brows, and he relaxes under my fingers.

"It's a bit weird looking at everyone now," I whisper while focusing on his brow. His hand captures mine, snapping my attention to his eyes. My stomach squeezes.

"It's all new. I know that, but you can talk to me." He's words are low, and I find myself moving closer when it's not necessary.

But I want to be closer to him. I close my eyes against all the irrational thoughts that are bouncing around. He is making me lose any sense of myself.

His hand still holds mine, and I try to focus on the touch, but I can't. It's Shane's touch, Shane's hand that has my pulse racing.

"Una." My name is whispered, and I open my eyes to stare up at him. "You have nothing to fear." His brows are drawn together as he speaks furiously.

I'm looking at this man, and fear of him isn't possible. I'm afraid of losing myself with him, in him. I'm afraid that he might not feel the same way about me that I feel for him. I'm afraid of the rest of his family. Once upon a time, they were mine, but I didn't know them.

"I know," I find myself saying. A door banging downstairs has Shane returning to normal.

"Are you ready to work on your bike?" The excitement in his voice has my mournful thoughts fleeing.

"Yeah, I would like that." Shane doesn't move.

"First, I want you to eat. You left your dinner behind."

I can't stop the smile that crosses my face. "Finn sure gave you a run down," I tell him, and one side of his lip lifts slightly, like he's fighting off a smile.

"He was concerned."

"About little old me," I tease, but my words seem to sober up the mood.

"You're safe with us, Una. We all care for you." His eyes roam my face as he speaks.

I bite my lip, chewing on it as I think of his words. Conflicting thoughts rattle around in my head. On one hand, I always thought they all cared for me in some way, but now I wasn't sure. Their intentions seemed different now that I knew what they were. As Shane continues to study me, I tell myself that I need to respond.

"Thanks, Shane," I answer, and from the tightness around his eyes, it's not what he wanted me to say. I'm not sure what he wanted to hear. Maybe that I knew I was safe? I'm not safe.

"Come on. We'll get you food." As he speaks, he turns around and walks down the stairs, and I follow.

***

When Shane flicks on the lights in the second garage, I roll my eyes, and he actually laughs. The sound scatters my nerves.

The garage would easily hold six cars or more, but right now, the center has a beige tarp, and standing on it, is my bike, all the parts laid out around it. I walk towards it with my hands behind my back. "You know, the size of this place is scandalous," I tell him.

Shane still wears a smile and places his hand behind his own back as he walks in the opposite direction to me. Both of us circle the bike, staring at each other. It's like a dance. "It's for our bikes," he says with a shrug and a grin.

"I only see mine," I tell him still moving, still smiling.

"I had the rest cleared out," he answers easily, like emptying the garage for me wasn't anything. The garage is virtually empty except for ten large stainless steel drawers that line the back wall. I'm assuming that's where all the tools are.

I stop walking, and so does Shane. My heart is pounding while I gaze up at him. "So where do we start?" I ask while being careful about how I breathe. I want to inhale quickly as my heart demands more oxygen, but I take slow, controlled breaths. When I look at Shane, I don't think I have any impact on him. He kneels down on his hunkers and stares at the bike. He's relaxed, and when I kneel down on my knees, he glances at me.

"We clean it," he says with a wink that nearly topples me over.

VI CARTER

CHAPTER SIXTEEN

SHANE

I leave Una to check out her bike that she seems pretty taken with as I get buckets and sponges. The cleaning isn't really necessary. It can wait until after, but the simple task with Una is all that matters.

When I return, she's sitting cross-legged on the tarp chewing her lip, and my heart stills. Her red fiery hair is like a halo, and I think again of what this place will do to her. Since arriving, she has lost weight, and dark circles have grown under her eyes.

She's been strong for all she has found out, but I'm not sure she's strong enough. I don't want her to have to strengthen herself to our way. This is why I never got close to her, why I never touched her, and now I'm terrified because I can't let her go, even if it damages her.

She looks up, and a smile lightens her eyes. She takes in the two buckets and sponges that I carry. Once I set them down, I take two pairs of rubber gloves from my back pocket, one yellow the other pink. I hold the pink pair out to her, but she nods while biting her lip.

"Nope, I want the yellow," she tells me, taking them from my hands. She's trying not to laugh as she puts on her yellow gloves.

"Put on your gloves, Shane," she tells me as she snaps the rubber band at the wrist before grinning up at me.

"You think I'm afraid of a bit of pink?" I ask her, and she laughs. I want to keep her laughing, so I put on the stupid gloves.

"I need to take a picture." She's still laughing as I kneel down and pass her a bucket and sponge.

I open out my arms. "By all means, snap away," I tell her, and she sticks out her pink tongue at me. I'm transfixed, and don't look away from it until she pulls it back into her mouth. My focus now is on her moist lips. My heart gives a heavy thump, and I glance away.

Dipping my sponge into the water, I start cleaning the frame. Una does the same. I follow her sponge hitting it with mine, causing her to laugh and telling me to stay on my own side. There is something amazing about being this close to someone but having a separation between us. I can see everything clearly, but I can't touch, and that makes me observe her and take every tiny detail of Una in. From the freckles that coat the bridge of her nose. The beauty spot under her left ear. Her lashes rise as she pins me with those eyes. Her beauty undoes me all the time, and I snap out of it when she flicks me with water.

"Oh it's like that, is it?" I say while wiping my face with my sleeve as she laughs. I'm quick to act and scoop up a hand full of water, soaking her jumper. She jumps back with a squeal, and I'm smiling.

"No, no," I tell her as she picks up the bucket. I'm standing hands held out, trying to make her put it down. The cold of the water pulls a screech from me along with a few curse words. She's upended the full bucket on me.

When I blink water from my eyes, her face is flushed with excitement. We both move for my bucket, and I get it first. She runs. I use one arm to grab her around the waist and pull her back.

"Okay, hold on. Hold on. Let's talk about this," she says straining to see me, and I entertain her pleas, moving her slowly towards the wall.

"Talk," I tell her once I have her back against the wall. I keep one arm close to her waist as I hold the bucket with the other. The bucket that she keeps looking at.

"I have a cold, and if you pour that water over me, I'll get really sick, and it will be your fault," she says it with a quick jerk of her head, like she's stating a fact.

Water is still dripping from my hair, but I don't wipe it from my face. I keep my hands firmly where they are. "Not good enough," I tell her lifting the bucket, and she holds out her hands, touching my chest.

"If you do that, I will run up to your room in my wet clothes and roll around in your bed."

I snort. "Mary will have more work. This is your last chance," I say with a shrug and lift the bucket a little higher. I love the way her eyes dart from the bucket to me. I'm not going to pour it on her, but seeing her trying to worm her way out of this is fun.

Instead, this time, she leans in closer to me, her hands still on my chest, her focus is on my lips now, and my heart beats faster under her hands. Her lashes rise, and there is something different in her eyes.

"I love you." Her lips tug down as she whispers it, like she might cry.

My heart is ready to come out of my chest, and I know she feels it. I'm frozen not sure what to do. I jump away from Una with a curse as water pours over our feet; I had forgotten it was in my hand. When I glance back up, Una isn't facing the door.

I want to tell her it all starts and ends with her. Seal it with a kiss. My mother's voice comes to me, her stupid saying that for some reason really sank in, took hold and has never left me.

The door opens, and it's like a bubble burst. Liam sizes up the situation. Una stiffens at Liam's arrival, and I don't like it at all. When he turns back to me, his words carry more weight than normal

"I need to have a word with you," he tells me.
I stare at Una, but she still is focused on the door.

"Now," Liam adds, and I grit my teeth at his
words.

"Una." When I say her name, she peeks at
me. The hurt that shines is quickly covered up
with a smile.

"Yeah go. We can do the bike later."

Like a coward, I nod and leave her. I'm
afraid in case she said it as a joke, but it didn't
seem like one. Once we leave the garage, I tell
Liam I will meet him in the library once I change
my clothes.

When I enter the library freshly dressed,
Liam stands with his back to me. "Your actions
have consequences."

My mind hasn't left Una's words. Her face is
there in front of me, her lips tugged down as she
said, "I love you." The longer I was away from
her, the more I questioned if she was messing.
That part of me that wanted to believe she meant
what she said was taking over.

"Are you listening to me, brother?" Liam
now faces me, one hand in his navy suit trousers

pocket. He was talking about father's source telling him Brian was out and looking for vengeance. I don't want to be here, but I will do this back and forth with Liam.

"I'm beginning to see the funny side of all this," I tell him, and Liam doesn't as much as shift.

"So father has a source who gives him information," I say taking a step closer to Liam. "Yet…" I hold up a finger. "Father has never mentioned this source to me, only you."

Now Liam exhales. "Your point brother?"

My point, I wasn't entirely sure I had one, but I knew something was off, or maybe I was being paranoid.

"I don't know, but why does he not tell me." Now I sound jealous.

"Because I am the next in line. You know this. You know you will be my right-hand man. You are already." Sometimes, I felt like a puppet. I never really cared. I just cared about my family. But Una? She was changing me.

"Either of you saw Darragh?" I turn to Finn who hasn't entered the room. The disdain in his voice drips into his words.

"Did you let him off his leash again?" I bark my anger at him, and Finn steps into the room.

"Actually, I wanted to talk to both of you about that."

Liam moves and steps up beside me like we are a united front. With both of us standing in front of him, Finn shrinks back.

"I'm moving in with Siobhan, so you'll have to hire someone else to babysit him."

"So you no longer want to be part of the family business?" Liam asks, and Finn folds his arms over his white t-shirt.

"I didn't say that…"

"You didn't have to. You leave this house, you leave this family." I glance at Liam, questioning when that had become a rule, but he holds Finn's steady eye.

"What, you want me to let Siobhan live here with you two?" His smirk is said with a shake of his head. I had no interest in Siobhan, so I step away and sit down.

"He threatened to kill her." Finn is pointing at me now, anger growing around him.

"You're still hampering on about that," I say with as much boredom I can muster.

"How would you like if I threatened Una?" I sit a bit straighter, but the way Finn says it, I know he never would, but Liam takes in my reaction. They are aware about Una and me.

"Make the threat," I demand standing, trying to clamp down on my temper. He won't, but even the thought has me wanting to reach him.

"You know he wouldn't." It's Liam who speaks, and Finn shrugs as if to say I might. "Also, Shane would never harm Siobhan. You have my word."

Finn glances from me to Liam, but his eyes settle on me. "I want to hear him say it," he says to Liam, but he's staring at me.

"Remember that story that Dad told you about him and his brother killing the boy." Finn's fist clenched at my change in topic, but he nods and says a quick yes and what.

"He lied to you," I tell him and can see color growing in his cheeks.

"When the police came, he told them that it was his brother who killed the boy. His brother Tom who spent ten years in prison for it."

"He said the father went down for it, that he was an alcoholic…" I wave off the fairy tale that Dad told Finn.

"He told you so you would always protect your brother." Liam is staring at me, but I hold Finn's gaze.

"So why are you telling me the truth now?" I didn't blame the suspicion that fills Finn's voice.

"Because father lying to you didn't keep you here, so maybe the truth will. Maybe working with us more would make you stay." Finn walks closer to us and I can see the want there. The want that we can never truly fill.

"But Darragh safety is important, and you are the closest to him," Liam speaks, and I glance at him as he touches Finn on his right shoulder. "Also Shane will give his word that he will never threaten Siobhan again."

"You have my word," I say the pointless words, knowing if she ever needed to be removed, it would be done, but Finn relaxes at my words.

"What else would I be doing?" he asks, and his blue eyes are shining eagerly. I never thought Finn wanted in. I never really thought about Finn, only for him to keep Darragh in check.

"I have a few jobs in mind. But for now, pick one of the outbuildings on the property. Do it up, and you and Siobhan can live there. You don't have to live in the house." I never thought about leaving our home, but the thoughts of us all on the same property didn't entice me.

"Yeah. Yeah. Okay." Finn smile is wide, and I can't help the smile that tugs at my lips.

"What about a drink later to celebrate?" I tell him, and once again, he seems uncertain.

"Okay," he finally says.

"We will speak to you later," Liam's gentle dismissal is a reminder of his place in the family. His eyes dim, but he nods and leaves us alone.

"Well played," Liam says, opening his suit jacket and sitting on the couch across from me.

"I wasn't playing," I tell him. I follow the pattern of golds and red swirls on the large rug under our feet.

"You were. You're that used to it, you were doing it without thinking." I peer up at Liam now, his heavy brown eyes taking note of my every move and reaction. "You need to repair the damage you did with Brian." I know I do, and I will, but right now all I can think about is Una.

"I will." I rise but sit back down as Liam speaks.

"You're too distracted, brother. That will cost you."

"I'll fix it, Liam," I tell him with a warning. I don't regret beating Brian. My only regret is not killing him. I have to fix it for the family's sake, and I will.

It's Liam who stands now and slowly buttons his suit jacket before pinning me with a stare. "Good," he says, and when he walks away, I find myself smiling. He's like father.

After checking the garage, stables, and my room, I find Una in hers. She's lying on her bed. She's changed her clothes to jeans and my green t-shirt. That pleases me. She glances up at me, and color enters her face.

"I'm sorry about leaving," I tell her walking around her bed, so I can see her face.

She glances up again, but her mouth is buried in her crossed arms as she lies on her belly. "It's fine," she mumbles. I don't want to sit on her bed. I can sense her upset, so I lean against the wall right across from her.

"It's just Liam…"

She's up now on her knees, her eyes alive and on fire. "I said it's fine. I don't really care what you and Liam spoke about." Her lips form a thin straight line.

"You're angry." I state the obvious, and she drops my gaze while shaking her head.

"No. It's not your fault," she says, sliding off the bed and sitting on the edge facing the door, with her back to me now.

I move around to her and can see her shoulders tense as I stand before her. "I know your family business, so it's no big deal. We can do the bike another time." I kneel down, and when she glances at me, I try to keep my focus on her words and not my desire to have her right now.

"I know, but my time with you is just as important," I tell her and she quickly drops my gaze before she returns my stare.

"Okay." She doesn't believe me.

I lean in and put my forehead against hers. "I mean it, Una. You are important to me," I tell her.

She leans away from me, and I give her some space but stay on my hunkers. "Summer is important to me."

"You're comparing yourself to a horse?" I ask, not liking that.

"Should I?" Her words are loud, and her anger is building to a point I'm not sure how to contain it.

"I don't know what you want from me?" I'm fucking confused with her anger. I'm telling her she's important, but I don't think she knows what that means. Saying anything else has me shrinking like a coward. I stand up and let her cool down. I tell her this, and she starts laughing.

"I told Darragh." I don't ask what as I face her now. She's standing, her anger moving her lips. "He knows that I know about your family. About you all being drug lords." I can't stop the words that bubble up her throat.

"Do you want to know what he said to me?" she asks, but I clench my fists not answering her. She doesn't want an answer. "Not to tell any of you. That I would get hurt."

"You think I'd hurt you?" I ask through clenched teeth.

"You already have," she shouts the words, and it's like a slap to my face.

"Is this about what you said in the garage?" I ask and her eyes blur.

"God. I'm not doing this with you." She storms into the bathroom, and I'm so fucking confused.

"Una, open the door."

"Go away," she screams back, but I can't leave.

"I'm sorry," I tell the door only to be answered with silence.

"Una, please."

"Please leave me alone." Her whispered words sound tired, and when she says please again, I give in and leave her.

CHAPTER SEVENTEEN

UNA

Tears fall quickly down my face as my heart threatens to come out of my chest. He has no idea how hurt I am. I told him I loved him, and he didn't say it back. I know it's not his fault, but it doesn't stop it from hurting. I needed him to leave before I said something I regretted. Like, begging him to tell me he loved me. God, no one tells you how much this hurts.

I hear the door close, and the fact he actually left hurts even more. I can't stop crying. When did I fall so deep? I knew this would turn out badly. If Liam hadn't arrived, would he have said it? I don't think so. Even coming into my room, I really thought he might, but instead, he acted like I was mad that we didn't finish the stupid bike. I'm half laughing half crying at how stupid I am. Getting up, I don't meet my eyes in the mirror. If I do, I will understand why he doesn't look at me the way I look at him. He's out of my league.

"You're so stupid, Una," I tell myself and leave the
bathroom, taking my phone with me. I have one
destination—the bar. After snagging a bottle of Jack
Daniels, I make my way out to the pool house.
Thankfully, Stephen is finished for the day; I don't
bump into anyone in the yard.

The pool house is empty as I suspected. I don't turn
on any lights. Instead, I sit down on the couch that's
against the wall and stare out onto the pool. I sit
until the night settles in with the bottle of JD still
tucked under my arm. I want to drink it, but another
part of me doesn't. In my other hand, I hold my
phone. It's sad; I have no one to ring.
Acquaintances, I have in the dozens, friends—zero. I
often thought I was born into the wrong era.

I set the phone down and unscrew the cap of the
bottle of Jack Daniels. The first sip burns, and I let
it dull my pain for a second before the pain returns,
and it seems worse, if that's even possible. Pulling
my legs up to my chest, I take another drink of JD
as my phone starts to ring.

I laugh when I see Darragh's name flash across the
screen. I turn the phone facedown. I lie back and
slowly drink from the bottle. The conversation with
me and Shane keeps going around in my head, and
no matter what way I view it, I can't seem to find
the good in it. I say I love you. He doesn't. When he
comes back to me, he tells me I'm important. Not

losing my ID is important or something as equally shitty as that. My phone rings again.

"Why are you being so persistent?" I answer the phone to Darragh.

"I need your help."

I sit up and drink from the bottle again, but I roll my eyes at Darragh's words. "With what?" I ask, ready to end this phone call.

"Please, Una."

"Are you crying?" I question, thinking he can't be. But he doesn't sound good now.

"Can you come and get me?" I lie back and take another swallow from the bottle.

"Can you not ring someone else?" I ask back. The JD burns a path of fire down my throat. It's nice now. It's starting to numb me.

"If I could, I wouldn't be fucking ringing you."

"Keep your knickers on. Fine, give me the address." I laugh at my little joke, and Darragh rattles off the address of where he is. He's in Kells and not far at all.

"Give me twenty minutes," I tell him, and he hangs up, not even a thank you. I take a final drink before I pocket my phone and creep out into the dark night. An idea starts to form in my head, a bad idea, but it's making me giddy with excitement.

Making my way to the garage, I open the box that holds spare keys for all the cars. I get the Audi unlocked with the second key. Sliding into the driver's side, my heart squeezes. Shane's car purrs when I press the button. The rational part of me says he is going to be pissed, but the reckless side of me thinks it's a bit of justice.

When I start to reverse, the garage door lifts up, and I back out without crashing the car. I floor it as I race up the drive, sending dust and stones against the side of the car. I'm smirking as I hit the main road. There's a sense of freedom as I keep changing gears. Once I shift into sixth gear, I let out a yell. Yeah, this was fun.

The estate I pull into is run down. Grey two-story houses are lined until I can't see them. They don't end, but keep going in some infinite line. There is a good chance if I leave the Audi and go and get Darragh, it won't be here when I get back. Darragh had said number three, and I pull up outside the house. No lights are on, and all the curtains are pulled. Several car tires are sitting on the lawn that's dead and bleeding out onto the cracked asphalt.

Pulling the phone from my pocket, I then ring Darragh. He doesn't answer. I'm peering around the estate. It's quiet around, but still, I don't want to chance losing Shane's car.

"Where are you?" Darragh asks when I ring for the third time.

"Outside. Why wouldn't you answer your phone?"

He doesn't answer me.

"I need you to come in." When I start to protest, the asshole hangs up on me.

"Shit," I say as I turn off the car and get out. Locking it doesn't make me feel any better as I walk up the driveway to the front door. I don't have to knock as Darragh opens the door and yanks me in.

"Does anyone know you're here?" he asks. "Is that Shane's car?" He spins around on me, and I shrug. "I'm alone, and yeah, it's his car."

He closes the door and scratches his neck. "This was a bad idea."

"Yeah, it was. Why couldn't you come outside?" I say, peering around the hall. It wasn't dirty, but the simple beige linoleum on the hall floor had lots of cracks and holes in it. The door to the right of

Darragh was pine and light enough that if you punched it, your fist would go through. A small lamp that was shining from under stairs was the sole light in the hall, but I could still make out the paleness of Darragh's face.

"I've fucked up." His words have dread dripping down my spine. The alcohol burns out of my system as he pushes open the sitting-room door. Three dark, stained couches fill the room. A TV that is showing static now is lighting up the room. The light bouncing off the face of the girl in the silver disk dress. Her purple lips and still chest have me frozen in the doorway.

"Oh my god, is she dead?" I ask not taking my eyes off her.

"Yes, she's dead." I glance at Darragh.

"You ring me?" I can't for a second understand this. My eyes go back to the dead girl. This isn't like the bathroom with the other girl. This girl is dead dead. Like really dead. My stomach heaves, and I turn, but nothing comes out.

"If I ring my family, they will kill me this time." The fear in Darragh's words isn't enough for me to not miss the 'this time.'

"You've rung them about a dead body before?" I ask. "Don't answer that," I say quickly.

"Oh my God, Darragh. She's dead." He sits down beside her, and when I shout at him, he gets up.

"Calm the fuck down, Una. I need you to stay calm and help me. Not fucking lose your shit over a prostitute." I stare at the girl again, and my pity for her increases.

"She's a person," I tell him.

But he doesn't hear me. Instead, he lights a fag. "First time, it's hard, but you're part of the family now, and family comes first." He's rattling off words while staring at the girl.

"First time for what?"

"We need to get rid of her." I could accept a lot of things, but murder wasn't one of them. I take out my phone to ring the Gardaí. The carpet scrapes against my face as my phone hits the skirting board. I didn't even see Darragh move.

"Who are you ringing?" He sounds calm now, but it doesn't match his actions. His hand is on my head keeping my face pressed into the carpet. A terrified part of me questions if he will kill me, too.

"No one." I try to peer at him, but he forces my face harder into the floor. "Please, Darragh." I whimper now. I was stupid for coming here. He releases me, and I sit up but don't stand. I don't think my legs could carry me.

Darragh is still on the floor. "They will kill me," he says now as he peers at me.

"Who Shane, Liam? They wouldn't," I tell him, and he starts to laugh.

"You have no idea." A shiver snakes its way around my spine. "Tell me," I say, but I don't want to know. My brain has short circuited on the fact that there is a dead body not ten feet from me. My ringing phone has both of us jumping, and I don't go for it. Feralness has entered Darragh eyes, and I'm afraid.

"Darragh, please, let me ring for help."

His eyes snap to mine. "Are you fucking thick?" he barks, and there is a huge part of me that shrinks back and shrivels up at his words. But the survival instinct kicks in, and I stand.

"What do you want me to do?" I ask but can't stop the tremble that's entered my voice and lips.

"We need to find something to wrap her in and then get rid of her." My phone rings again, and Darragh marches across the room and picks it up. His back is to me. I could make a dash for the door, but he's too close. My eyes dart to the dead girl and my stomach rises and falls. This isn't happening.

"Fuck!" his roar has me frozen as his eyes snap to me. "Did you ring him?" he asks marching back to me.

"You need to calm down." I push as much authority into my voice as I can. My phone is being waved around in his hand. "Did you ring Shane?"

"No, Darragh." The fear and upset is in my words, and Darragh pauses his raving and exhales a breath.

"I'm sorry," he tells me pulling me into a hug and every part of my skin crawls. I want him away from me, but I force myself to wrap my arms around him, I hope he can't feel the dampness on his neck as my tears trickle down my face. I squeeze my eyes as his phone starts to ring. When he peers down at it, he pulls his hair, but I'm surprised when he answers.

CHAPTER EIGHTEEN

SHANE

"Do you have Shane's car?" Liam asks as I sit back on the couch. My head is pounding. An hour ago, I found my car missing and also Una and Darragh. It's a bad combination. Liam has insisted that he will ring Darragh before I jump to any conclusions.

"Have you seen Una?" I stare at Liam now as my heart starts to pick up it's pace. I'm checking his features for any change, and when he turns his back on me, he's hiding something. I'm standing now, and when I reach him, the call ends.

"Our brother needs us," Liam says as he turns to me. "He needs us to be calm."

We take Liam's Range Rover. "Are you sure Una wasn't there?" I ask him again as I glance out the window. He's withholding something from me.

"I told you, Darragh wasn't very clear. Just he needed us." I hate being the passenger. Liam is a careful driver, and I'm trying not to tell him to stop the jeep so I can drive.

"Our brother needs us," Liam speaks again when I don't.

"That's the problem. He always needs us," I mumble.

"Family comes first," Liam says our family motto with a ferocity I understand.

"If she's here, I'm going to kill him." This time, I stare at Liam, but he doesn't flinch. "She may have decided to go with him. You don't know the facts." I get a flicker of his attention before he focuses on the road again.

"She's with him isn't she?" I repeat and clench my fists. I should never have left her. She must have gone drinking with Darragh, and he wouldn't take care of her.

"Family comes first Shane."

I snap my attention to Liam. "She is family," I tell him, and he glances at me. "She's not blood."

He reminds me, but she's more than that to me. Fuck. She takes place over Darragh any day.

We pull into a rundown estate, and my car is parked outside the third house. I'm surprised it's still sitting there. My focus goes to the house.

"I'll go in first," Liam speaks as he pulls up behind my car. I jump out but wait for him to go first. Darragh opens the door, and Liam steps through. He goes to close it, but I push it open. There is a change in his face. He pales. He wasn't expecting me.

Liam enters a room, and Darragh skips ahead of him, and I tell my heart to slow down as a horrible thought comes to me. What if he has hurt Una? I step into the room as Liam speaks. "Everyone needs to remain calm," he says, but my sole focus is sitting on the couch.

My heart gives a heavy thud as I skim over the dead girl and take in Una. She's sitting on the couch with tears streaming down her face. She's staring at her hands that are folded in her lap. Her face is obscured from her hair. I can't take my eyes off her. I can't breathe. Air gushes from my nose.

"Shane, calm down," Liam speaks again, and Una's head snaps up, her lip trembles, and all I can do is uncurl my fist and stretch out my hand for her to take. She steals a glance at Darragh and Liam but stands quickly, ducking her head as she comes to me.

Pulling her into my side, I glance up at Liam. I can't speak. If I do, I will kill Darragh. I'm not sure what Liam sees on my face, but he turns to Darragh. The contact isn't enough for me, but the slap has Una tightening herself closer to me. I wrap my hand more securely around her frame.

"All the stupid and reckless things you have done. This is the worst." Darragh holds his face. His coloring darkens to a grey. Liam has never put his hands on any of us, so this tells me he's angry.

"I didn't mean for her to die." Another slap is delivered to Darragh's face cutting off his words.

"I'm talking about Una. You had no right involving her in this." Liam's raised words are feeding into the want to hurt Darragh myself. But I'm unable to move. I can't let Una see that side of me, and I can't let her go right now.

"I knew if I rang you, Liam, that you'd kill me." Darragh's throwing his hands in the air, a shiver in his tone. He's avoiding eye contact with me.

"It's not me you should be worried about," Liam informs him as he glances at me.

"I know." Darragh still doesn't meet my eye, but I can't stand here any longer and not kill him. I turn and take Una with me out of the sitting room and enter a clean but scarcely furnished kitchen. A large table takes up most the room, and I pull out one of two chairs that remain tucked under it. Once I have her seated, I kneel down in front of her.

"I'm sorry." She swallows her tears as she speaks. My fingers cup her chin and gently tilt her head up. She meets my eyes.

"You have nothing to be sorry for," I tell her, holding her face as gently as I can.

"I stole your car." Her lips are in a frown as she speaks, and my thumb strokes her lips gently. They turn up slightly.

"It's only a car," I tell her, and she shakes her head.

"I was stupid to come here, and there's a dead girl in there, and I don't think he cares." Her words hitch at the end, and her eyes blur before tears start to fall again. Pulling her into my arms, I hold her, and she shakes with large sobs.

I was going to fucking kill him.

"I tried to ring the Gardaí, but he wouldn't let me." Her words have me closing my eyes briefly. She sounds stunned that we wouldn't ring the Gardaí. Her innocence is refreshing, and also a reminder of what our life will do to her. She sits back and sniffles, her face flushed.

"You'll ring?" she asks, but she's nodding as if to say of course I will. I don't want to lie to her, but I'm also not going for the truth.

"Let's find out what happened first. Okay?" I tell her, and she nods.

"He rang me. I thought it was to pick him up. I didn't think it would be this." She flicks her head in the direction of the door.

"It's okay now," I tell her, brushing back some red curls from her face.

"I'm going to go in and see what's happened. I want you to stay here," I tell her, wanting nothing more than to scoop her up and take her from this place. But she gives me a little nod, and I press my lips to her forehead before I rise.

I enter the sitting room, and Liam takes a step towards me. The girl is still where she was, and Darragh is sitting on the couch smoking.

"It wasn't his fault. She overdosed. He had sex with her, so was worried about his DNA." Liam is explaining the stupidity that is our brother.

"Shane," Darragh pleads my name, and I manage to raise one finger.

"Not a word," I tell him, and he gives Liam a final glance before his eyes settle on the floor.

"I'll get him to ring it in and report it," Liam tells me, stuffing a hand in his pocket. Darragh's head snaps up to Liam, but he has the sense not to speak. Liam's handprints are still on Darragh's face, but it's nothing compared to what I want to do to him.

"Darragh, go wait in my jeep." Liam speaks to Darragh, but he's focused at me. Darragh gets up and gives me as wide a birth as the room will allow.

Once he leaves, Liam opens the top button of his shirt. "I've never asked for anything from you. I beg you, leave him alone. You have my word he will never go near Una again." It means so much coming from Liam. If this were for anyone else, I would agree. But right now, at this given moment, I can't.

"No," I tell him and leave the room to go get Una. When I walk into the kitchen, her head snaps up to me. She's stopped crying, but the circles under her eyes have grown darker.

"Liam is ringing the police now, so we better go." I've never seen Una appear fragile. When I reach out my hand, she takes it easily and twines our fingers together. Her face is still tense.

I remind myself I am doing this for her as I speak. "She overdosed. Darragh didn't hurt her. He panicked because he was intimate with her." My words don't come out as soft as I hoped, but when Una glances up at me, I see a spark there, like everything is going to be okay.

"He didn't hurt her," she says like she's waking up from a dream. I squeeze her hand.

"Of course not. He just panicked." I open the passenger door for her and don't glance back at Liam or Darragh. Liam has started the Jeep but hasn't pulled away.

Once Una is safely inside, I move around to the driver door. It's then I peer up to find both of them watching me. Once I climb into the car, I turn on the heat. She's shivering. It's not the cold, but I'm unsure what to do.

"God, I'm so, so sorry for everything. I acted like such a child earlier." The car has been moving for a few moments, and I thought she had fallen asleep.

"Una, everything is fine. You did nothing wrong," I tell her, and she falls silent.

I have a pain in my hands by the time I pull into the garage. I unclench my fist from the steering wheel, and once I knock off the car, I turn to Una.

"He scared me," she tells the window. "I tried to leave, but he wouldn't let me. Only for Liam

ringing, I don't know what would have happened."
Her lips tug downwards as she blinks back tears.
She doesn't cry, but her gaze becomes more focused
on me.

"He's your brother. I'm sorry." She frowns and
shakes her head, like trying to stop herself from
talking. My silence isn't helping, but the idea of him
not letting her go is killing me. "I'm just tired," she
says and reaches for the door handle.

"I wish you didn't have to see that tonight," I
manage to say, and she glances back at me over her
shoulder, her eyes blinking with exhaustion.

"Me too."

Una changes her clothes, and I wait as she gets
organized before she slips into the bed. After
tucking the surrounding covers, I trace the darkness
under her eyes. "You need to sleep. Everything will
be better in the morning," I tell her.

She manages a weak smile. "Liar," she says, but
I'm smiling because so is she.

The relief has me almost thinking of getting in
beside her. But I don't. I can't.

Kissing her on the forehead, I leave on the lamp light before making my way to the library, where I know Liam and Darragh will be.

The door is closed, but I can hear them behind it. Once I enter, they stop talking, and Darragh moves behind Liam. That sets me off.

I grab him by the shirt and drag him out.

"Shane, don't."

Liam's warning I don't pay any attention too.

"Jesus. Please..." Darragh, the coward, covers his face, but I put as much force as possible into the punch. Holding him with my other hand, I don't let him fall. Liam drags me off him after three punches. I'm only getting started.

"Family comes first." Liam's holding me around the chest. His words are spoken harshly and close to my ear. Darragh is lying against the bookcase, his face a bloody mess.

I'm breathing fast with adrenaline and I'm not satisfied, but Liam repeats his words again, and I try to bring some calm back to me.

"Let me go," I tell him, but he doesn't immediately. "Liam, let me go. I won't touch him." He releases me, but I don't release Darragh from my stare. A shaky hand rises, and he wipes blood from his mouth and nose. Liam walks over to him and drops a white handkerchief into his lap. Darragh picks it up and starts wiping at his face.

"Are you done?" Liam asks me, and I flex my fist, my knuckles burning. I don't answer his stupid question.

"Have you wondered why he rang Una?" Liam asks while he glances back at Darragh who's still trying to clean his face.

"Because he's a spoilt little prick who thinks he can do whatever he wants," I say, but my stomach tightens at the question.

"Someone told her about us."

"Is there something you want to ask me?" I shoot back to Liam, his words sound like he's implying I told her.

"Is there something you want to tell us?" Liam sounds righteous.

"Yeah, that he is always high. Maybe he told her and forgot."

"No, I didn't." I take a threatening step towards Darragh, and he shuts up, but Liam moves closer to me.

"Liam won't always be here to protect you, Darragh. You're such a fucking disappointment to us. To Dad."

"Shane, stop." Liam the peacekeeper speaks again, but I don't as much as give him a glance I keep Darragh pinned to the floor with my stare as I speak.

"It's only a matter time before we are pulling you out a ditch as you rot away like a sheep." My words have him standing, fire in his eyes, and I grin at him.

"Look, I know I fucked up…"

I have to walk away from his pathetic words. But as he keeps speaking, I turn back around. "I never put a hand on her." His words have Liam closing his eyes, but my whole body tenses.

"I never said you did, so why would you say that." I take a step back towards him.

"I'm just saying because I don't know why you're so angry." He's still dabbing his nose with his little white handkerchief.

"Shut up, Darragh," Liam tells him, and his eyes widen.

"No, it's fine, Liam." I hold up a hand towards Liam to let him know to say silent as I educate my dimwit brother. "You rang an innocent girl who, number one is a girl, number two, has no dealings with our world. You don't just ring her to pick you up from a junkie's house, but you what? Expect her to help you get rid of a body." I'm laughing again. "Are you that fucking stupid?"

"I panicked." He's acting like a victim.

I move quickly and slam him against the bookshelf. "You're a self-centered little prick." My hands go to his neck, and I squeeze. He's trying to claw my hands away from his neck. His eyes widen as he stares at me.

"Shane, let him go." Liam is there now, but I don't. His words have me squeezing tighter. Darragh's eyes grow wider. Liam grabs my face. "You're going to kill him. Let him go." His calm words in a moment of chaos have me releasing him. Darragh falls to the floor, gasping and retching for air. But once again, I'm not satisfied. I can no longer stay in the room with them.

CHAPTER NINETEEN

UNA

I wake up with a racing heart. All I see are silver disks that belong to the dress of a dead girl. Tears leave the corners of my eyes, and I blink quickly wanting them to stop. As I sit up slowly, I'm faced with Shane's back. He's sitting on the bed, his head bowed. I can't see his face.

"Shane?" I whisper, and his head shoots up. The strain on his face disappears, and his eyes grow lighter.

"I didn't mean to wake you," he tells me as he gets up and makes his way around the bed.

"You didn't." I don't tell him what did. "Are you okay?" I ask. Dark circles under his eyes are worrying me. A frown appears on his face as he sits down on the bed.

His eyes roam my face, and my stomach squeezes.

"You're too kind, Una," he says, and I'm not sure why. But I don't object as he moves closer and pulls me slowly into his arms. I come out from under the covers and wrap myself around him while inhaling his scent, and it relaxes me. In his arms, I feel safer. "I keep seeing her face when I close my eyes," I tell him like a confession, and his arms tighten around me. "What happened with her?" I ask him.

"Her family has been notified. She's in good hands now. Poor girl was an addict." Shane doesn't sound like he thinks she is a poor girl. His words are robotic, and I try to see his face, but he holds me closer. "Just let me hold you for a while longer." His request scares me.

Every few seconds, Shane plants a kiss on my head, and I'm sure his hold grows tighter to the point of being almost crushing.

"Shane." When I speak his name he loosens his hold on me, but doesn't release me, and the longer he keeps me in his arms the bigger my fear grows. It almost seems like a long goodbye.

"When I saw you sitting on that couch…" He stops speaking and releases me, allowing me to sit back.

I'm on my hunkers in front of him. He won't look at me, and I swallow the ball of fear that has lodged itself in my throat.

"You don't belong here. I've been so selfish holding on to you." His eyes hold such conviction, and my heart slams against my ribcage. "If you want to leave, you can." I'm gaping at him and struggling to breathe. He was trying to get rid of me. Telling him I loved him seemed to have messed everything up. I want to take it back, but looking at him, it hurts too much to speak.

"Una, don't look at me like that." He reaches for my hand, and I pull it back.

Tears fall quietly. "I've been forward with you." My nose, throat and eyes burn, and I have to stop speaking before I bawl cry. "Too forward," I whisper and wish my stupid emotions would stop until I got the words out.

"I can take a step back," I tell him with a shrug and I sound pathetic. The pity in his eyes has heat travelling up my neck. Oh, God. Was everyone laughing at the lovesick fool, pining after Shane?

"It's not you, Una."

I laugh at his words; my laughter dies down and ends on an angry sob. Climbing off the bed, I need to get away from him.

"This is coming out all wrong. You're picking me up the wrong way." His words are barked at me as he gets up too.

"Tell me, Shane. Do you and Liam laugh about how stupid I am?" I question, and Shane tilts his head with narrowed eyes.

"What has Liam got to do with this?" He takes a step towards me, and I ignore the tightness that enters my stomach.

"He warned me away from you. Did you ask him to do that because you're not man enough?" Shane's eyes widen, nose flared, and I'm surprised at the frozen stature of his frame.

Shane clenches his fist. I see the red and swollen knuckles. I'm there beside him, taking his damaged hand in mine. "What happened?" He didn't have this before I went to bed.

"What did you do?" I ask him quietly. His chest rises and falls quickly, and when I put my hand over his thundering heart, wild eyes meet mine. I want to know what the hell is going on inside his head.

"What I had to," he answers through clenched teeth. I'm shaking my head.

"Shane." He tries to move past me, but I race to the door. I don't have a clue what I'm doing, but the violence in his eyes is scaring me.

"You hurt Darragh?"

His eyes snap to me. "Move, Una." I'm shaking my head again.

"You can't go around hurting people," I tell him and force as much authority as possible into my words.

"They can't go around threatening and terrorizing you," he shouts back, and I jump slightly.

"It wasn't like that. He was concerned for you." Now Shane is shaking his head. He's in front of me, a head taller as he stares straight ahead. "Move, Una," he tells me again.

He glances at me as I place a hand on his chest. "I'm begging you, for me. Don't leave this room. Not tonight." His eyes roam my face, jaw clenched. He doesn't answer me, but he doesn't ask me to move again either. I'll take it as a small victory.

God, my love for him is affecting my judgment. Anyone else, I would be long gone. I can't figure him out. I tell myself I'm doing it to calm him down, but I can't manage to keep away from him. My hands leave his chest and roam to his shoulders, I want to pull him into a kiss, but something stops me. Slowly, moving him back towards the bed, he lets me. My heart picks up. Every part of my body squeezes at the thoughts of having him again.

VICIOUS IRISH

The weight of his stare nearly undoes me. But I keep some form of control as he sits on the bed. Pulling his jumper off, I inhale the scent of him as my eyes devour his flesh. His muscular torso has me squeezing my legs together.

I kneel in front of him and spread his legs. Shane doesn't stop me as I move close to him. When my lips press against his stomach, the muscles flex and tense under each kiss I plant there. I trail kisses up his chest and along his neck; I have never been so taken or consumed with someone before.

Holding his face, staring into the darkest brown eyes ever, I flicker a glance at his lips. He tenses when I move close, I place the kiss on his shoulder instead. His hands move now and pull off my top. The cream bra that I wear is unhooked quickly and finds itself on the floor.

I don't cover myself but allow Shane the same access as he gave me. My fingers sink into his hair as he starts a trail of kisses down my neck. Stomach twisting and the yearning that was building in me, I wasn't sure I could hold on. The intensity grows on Shane, too, as I find myself on my back on the bed. His strong hands and damaged knuckles graze my thigh as he pulls off my trousers. His eyes devour me, and I arch my pelvis up.

It seems forever as he removes his trousers and boxers. His erection springs out, and I'm spreading my legs for him as he moves on top of me. Pulling my underwear aside, Shane places his erection at the opening. His focus is back on my face. Biting my lip is the thing that stops me from shouting out that I need him now.

When he enters me, I let out a long moan. His thrusts are slow and deep, but I want it quick. I want all of him in me. Pulling him down closer by the shoulders, I widen my legs even further, and Shane plunges deeper, faster, and I close my eyes as each roll of ecstasy courses through my body. The final one ends when Shane slams into me and pauses as he releases before moving out slowly and back in two more times.

Slipping out of me, he moves down until his head rests on my stomach while he still lies between my throbbing legs. We stay like that as we catch our breath. A kiss to my stomach has my heart picking up speed again. Watching Shane now as he hoists himself off me, my stomach twists and dances. It's there, those stupid three words that I want to tell him. I drop his gaze.

I don't know what to do as he arrives back from the bathroom with a face cloth and cleans me down. I bite hard on the inside of my jaw so I don't cry. How could I let him go? Once he has me cleaned, he goes into the bathroom and turns on the shower. It's then I get up and put on his green t-shirt and a clean pair of underwear before climbing back into the bed.

When Shane climbs into the bed, my breasts swell in his t-shirt with a want to have him again. The need has me almost turning around, but I don't. He's beside me, and the heat off his body sends me into a slumber. I'm nearly asleep when his arm drapes over my stomach, and a kiss is left on my cheek.

***

I wake. My body tells me I had sex last night. I still throb. Opening my eyes, my stomach sinks. Shane isn't here. While sitting up, I stare at his side and find a small note sitting on his pillow. I'm smiling like a fool as I open it.

The sun is shining, so get dressed. I'm taking you off.

One line has me racing from the bed, like a kid on Christmas morning as I jump in the shower. I spend time picking out a nice cream lace summer dress. It's really pretty, and this was the perfect occasion. The buttons start at my belly button and go the whole way to my neck. I leave the top two open and grin at myself in the mirror.

My hair is wild today, and no matter how I try to tame it, curls stick out and spring wherever they want. Today was going to be warm. My hair was telling me that. It never behaved in good weather. Oh, well.

After grabbing a pair of green runners, I slip them on. A bit odd with the dress, but I wanted to be comfortable.

When I enter the kitchen, Mary gives me a smile. "He's waiting out front for you." Her words have my chest swelling, and I can't stop the ridiculous smile that's plastered across my face.

A squeal tears from my throat, and Shane's lips lift, dimples appearing. I would be consumed by him, but the Cadillac that he stands beside gets most of my attention. But not all.

"Where have you been hiding this beauty?" I run my hand along the leather roof that's rolled back. I can see my reflection in the black Cadillac, my eyes are huge, and I'm still smiling.

"She's new," he tells me, removing his hand from his trousers pockets. The short-sleeved navy t-shirt is allowing me to see his tattoo in the light of day. The thick black bands are such a statement.

"You like her?" he asks, and I snap my attention back to him.

"It's a 1941 Convertible Cadillac. I mean, what's not to like." His smile turns into laughter at my enthusiasm.

Moving around to the passenger door, Shane opens it, and I climb in. I don't say anything about the wooden weaved picnic basket in the back seat.

Shane starts the engine, and I close my eyes in bliss as the engine rumbles under us. "Will I give you a moment?" Shane teases, and when I glance at him, I want to tell him how much I love him. How he undoes me every time I set eyes on him.

"No," I answer, and he takes in a deep breath through his nose like he heard my three words on that one answer.

The wind whips my hair around my face. It's not a pretty picture. It's most certainly not like the movies. It's like a sheep slammed into my face, and Shane has been proper laughing for the last few moments as I battle with the red curls.

"I'm cutting it off," I threaten as it settles. Shane knocks off the engine as we pull in at Dun Na Ri Park.

"Don't you dare," he warns.

"You laugh at me again, and I will," I threaten. A yelp jumps from my lips as he pulls me close. My heart slams into my chest. When Shane presses his forehead against mine, I'm disappointed, but also, I'm beginning to think this is how he kisses. Like penguins use their noses. Shane uses his forehead. A quick abrupt laugh leaves my lips. I don't answer Shane's raised eyebrow. Instead, I jump out of the Cadillac.

The grass under my feet has recently been cut, the ends of the grass sending small shock waves up my legs. I glance at Shane as he sits on the rug and eats grapes out of the basket. He had packed our breakfast, and it was perfect.

With my stomach full and my soul light, yesterday seemed like a distant dream. "I don't know how you are doing that?" Shane says again, and I lift a leg before slowly lowering my bare feet into the grass. He visibly shivers.

"Come on, try it," I tell him, but he's shaking his head.

"No grass and sand are two things I don't like touching my skin."

I roll my eyes. Bending at the waist, I pull out a handful of grass.

"Oh, Shane O'Reagan is afraid of a bit of grass." I throw it at him, and one piece manages to float into his mouth that he spits out, and I laugh. Laughter turns to yelp as he gets up off the grass and chases after me. My destination is a large oak that stands in the middle of the park. My feet leave the ground as Shane grabs me and spins me around. The world halts as he drags me down onto the grass.

I'm laughing as he pokes my stomach, and when he stops, all I see is the blue sky and brown eyes, and it squeezes my heart. Shane is above me, resting on his tattooed arm, and I don't move. There is such a seriousness in his eyes that I hold still.

"When you first came to our house, I hated you." Not what I was expecting. His confession has me wanting to rise, but he continues speaking. "I hated you, because I wanted you. I wanted you like I've never wanted anything." His brows pull down as he speaks. His focus is on my shoulder. "I didn't want to ruin you," he says and glances at me.

My heart gallops as he reaches out and moves a curl off my cheek. "I know the right thing to do is to convince you to leave…" I try to sit up, but his free hand on my shoulder stops me.

"Not this again," I tell him as my heart thunders in my chest. He was going to tell me to leave again. My heart couldn't take this.

"Please, let me finish." He closes his eyes on the word please. I try to remain quiet. "The right thing would be to tell you to leave, but I'm too selfish to give you up, Una." Heat rises in my cheeks at his words.

Reaching up, I hold his face, and he leans into me. "I won't leave, anyway. I'm like a bad infection." He snorts a laugh at my words before turning my hand around and kissing my palm. Electricity zings down my arm and goes straight to my heart.

"My mother, she had this funny saying. 'Seal it with a kiss.'" At the mention of a kiss, my heart grows almost frantic in my chest.

"At night, when she tucked us all in, she would tell us how much she loved us. A kiss to the lips was the final part. She said it sealed in her love. She said that when we truly love someone, it was so important to seal it with a kiss." I nearly can't breathe at what he is saying. His eyes flicker to my lips that I must have wet a million times since he started talking about kissing.

"I'm going to kiss you now," he tells me.

I'm shaking my head. "Wait." My one word is breathless, but I can't stop the panic that races through me.

"What if it's not good?" I ask, my insecurities rising like a tidal wave to the top. "What if I'm too sloppy, or too dry?"

"Una," Shane says, but I cut him off.

"There's too much pressure, I don't know if I can live up to such…"

"Cunas, Una." The softness and the Irish word for quiet has my words silenced as Shane moves closer to me. A sense of sinking into the grass, and going deeper down the rabbit hole has me holding my breath. His breath brushes my lips, and my hands sink into the grass.

"You look terrified," he says, and I'm blinking, thinking why the hell is he talking, why are his lips not on mine.

Our breaths mingle together, and I flick out my tongue one last time as his lips brush mine, and my whole body seems to sigh before a drum beats within my veins, pushing the blood around my body way too quickly. A sense of swaying as Shane parts my lips with his tongue makes this all seem unreal.

His kiss is full but not urgent. It's slow and perfect, and I can't get oxygen into my lungs. Shane's smell, taste, his mouth is taking over every part of me, and I give myself up to him.

CHAPTER TWENTY

SHANE

Una under me is as I had imagined. Kissing her is a high I've never felt before. I deepen the kiss, forcing my tongue deeper inside her mouth, and she gives me entry easily. Her hands grip my shoulders as she pulls me closer. I have to pull back. My body is demanding more, but I remember we are in the middle of a park.

"Wow." Una's swollen lips move, and I smile down at her.

"Yeah, wow," I repeat, and her lips tug up into a smile that shows me a set of perfect white teeth.

"Can we do it again?" Her wide eyes and eagerness has me giving her a soft kiss on the lips.
"Anytime"—I kiss her again—"you want." Another kiss, and this time, she forces her tongue into my mouth, and I pull back again.

"There could be children around," I tell her, and she nods, fixing her dress.

"Yeah, you're right." Color coats her cheeks as I sit up and take her hand, helping her sit up too. Pressing a kiss to her shoulder, I glance up at her from under my lashes, and there is pure awe in her eyes.

"Tell me about your mum?" she asks.

The question surprises me. "She was really great." Great doesn't even cut it. "She was fun." I'm smiling at the memory of her waking us up at six in the morning. She had spent hours filling water balloons up. She must have filled hundreds of them. Taking us outside, we had the biggest water fight ever.

We were all red and marked when we came inside later that morning, but we all were smiling. Even Liam used to smile then. My smile must falter as Una squeezes my shoulder.

"Are you okay? I'm sorry if I pried." I cover her hand with mine.

"I was thinking about how Liam used to smile more when mum was alive."

"Liam and smiling in one sentence? Never." Her wide eyes and exaggerated surprise has me smiling again. My lips find hers, and my fingers sink into her hair. Her lips are warm and moist and fit perfectly against mine. She was created for me.

My heart thuds as I think of what she means to me. "I don't think I could ever get used to this." She speaks in-between kisses.

"Stay with me," I ask, and she leans out.

"Like in your room?" She seems confused.

Holding her face, I swallow before speaking. "No, stay with me forever."

Her chest rises and falls quickly. "Forever is a long time." Her whispered words are accompanied with blurred eyes.

"Not long enough with you." I wipe away a falling tear. Turning her face, she kisses my hand.

"Forever," she says, and my heart swells.

My phone ringing can't be ignored. I kiss Una on the nose before getting up to take the call. It's Neill, and I have been waiting on any word from him about the new supplier. This is one call I can't miss.

"What news do you have?" I ask after taking a few steps away from Una. Glancing back at her now, she has her hand covering her swollen lips, but I can see the smile in her eyes as she gazes up at me.

"Brian is out of hospital and meeting with the new supplier today." The little prick. Liam warned me about this happening.

"Where?"

"Smiths in the next hour." Brian had to know that word would get back to me.

"Thanks, Neill," I say and hang up. Each step towards Una makes guilt churn in my stomach. I hate that I have to cut our first proper date short. But we have forever to make up for it. I sit back down and kiss her on the shoulder again. Her eyes roam my face.

"What's wrong?" she asks as I kiss her again on the shoulder.

"I have to go to work," I tell her. "But I'll make it up to you." A spark of desire flares to life in her eyes.

"I can think of a lot of ways that you can make it up to me," she says, and I kiss her softly on the lips.

"Care to share?"

She bites her lip. "I'd rather show you later."

VICIOUS IRISH

My trousers tighten at her words. "You're killing me," I tell her.

She gets up while wiping grass off the back of her dress. "Good." She winks before strolling back to our picnic basket. She throws a smile over her shoulder, making all her red curls bounce, everything about Una takes my breath away.

I hadn't told Una that I bought the car for her. I know she won't accept it, but it's in her name. I put the roof up this time but leave the windows down. Watching Una glance around the car while she touches it like it was a pet lets me know I made the right decision buying it.

Once we get home, I switch cars and give Una one final kiss. "I'll try not to be late," I tell her as I climb into the Audi but roll down the window.

"I'll wait for you." She is swaying like an innocent girl would, but her words and eyes are full of devilment.

I leave before I change my mind. Twenty minutes later, I pull into Kells. It's two in the day. The pub won't be an opening for another two hours. I take my handgun out of the glove compartment. Checking to make sure it's loaded, and the safety is on, I push it into the waistband of my trousers.

I knock three times before Michael opens the door. He quickly steps aside before closing the door behind me. "Shane, this is my livelihood. Please don't wreck it." His words have me pausing, and I give him a curt nod that seems to relax him.

I'm not sure what exactly I'm walking into. I go into the lounge knowing it will be empty before jumping the counter. Moving down the bar, I ring the bell as I enter the bar area. Two men sit at a corner table both face me and I force a smile. "A drink?" I ask. Brian's face is covered in a white cast that covers the top part of his face showing his eyes.

"A whiskey," a Northern Ireland accent says. I pour out three whiskeys. Bernard gets up from the table and sits at the bar picking up a whiskey. He holds it up to me. "To family," he says, and I knock my glass against his.

"To family," I repeat.

"You know each other?" Brian speaks now for the first time, getting up, and I slide the glass down to him. He's too slow, and it slides off the end of the bar and smashes on the floor.

"How's your face?" I ask him, and I'm not sure, but I think his eyes narrow. Hard to tell with all the bandages.

"Michael's not impressed with you crossing the line," I tell Bernard as he finished his drink.

"Michael? That's what you call him now. I call mine Da."

I smirk, but it's stretched across my tense face. "You've no right to be here," I tell him.

"You think your family is better than mine." It's not a question but a statement.

"At least my Da isn't a rat." My heart thumps wildly in my chest.

"You know each other?" Brian parrots again.

"He's my cousin," I say, not looking away from Bernard.

"They were kids, and name calling isn't very smart of you," I say through gritted teeth.

"What are you going to do, Shane? You touch me, and the RA will be down here tearing this place apart."

I force a laugh before refilling my drink slowly. "Trust me Bernard..." I say and take a drink. "You're not important," I tell him, and his annoyance grows.

"I've every right to be here. You treat your men like animals, so I'm taking over."

I finish my drink, tired with this conversation.

"I'm not looking to get employer of the year. But you taking over? Let's see," I say and decide that he's no real threat. Gary in Dublin would never bend to Bernard's terms. He's too cocky. The problem that really was here was Brian. I needed to get him on my side. I refill two glasses, and this time, I walk down to Brian and place a drink in front of him.

"Water under the bridge," I say holding up my glass like I hundred percent expect him to the same. Relief swims through me as he picks it up and clicks glasses with me.

"You can't do that. We made a deal." Bernard is standing now.

"The deal is off," I tell him, and his face grows red.

"You can't do that."

"I just did."

"You do know who I am?" His arrogance is pissing me off.

Moving back towards him, I lean across the bar. "No, Bernard, do you know who I am?"

"Yeah, I do. You're a whore's son." I look away before snapping back and slamming my fist into his face. He falls back onto the ground as I hop the bar. Spitting out blood, he laughs as he stands and wipes his mouth.

"You know she was giving my Da head." My head connects with his nose, and he hits the counter before the ground. I'm down on my knees my fist hitting his face.

"Stop! Shane!" Brian doesn't touch me, but he pulls me back from the edge of darkness that was threatening to consume me. A pool of blood is growing under Bernard's head. His still chest has me sitting back. I hit him a few times. His head had collided with the counter, obviously harder than I thought.

"He's dead," Brian says as he places his hands on his head and walks away from me before returning.

"Help me get him out back," I say, getting up and pulling Bernard with me. "Just open the door," I tell Brian as he stares at the pool of blood. I take Bernard out back to where the smoking shed is.

"Get me a towel," I tell Brian. When he returns, I tell him to keep the towel to Bernard's head to stop more blood leaking everywhere. After leaning him against the tin structure, I go back into the pub and start to clean up the blood. I don't think about what happened; instead, I just clean.

After scrubbing the floor twice with bleach, I gather all the glasses and take them with me. "Are you still there?" Brian shouts in from the back, like a moron.

I take a final look around. It smells funny, but nothing appears out of the ordinary. Going out back, I give Brian the glasses to hold and take the towel and Bernard from him. I need to get my car around back. I'm about to tell Brian when the back door opens. "Who's been pouring bleach..." I don't turn as a girl speaks, but her words are cut off.

"Ava. Yeah, our friend here pissed himself. We are taking him home."

"Is he bleeding?" this is too risky, letting her see so much. I shift, and Brian must sense my urgency.

"Yeah, he fell over, but fit you better to go inside and do your job." She must be able to see half of Bernard's face, and that's making me nervous. But when the door slams, I glance at Brian.

I leave Brian with Bernard's body and make my way out the back of the building. The girl is annoying me. She saw Bernard and me. She needed to be eliminated. Getting the car, I drive around back. My eyes scan the area for cameras, but I know there are none. That's why I picked this small pub. There is no surveillance in this area.

Opening the double green doors that have no parking in white painted across them, I reverse the Audi in as close as I can and pop the trunk. Once I have Bernard, the towel, and glasses in the boot, I tell Brian to get in. He hesitates but jumps into the front seat. Closing the gates, I pull away from Kells and drive towards home.

"Who was the girl?" I ask Brian who hasn't spoken a word.

"Shane, she can't be touched." I glance at him.

"What, is she your sister?" She didn't resemble him, but I could tell they knew each other.

"No, it's complicated. But she thought he was drunk. There is no need to go near her." Panic is rising in his voice, so he was intimate with her.

"She's a loose end," I tell him while making sure I'm keeping within the speed limit. I don't need to attract any unwanted attention.

"Shane, you have my word she will never tell a soul." His word means nothing to me. We reach the bog land fifteen minutes later, and I back up my car into the mud.

"It's too risky, Brian," I say, opening the trunk.

"Leave her alone, and you have me, I will never look at anyone again. You will always come first. If I break my word, you can kill her." I mull over his words. It would be something to have that power over him.

"I'll think about it." My words seem to satisfy him as I start to pull the body out of the car. I should have waited until nightfall, but we don't have that luxury.

Brian follows my steps as we make our way carefully across the land. I send him back for the shovels as we start to dig. I don't bury the towel or glasses with him. Once he's covered over, I take a breather.

"I'm going to drop you back to the bar. You make sure Ava saw a very drunk guy." He's nodding like a fucking dog, and I don't like how over eager he is. But if he betrays me, I'll kill her first and make him watch. "Clean the bar every single place he could have touched. If I go down for this, so do you," I tell him as I start back to the car. "Burn your clothes," I tell him, and he nods.

"Okay, I got it. Don't worry." Worry is exactly what I'll end up doing.

CHAPTER TWENTY ONE

UNA

It's three in the morning when the bedroom door opens, and I question for the hundredth time tonight if this is going to be my life. I don't want to be all, "where were you," but I'm curious about where the hell he was until three in the morning. I can see his outline as he creeps to the bathroom. Clapping my hands, the room floods with light, blinding me momentarily. Once I open them, I wish I hadn't.

"What the hell?" There's blood again on Shane's clothes and arms. My eyes travel to his feet. "Is that mud?" Muck coats the side of his black boots. *Had he trekked through a muddy field?*

"It's okay. My car got stuck." His explanation has me folding my arms across my chest. The silky, small nightdress didn't cover much, and right now Shane was taking me in, but for once, I wouldn't be distracted.

"Was the car bleeding?"

Hanging his head, Shane takes a deep breath. When he peers back up at me he seems more composed. "I don't want to lie to you," he says pulling his top off, and it's all flesh and muscles.

My eyes roam his body. There isn't a mark on him, and I'm grateful that he isn't hurt.

"Then don't," I tell him as he opens the belt of his trousers. Pulling them off, he turns to me in his boxers, and it's not fair.

"Una, I do things in my line of work that aren't easy to do."

I tighten my arms at his half explanation. "The other person? Are they okay?" I can't look at him now. What would my dad think of me? I know he's hurt people. I've seen the blood, the anger, yet I love him. What kind of person does that make me? There is a lull, and that's what makes me glance at Shane.

"No." It's stupid of me, but I'm shocked. Taking a step away from Shane, I need to think. I also need more answers, but I'm not sure I can take it in right now.

"No as in he's in the hospital, or not as in he's…" I can't finish my sentence.

Shane glances away from me. A muscle twitches in his jaw, as he debates what to say. I want the truth, but that terrified part of me hopes he lies.

"I don't know what you want me to say." He settles on, and my stomach twists.

"I don't know either." I swallow the lump in my throat. But I have my answer. Whoever's blood is on him is dead. As I sit down on the bed, I try to process this.

"I thought it was just drugs." I ask the stupid question, and I can almost see Shane grinch at my naïve question. He runs his hands through his hair before coming to me. His muscles seem to flex and roll as he walks, and I think it's a nicer thing to focus on. Kneeling in front of me, Shane takes my hands in his bloodied one. We both stare at the blood for a moment.

"Una, I know this is difficult for you. But I would never harm someone for no reason." His brown eyes hold mine, and I nod.

"But sometimes, in this job, there are losses."

"I can't bear to think one day it will be you." I swallow the tidal wave of emotion that wants to consume me. He pulls me closer to him and lays his forehead against mine before kissing me softly on the lips. I melt into his arms and kiss him like its oxygen for my screaming lungs. "It won't be," Shane tries to reassure me as his hands roam into my hair.

"You can't promise me that," I say, and he holds my stare.

"If you keep dressing like this, I will always come back to you."

I give half a laugh and half a sob at his stupid statement. He can't actually promise me his safety. All I can do is hope and pray that God keeps him safe. As I flicker my gaze to his lips, I stroke his face, my thumb moving back and over his cheek.

I give a quick glance up at Shane. He hasn't taken his eyes off me before I close the distance and kiss him. My tongue gains entry easily into his mouth, and I give him the same access into mine. My skin burns as his hands leave my hair and roam my body. His touch isn't gentle, and the kiss has grown in intensity to an almost frantic rhythm. We break the kiss as Shane yanks my dressing gown over my head. Our lips smash back together as I move further back on the bed.

My hands roam his wide back, and a pool has formed between my legs. When Shane enters me, he lets out a moan. His thrusts are as frantic as his kisses, and it doesn't take long before I release, and Shane follows shortly after. His head is on my chest now as he breathes fast, and I kiss his hair, running my hands through it, fighting for air too.

"I love you," I tell him as my heart thunders in my chest. It's the type of beat that almost hurts as it slams against my chest.

Shane raises his head and removes himself from me, but climbs up to me. He doesn't say anything, but he kisses me, and I can feel the seal.

***

The next morning, I wake up to an empty bed. Things always seem better in the morning, but honestly, I'm questioning if going to bed alone and waking up alone is something I can get used to. Do I really have a choice? The idea of not having Shane at all causes me to pull my knees up to my stomach. I can accept having a small bit of him rather than none of him. With that thought, I get out of bed and shower and get ready for work.

After putting on my work clothes, I go downstairs and smile when I can smell the pancakes wafting from the kitchen. "They smell." my words fall silent.

"Delicious," Liam finishes for me, and I don't smile at him as he cuts up a pancake. Mary isn't here, but

I know Liam didn't make the pancakes. A plate is sitting across from him.

"Sit, Una," he tells me, and I reluctantly sit down. The pancakes aren't as enticing now as I glance up at Liam. The hairs stand on my arms as he assesses me.

"How are you?" The question has me narrowing my eyes, but Liam doesn't react to that. Instead, he waits with his knife and fork poised.

"Fine," I answer, and he continues cutting up his pancake in tiny little pieces. That he chews like fifty times before swallowing.

"How was Shane this morning?" he asks, and I try not to let him see how much he bothers me as I place a piece of pancake in my mouth. "I don't know. He wasn't there when I woke up," I bite out.

"I'm worried about him." I'm not sure if Liam is being sincere or not, but this is about Shane.

"Why?"

"Because, Una, he is acting out against anyone who looks at you funny. I fear you have cast a spell over my brother."

I drop my knife and fork at his words. "No one looked at me funny. Darragh wouldn't let me go.

That's not a look, and Brian was an asshole. I don't want Shane go around beating anyone up, but don't make it out like I'm whispering lies to him." Liam continues to chew slowly not reacting to my words.

"Screw you, Liam," I bark when he doesn't respond. While taking half the pancake, I jam it into my mouth unable to press my lips together, but I chew and swallow the lump, washing it down with a glass of OJ that had also been left out on the table for me.

"I wasn't insulting you. I was stating a fact." The want to stick my tongue out at his righteous tone is squashed as he stands.

"That's not a fact, Liam. You know what? I used to think your weirdness was cute. Now I see you for what you are."

He places his knife and fork on the plate. "And what's that?" I'm honestly surprised he asks, and I have no problem delivering my answer.

"An asshole," I tell him standing too. Taking my plate, I leave it in the sink before going into the wet room. It's there that I slip into my wellies and take my coat off the hook. Leaving the house, I slide my phone out of my pocket and ring Shane. No answer. I honestly don't know what he has a phone for.

I don't see Stephen around the stables. He could be over at the cattle sheds; I feed and bed all the horses. I leave Summer until last so I can spend some time with her. The noise of a quad has me smiling. Stephen must be back. Leaving Summer, I close her stable and make my way to the front yard. But it's not Stephen. Darragh falls off the quad. His face is black and blue. As his eyes snap to me, he glowers at me. I'm not surprised, but it still hurts. He gets off the ground and makes his way to the shed. I know what's in it, and against my better judgment, I follow him in.

"Darragh." I speak his name gently as he removes a gun from the wall. The double barrel is empty. I know because I checked them yesterday.

"Go away, trouble maker." He's not just drunk. I'm pretty sure that Darragh is high. The way his eyes grow and shrink rapidly tells me it isn't that long ago since he got high.

"You're in no fit state to take a gun." I'm not rushing towards him, as he doesn't have any bullets.

"You sound like your mother, a broken fucking record. That's why my Da had to get rid of her just like Shane will get rid of you." I force a smile even as Darragh's words sting. He isn't himself, and Shane did a number on his face. I had to remember he had a right to be angry with me.

"Okay. I'm not fighting with you, Darragh," I tell
him as he starts opening the press close to the gun
rack. He rattles the locked doors.

"Give me the key," he says, and I fold my arms
across my chest satisfied that he can't get the
bullets. "Nope, and I'm doing this because I care," I
tell him, and he snorts.

"You are trying to control me like everyone else."
The gun is making me uncomfortable as Darragh
waves it around, and I have to keep reminding
myself that it isn't loaded. Yet, a saying my father
used to say is playing around in my head. "The
devil puts a bullet in a gun every ten years." Not a
clue where the saying came from, but I'm moving
every time the gun is pointed in my direction.

"Give me the key now, Una." Once he doesn't have
ammunition, not much can go wrong. I leave the
shed, as I'm too uncomfortable with him waving it
around. The sound of shattering glass causes a
shiver to skitter up my back.

"There's more than one way to get in," Darragh
says while taking a hand full of bullets and shoving
them in his pockets.

"Darragh. You're being stupid," I tell him trying to
get him to put the bullets back. But that's not
happening.

"I'm going to shoot the pheasant who keeps stealing my boots." He's on the quad, with the gun in his hand.

"Darragh seriously…" My words fall on deaf ears as he kicks the quad into gear and races from the farmyard.

"Shit."

***

"And you let him leave?" The question that Liam asks me has me tightening my fists.

"I couldn't stop him." His back is to me as he checks the cabinet for the missing gun and bullets.

"You're wasting time. I told you the gun he took," I say, but he isn't listening to me. Once he finishes searching, Liam leaves the shed and starts in the direction of Darragh. I'm on his heels.

"Should you not ring Shane?" I ask, and Liam glances at me sideways. He's walking fast, and I have to walk/jog to keep up.

"I assume I wasn't your first choice. So I can also assume you have already rung him, and he hasn't answered."

Liam and his know-it-all ways. I don't answer. He's right I did ring Shane first, but once again, his phone is going straight to voicemail.

"Go back. I don't need you," he says, and I jump over a log that was hidden in the long grass.

"I don't feel comfortable leaving you alone with Darragh," I tell Liam, and it's weird when his lip twitches.

As we approach the tree line, Liam pauses, and it takes a lot of control not to take a step back from him when he levels me with a stare. "I want to make it clear, I've advised you to go back."

I roll my eyes at his words and move past him. Fingers that are long and cold circle my upper arm, and my eyes snap up to their owner.

"I'm not joking, Una. You're responsible for you." I swallow and nod, and Liam releases me. As we enter the forest, I sound like an ogre moving through the debris. I have to keep checking behind me to make sure Liam is still there. He doesn't make a sound. Lucky for us, Darragh is nearby, and he's making plenty of noises.

"Here, here little pheasant." He's calling it like you might call a dog.

"The gun isn't loaded," I tell Liam as the world shatters. I'm on the ground covering my head as the world explodes for the second time. My heart pounds in my ears, and when something touches my leg I scream. Looking at my leg, I see a black shoe and my eyes move up the trouser leg until I stare at Liam who stands over me.

"Are you okay?" Am I okay? Two rounds had been fired. I'm thinking about how they could have hit us. I'm not sure where Darragh was pointing, but my hands are patting my body down, looking for holes. Thankfully, I find none. I can see the amusement in Liam's eyes. I'm about to tell him that I'm glad I amuse him when a third shot is fired. This one is too close to home. Liam throws himself beside me as wood from a nearby tree sprays us.

"Darragh," Liam's raised voice makes me still.

"That little bitch get you?" Darragh asks while re-pumping the gun. He has lost his mind.

"Stay down," Liam says.

He doesn't have to. I have no intentions of standing up.

"Darragh, I'm going to stand up. So don't shoot me." Liam rises slowly. I can't see his face.

"I'm so sick of being the last one." Darragh's voice carries such a note of despair that as I lie here on the floor of the forest, something inside me twists for him.

Liam ducks again as Darragh fires, and that has my sympathy fleeing. Was he trying to kill Liam?

Liam's eyes clash with mine. "How many bullets did he take?" my mind races back to the moment in the shed.

"I don't know four, five maybe." Liam rises quickly as Darragh re-pumps the gun. I'm moving, reaching for Liam's leg to pull him back down. Four rounds have been fired. There could be one more. The tips of my fingers skim Liam's trousers as he charges towards Darragh. The noise of their struggle has me sitting up. Liam has wrestled the gun out of Darragh's hands.

"Did you just shoot at me?" Darragh is pinned under Liam, shaking his head, but it's Liam's fury that seems to be multiplying and growing around us. My lungs squeeze.

"I'm the only one who cares." Each word that Liam is shouting is like a punch in the stomach. His own pain, I don't understand, but it's etched like a name would be into wood.

"I'm the only one." He's breathing heavy, still holding Darragh down, and I stand up now, but I try to make myself as quiet as possible. Tears run out of the side of Darragh's eyes as he battles with the war the rages inside him. I have no idea what passes between them, but seeing Liam lose control is unsettling. As if my thoughts summon him, his head snaps towards me.

CHAPTER TWENTY TWO

UNA

"You let him beat me." Darragh recaptures Liam's attention.

"I stopped him." Liam's voice has calmed now, but he hasn't let Darragh up.

"You stood there." Darragh's voice is quivering as he shouts at Liam.

"What do you think would have happened if I wasn't there? I pulled him off you." Darragh is shaking his head and turns his head away from Liam. Now his focus is on me.

"Since you arrived, everything has gone to shit." Liam releases him as he starts at me. My gaze flickers to Liam, wondering what the fuck he is doing as Darragh walks towards me.

"Liam!" I shout his name, and he doesn't even blink. The bastard. I return my focus to Darragh.

"That's not true," I tell Darragh and hate how my voice trembles. I turn and start to leave with a thundering heart. I hold my shoulders high, like they might protect me as Darragh follows me.

"Yeah, you fucked everything up for me. With Brian, Shane, and now even Liam."

I spin around, my temper taking over. "No. You did that. That's all on you, and your drug habit. I have nothing got to do with any of this," I tell him, and there is some part of Darragh that I can sense peeking out at me behind the madness.

"You're like my brother," I tell him trying to restore some sense to this.

"What, like the way Shane is?" His sneer has heat rushing to my face. "You fuck all your brothers?" My throat burns. Liam stands behind Darragh not intervening. My temper flares again. "Just the good-looking ones," I tell him as I force a smile.

"Keep away from me." Those are Darragh's departing words as he walks out into the field.

"Gladly," I shout after him.

Liam has paused beside me, the gun in his hand, and now it seems more dangerous than it ever has before.

"Burning the candle at both ends will soon leave you without a light." My attention snaps up to Liam.

"What?" I question.

"Go home, Una." Liam steps out into the field, and I stare at him as he departs. I don't think he means his home. He wants me to leave. I march across the field, so done with today.

***

After a shower and pulling bits of twigs out of my hair, I go to the sitting room to try to do something normal like watch TV. The blue suite of furniture is velvet and has been brushed recently. The marks are visible.

I love the smell of this room. It's like lavender mixed withfreshly cut wood. The wood smell is coming from the logs that are stacked either side of the fire all the way up the wall. To get to the top of the pile would require a ladder. But that wood is never used. A wicker basket holds the wood for the fire that isn't lit. I could call Mary. I could light it myself, but I don't. Opening a large beige trunk that is behind the couch, I take out a floral throw and take it with me to the couch.

I haven't been in this room since I was a child. I spent so many hours in here with Connor. He was such a movie buff and easy to be around. He was always kind to me. I put on one of his favorites, Rambo. Not one I particularly like, but one that gives me happy memories.

The credits roll, and I end up putting on Taken, another favorite of Connor's. This one, I actually love.

I'm at the part where the hero is on the boat, and I love when his daughter finally sees him. A knock at the door has me pausing the movie. I'm being hopeful that when I turn around, it's Shane, but no, it's Liam dressed in a suit and looking perfect again. I turn back around to my movie.

"Una, someone is here to see you." I glance over my shoulder, and my stomach twists. My mother's here. My eyes snap from her to Liam's, and the soft smile she wears worries me.

"What's going on?" I question standing up. "What are you doing here, Mum?" She walks to me before pulling me into a hug. I'm staring at Liam over her shoulder.

"I saw the signs but ignored them." I lean out at my mother's words.

"What are you talking about?" I ask as Liam closes the door and moves towards us. "What is going on?" I untangle myself from my mother. I don't like Liam being here. It's making me nervous.

"I told her about your drug problem." The color drains from my face.

"I'm going to get you help." My mother is nodding as she reaches for my hand, but I pull it away. I can't stop staring at Liam.

"Don't be mad at Liam, sweetheart. I'm aware that Darragh got you into it." I'm shaking my head trying to make sense of this.

"I don't have a drug problem." My words fall on deaf ears. It's funny, I knew they would.

I'm clutching my neck trying to wrap my mind around this. "You did this, to get rid of me?" I take a step toward Liam. He puts his hand in his pockets.

"Darragh is on his way to rehab. He's getting the help he needs."

"Darragh is here, after his little episode in the forest."

"What episode, sweetheart?" my mother asks, and Liam is acting like a normal person would to reassure my mother that the drugs have warped my mind. He's convincing. I'm actually pondering if I am losing my mind.

I have to step away from both of them as I try to gather my thoughts. "This is ridiculous. I'm not on drugs. I'm fine," I tell my mother, but when she reaches out her hand to me like I'm a child. I know she is listening to Liam's lies.

"Come home, sweetheart."

"No." I shake my head while folding my arms over my chest. "You need to go home," I tell my mother and hate the hurt that flickers in her blue eyes.

"You need help." My mother keeps protesting, and I throw my hands in the air.

"He is lying to you. I don't have a drug problem."

"So you are telling me you have never taken drugs." The lie is on my tongue. I know how the truth will sound.

"I have…"

"Oh dear God." My mother's acting like I'm the addict that Liam is trying to paint.

"Am I that much of a threat to you," I grin at Liam, but my temper is flaring. "Are you that insecure about me and Shane that what? You lie to my mother, thinking she will take me home and your problem is solved." I'm hitting a nerve, as Liam remains silent.

"Oh, you're not with that boy."

I rub my forehead. "Mum, not now. I'm not doing this with you," I tell her as I turn and knock off the TV.

"He is no good for you. He's a thug." I clench my fists. "So was Michael, but you married him," I tell her, and she pulls at her ear. A tick I'm used to seeing when she's uncomfortable. She is here because she has been lied to.

"Mum, I love him, and I'm not leaving him," I tell her gently, hoping she can understand.

Tears brim in her eyes, and I hate seeing how upset she is. "Your father," she starts, and my heart slams against my chest. "Would be so ashamed of you."

My nose burns, and my lips tug downwards. "Don't bring dad into this." It's whispered.

"Shane is no good for you. You can do so much better. An accountant or a doctor."

"My brother is as good as any other man." I forgot Liam was here. His words annoy me.

"We all know what Shane O'Reagan is." My stomach twists at the viciousness of her words.

"What is he?" I'm looking from her to Liam, and they are having a stare-off.

"Not good enough for my daughter." My mother's words seem final. "Come on," she tells me, and I can't understand why she won't listen.

"I'm not leaving him," I tell her more firmly this time. Her lips twist into a snarl.

"If you don't come with me now, you can stay here for good." I stand my ground even as my heart pounds. "You stupid girl," are my mother's departing words. I'm still standing in the same place after she has left, and my mind is caught on one thing.

"Your father would be ashamed of you." She voiced a fear of mine. My lip trembles, and I bite it. I exhale a deep breath as my vision blurs.

"I know you don't understand, but I love him, Liam." Tears fall as I face Liam. "I know I should leave, I know that…but I can't leave him." The thought is twisting my stomach painfully. Tears continue to trickle down my face. Liam doesn't react or say anything. I didn't think he would.

"I hope, one day, you find love too," I tell him
before leaving the room, feeling crushed.

Flickering on the lights in the garage, I focus on my
bike. I bought this because of my dad's love for
bikes. Right now, I want to be as close to him as
possible. I want him to tell me he isn't ashamed of
me. Kneeling on the tarp, I run my fingers along the
frame of the bike.

It's clean from the last time that Shane and I worked
on it. In my head, I think my dad would have loved
Shane. But if he knew what he did, he would have
been more afraid for me. I'm shaking my head as
the bridge of my nose aches, sitting back on my
bum; I bury my head in my knees and cry.

I want my dad back, even if it's only for a moment.
I want him to hold me and call me his girl like he
always did. Dreaming of him used to ease my
yearning. Now I hate how his face is fading.

"I miss you," I tell the empty garage. My tears come
heavier, and I hate this place. I hate everything right
now. It all seems unfair. I want to scream or smash
something, but I don't do either. I get up and leave
the empty garage. Right now, I need him.

***

He's the fifth headstone down under the weeping willow. Wiping some falling leaves off his grave, I sit down. I haven't been here in a while. The white pot that holds dead flowers tells me no one has. I remove the flowers and sit back down, staring at the headstone. At the start, it was nearly a daily journey for me where I would tell him all about my day, but these days, it was getting less and less.

"I'm sorry I haven't been around much." I sit on the curb now with my back to the headstone and stare up at the tree. "Everything is a mess, and I'm worried that it's my fault." A shiver assaults my body, and I bite my lip.

"I met someone," I tell him with a smile, opting for a happy story. He didn't need to hear my woes. "His name is Shane. You'd really like him. The man that Mum married after you, it's his son. So." I trail off. "But that's neither here nor there. Anyway, his brother Liam is being a pain. He wants to get rid of me. Darragh, who's Shane's other brother, is mad at me too. Oh," I give a little laugh. "So is mum, no surprises there."

I focus on my fingers, my ramblings not over, "I left my job, got the courage to walk away. I'm working with horses now." I start crying again. I'm not entirely sure why this time. "I named my horse.

She's Summer. You would have loved her. She's real feisty, a bit like me." I snort a laugh again. "I think she's pregnant, but we'll find out soon."

Wiping away tears, I stop beating around the bush. I know why I'm here. "I'm so afraid, Daddy." I snivel a cry. "I don't want you to be disappointed in me." I'm hiccupping and bury my head in my knees as I bleed my soul on my father's grave. He doesn't answer me, but being here and telling him my fears gives me some comfort.

CHAPTER TWENTY THREE

SHANE

The water is silent as I sit on the bank of the lake. I used to come here as a child with Liam and Connor. That was before we found out he was our half-brother. Back then, you couldn't separate us. A smile tugs at my lips now as I picture the three skinny kids in white vests jumping into the lake. We were happy until we had to leave and go home.

The walk back was filled with skitting and laughing. Connor was the comedian then. Liam smiled then. Back then, life had more meaning. The clay on my shoes mocks me. The man I have become isn't what I wanted.

I exhale and stare out at the lake, trying to find a peaceful place in my mind. I always had to be ten steps ahead of everyone else, and it was exhausting. Leaving last night, I dug up Bernard's body and reburied him on different land we owned near the Loch Leigh Mountains. It wasn't far from us, but after digging up Bernard's rancid body and reburying him, I was exhausted, and not just my body but my mind. I couldn't have Brian with the knowledge of where the body was. That was my only reason for moving it. I knew I would have to move Siobhan's auntie, too, and the girl from the house that Darragh had killed.

I think that's what hurt the most. They lied to me. They told me they were ringing the Gardaí. I laugh now at my own stupidity. Since when did we hand over bodies? We buried them.

Rubbing my forehead doesn't ease the ache there. It made me question what other secrets Darragh and Liam carried. Why Liam protected him continuously. They shared something that strengthened that bond, and now they had another secret that they had kept from me. But soon, they would know I knew. Once the body was moved, they would figure it then.

Standing, I move around the lake. I want to go home to Una, but I also don't. I don't want to see her questioning eyes when I came in late. Worry was gnawing at her, and it killed me. If I was going to keep her, I needed her away from the house.

She would end up too damaged with all of them. Even with me. But I couldn't let it go. Tomorrow, I had an appointment to view Deerpark Stud farm, and the idea of owning it was exciting. That's where I would place Una. She would have a home, a job.

She would be safe from my family. It was still close to our home, because no matter what, family came first. That was in me, and no matter what, I couldn't let it go. No matter what my brothers do, I will be there to help them. When you bury a body with a person, you're tied to them for life.

Returning to the car, I take my phone out of the glove compartment. I have two missed calls from Una, one from Liam.

My stomach twists as I dial Una's number, and it goes to voice mail. The engine starts as I turn the key. That's another thing I need to do is burn this car, and I actually like it. I ring Una again, and she still doesn't pick up. I don't ring Liam back. I'm too pissed at him right now after lying to me. Instead, I ring Neill. He answers on the first ring.

"Any word?" I ask leaving the lake.

"All quiet. Brian is back to business as usual." I'm nodding at Neill's words. I can breathe for the moment.

"Anything on Connor?" This is something that shouldn't have taken so long, but it's like he's gone.

"Not a thing, but I'll keep my ear to the ground."

"Thanks," I say before hanging up. When the car settles in the garage, I want to find Una straight away, but I don't want her to see me covered in mud. Showering in my room isn't an option. There's a shower room off the garage that holds fresh clothes also in case of emergencies. I make it quick. Once showered and dressed in a fresh pair of jeans and red t-shirt, I go and look for Una. I ring her three more times as I search the house. I get no answer. My stomach tightens.

The intensity of her stare as she focuses on the bike has me pausing in the doorway. Red curls are piled on top of her head as she sits barefoot on the tarp. An oversized brown jumper and cream leggings make her look a picture. I'm not sure what's she's trying to do, but I could stand here all day watching her. Her eyes grow wide, and a smile shows a set of perfect white teeth.

"Hi." She's beautiful.

"Hi," I say back, stepping into the room. "I've been ringing you," I tell her, waving my phone at her, and she tilts her head.

"Funny, that is. I've been ringing you too." Sitting down beside her, my fingers find her hand, and I entwine them. "Yeah, I'd left the phone in the car," I tell her. Her smile widens as she looks at our hands before her gaze travels up to my eyes.

"You showered." My heart gives at a heavy thud as I see that uncertainty in her eyes again.

"I did," I tell the bike now as I clench my jaw. I hate this. Hate how she is looking at me. Her small, pale hand takes my face making me look at her. "You smell lovely," she says, her eyes lighter as she dips her head towards me and places a soft, precise kiss on my lips.

"I love you, Shane O' Reagan, in every shape and form." Her eyes shine as she tells me this, her hand clutching my face, like by sheer force that I will hear what she is saying, and I do.

She's telling me she knows what I do and that she still loves me, regardless.

"This life that I live is dangerous, but I love it. I love my family, and I know I could never walk away."

Una's eyes are wide as she takes in my words. There is such a look of fear on her face that I pause and press my fingers to her cheek, I'm smiling now at a warning that Liam always gave me. "Liam used to say that love makes a man weak." At the mention of Liam's name, her eyes close slightly, and that makes me smile more. She wasn't a fan, but who could blame her?

"Your love makes me stronger," I admit, and her lips form a small o and her chest starts to rise and rise and fall wildly. "You're intoxicating, Una, and I want to share all of this with you. The moments that

I hold on to the most are the ones with you in them.
I love you." Her vision blurs, and a tear trickles
down her face.

"Wow," she says through a half sob half laugh.
"Seal with a kiss," she tells me.

My chest tightens, but I don't hesitate. I seal our
love with a kiss that reaches inside me and heals
some dark part of me that had me keeping Una
away. Now she was in fully.

The clearing of a throat is what breaks the kiss. Finn
is wearing a goofy smile, and I can't hide my own
smile.

"Dads surprised us all with a family meal." I raise
my eyebrows, hoping that Finn can shed some light
on this family meal. Dad doesn't do anything for
nothing, but Finn shrugs.

"Siobhan's coming." Finn sounds nervous as he
tells Una, who still clutches my hand.

"She's so sweet, Finn. This is going to be fun." Her
words have Finn relaxing, and when she rests her
head on my shoulder, I can't help but relax even
further.

Liam and Dad are the only two in the dining room when Una and myself arrive. Liam looks up, and there is something in the way he looks at Una that I don't like.

"Liam," she greets him sharply with a raised chin.

"Una," he responds, but he adds a nod of his head. Like approval or something.

Dad has been looking at mine and Una's joined hands, and when I meet his eye, he doesn't show what he feels. Releasing my hand, Una sits down beside Dad, but first kisses him softly on the cheek. His face melts, and a smile is there just for Una. I don't mind. As long as he is kind to her, that's all that matters. I sit beside Una and across from Liam, who stares at me.

"Hi." A shy voice at the dining room door has us all looking to Siobhan.

Una gives a seriously enthusiastic wave beside me, and I can't stop smiling. Siobhan slides in beside Liam without hesitation, and sitting opposite him, seeing him sitting beside a girl, is almost amusing. Has he ever pictured himself settling down? He was too used to the whores he managed.

"Siobhan, I'm glad you could come." Dad sounds like he means it, but I'm still nervous about why we are all gathered around this time. It's like the last supper. Finn nods at everyone, hands jammed in his pockets, before he sits down beside Siobhan.

"Thank you so much for the invite. You have a beautiful home, Mr. O'Reagan."

"Please, it's Michael." We are all waiting for Darragh, but when Mary enters and places plates in front of us, I look to Liam. I don't know why.

"Where is Darragh?"

"Darragh is gone away for a while," Liam speaks, looking at Finn before facing me and finally Father. Una seems to be frozen beside me.

"Gone where?" I ask, and from the look on Finn's face, this is news to him as well. My attention goes to Liam.

"What happened?"

"Please, we have two ladies at the table. Can we just have this meal?" No we fucking can't. Now all I can think of is the dead girl. Had this something to do with Darragh's disappearance? Liam is eating his dinner, and Finn is too, along with Siobhan.

"I'll tell you later," Una whispers to me, and I steal a glance at her. She knows? So it couldn't be about the dead girl. That makes me breathe a little easier, and I give her a nod. She squeezes my leg under the table, and I suppress a smile.

"So you two are a thing?" My attention snaps to Finn who is smiling at me, delighted at how uncomfortable things at the table just became.

"Yes, we are."

Siobhan gives a big smile, and I nod at her in response before turning to Una who has an eyebrow raised. "We are?" I say, and it sounds like a question.

Una tilts her head while smiling. "Yes, we are." I want to kiss her, but everyone is staring at us.

Dad is waiting for me to explain. I cut into my chicken. A kick under the table from Una I ignore and grin as I continue to eat. Her heavy sigh has my lips tugging.

"Michael, I hope you're okay with this?" Una's voice is so sweet, and I take a quick glance at Father.

"Are you happy?" he asks her, and she doesn't hesitate much to my delight.

"Very."

"Well, then it's okay." His blessing does mean a lot, and when I glance to Una and see the large smile on her face, it means a lot to her too.

I surprise her when I place a gentle kiss on her lips. Her cheeks turn pink, but she's still smiling. A snigger from Finn has me returning to my food, but I can't get rid of the stupid grin I'm wearing.

The conversation flows easily around the table that's down to the two girls who chat about movies. I knew Una had loved watching movies with Connor, but I didn't know she was that into it.

Her biggest love seemed to be Denzel Washington. "I cry every time," Una tells Siobhan who's nodding before Una can even finish.

"Me too." It looks like a friendship is blossoming.

"But if you saw it already, why would you cry?" I ask once Mary has set out the dessert, tea and coffees.

"He dies for her," Una says like I'm stupid. I love her feistiness.

"Yeah, but you already know that." I seriously can't understand this.

"It's just Denzel's acting." Siobhan interjects and Una is agreeing. It's fun at the table. It's different.

The only person not taking part is Liam, but that's not unusual. What is, is how distant he is. His mind isn't here, and that makes me think of Darragh.

"I think the girls make a great point." This is the first-time Father has spoken through the meal. He's nodded and smiled but hasn't spoken.

"The kidnappers didn't do their homework. If they did, they would have never taken that girl. Denzel does a superb job. There are people in life that you shouldn't hurt." I glance towards Liam, but he's focused on Dad.

"It's like the most recent news," Dad says, putting down his spoon. "A young Northern Ireland boy, I think connected to the IRA, is missing, presumed dead. Whoever made the mistake of hurting him has messed with the wrong people." Silence fills the dining table, and I remind myself that he doesn't know.

"Oh that would make a great film." Una's words are like water on flames, and she jumps right into a film about the IRA she saw and was disappointed in. I'm not sure if she's aware of what she is doing, but Father isn't finished, not by a long shot.

"Does the IRA kill the man's family for hurting one of their own?" I clench my jaw.

"I don't think so." Una shakes her head, and she's really thinking about it. "No. No they don't," she answers with more certainty.

"In real life, they would." Dad smiles after that before returning to his food.

"I didn't hear about that," I say before taking a drink of tea. Liam and Dad are observing me way too closely, but I make my mind go blank.

"Oh I did hear about the house that burned down in Kells." That causes a flicker of fear to ignite in me.

"Oh no, what happened? I hope no one was hurt?" Una asks, her voice so kind.

"My friend who works with me in Cavan, she lives there in black water heights. She said no one was hurt, but the house burned right to the ground, the houses either side didn't survive either. But thankfully, no one was hurt."

Una is frozen beside me, and my eyes snap to Liam who doesn't seem to give a shit. "I wonder what caused the fire?" I'm asking Liam.

"A cigarette not put out. Faulty wiring, cooker left on. The list is truly endless." I'm trying not to snap at him. Glancing at Una, she's as white as a fucking ghost. She's putting two and two together.

"Are you alright, Una?" Dad's hand covers Una's, and I want to rip it from hers. His patronizing words grate on me.

"Why wouldn't she be?" I snap, and silence fills the room.

"Shane." Una's surprise at me raising my voice has me reeling in my irritation. "I think I need some fresh air," she tells him, and Father smiles at her.

"How about a swim?" This suggestion comes from Finn, and Siobhan is nodding beside him.

"I don't have a swim suit," Siobhan says with disappointment in her voice.

"I don't mind," Finn says, and she nudges him with her elbow.

"I can give you one, and a swim actually sounds good." I'm surprised when Una speaks, and she looks up at me with such an innocent look on her face. "Are you coming?"

"You go ahead with Finn and Siobhan. I'll catch up," I tell her.

She hides her disappointment well before giving me a kiss on the cheek.

Once Finn, Siobhan, and Una leave, I ask about Darragh.

"He's in rehab, where he should have been a long time ago." I agree with that assessment, if it's true.

"I have work to do." Dad stands now, his focus on Liam. He ignores me as he leaves. Angry, I suppose, that I raised my voice.

"You burnt the house down?" I say the moment Father is gone. Liam pushes his chair out slightly from the table.

"Darragh left a cigarette lit." I wasn't buying it. He didn't know that I found the body, but I don't say anything about it. It's small compared to the other topic that Father brought up.

"Any idea who this boy is that Father was talking about?" I ask while placing my elbows on the table. I'm observing Liam for any signs at all.

"No, but it sounded like he was asking us."

I nod. That's exactly what it sounded like.

"Do you know who the boy is?" The question is delivered with a slight raised eyebrow. He thinks I'm involved, but he's grasping at straws.

"No, not a clue," I lie.

VI CARTER

CHAPTER TWENTY FOUR

UNA

I'm glad when Finn suggests swimming. Really, I would have grabbed any excuse to get out of that room. After coming back from my dad's grave and having a shower, telling Shane about Liam and my mother wouldn't help anyone.

It would cause more rows and more hate. I hoped that Liam would take my silence as a peace offering. I would find out in time if he accepted it or not.

Siobhan comes out of the bathroom in the pool house in the red bikini I gave her, and she looks like a sun-kissed goddess.

Her tanned skin seems to glow. Brown eyes smile at Finn as he appreciates each step she takes towards the pool. She's beautiful. Finn's very handsome. All the O'Reagans are. Too much, at times. Growing up around such stunning men had my expectations for the real world set too high. I think that's why I spent far too much time alone. Coming here in the summer was spent swooning over Shane. Now to think we were together was crazy.

"What are you smiling at?" Siobhan asks me as she swims over the side where I relax. "Shane," I admit, and it's nice to say it out loud to another girl.

"I'm not going to lie. He scares me." Siobhan's voice is still light as she confesses how she feels.

"Liam scares me, but I get why Shane would."

"Liam is strange," Siobhan adds with narrowed eyes and I laugh.

"Finn's a great guy."

"I can hear you," Finn says as he comes out of the changing room in a pair of white long shorts that ride low on his hips. He's all abs and wide shoulders, and Siobhan drinks him up.

I'd roll my eyes, but I can imagine that's how I view Shane too. Ducking under the water is nice. The water temperature is warm, but still, the initial sensation of being covered sends a shiver through me. Breaking the surface, I push my wet hair out of my face. Siobhan is swimming while Finn relaxes along the edge. I swim over to him. "Did you know about Darragh?" I ask treading water.

"No. I can't believe he's gone to rehab." Finn's face grows serious, and he scratches his brow. "It was sudden, because I'm sure I saw him this morning."

"Well, he's in the best place I suppose," I say while moving to the side of the pool. I'm facing out towards the large windows.

"When was the last time you saw him?" Finn asks, and I pretend to consider his question.

"Yesterday, I think," I tell him with a nod. "What do you think about your dad saying that about the Northern Ireland boy?" My question I thought sounded simple, but Finn looks at me differently now as he moves around to face the window too. Glancing over my shoulder, I see the red bikini down the far end of the pool.

"I don't think anything about it. Why do you ask? You know something?" The suspicion is growing in his voice and the way he stares at me.

"I thought it weird, that's all," I answer while giving him a nudge, and he grins.

"You're starting to sound like one of us."

Flicking water at him, I laugh. "Shane is rubbing off on me," I say, and even as Finn laughs at me, I can see the question in his eyes. He's wondering what I really know.

For me, I can't help but think Michael was asking his sons, and it was last night that Shane had killed someone. Instead of letting the fear fester, I dive under the water.

Swimming relieves some tension that had been building inside me. Today had been crazy. Chatting with Siobhan makes me feel normal. I'm not sure she could ever understand what her presence does for me. This big house with so much time on my hands can drive me a little crazy.

"Anyone want a drink?" Finn asks, climbing out of the pool. Siobhan takes the moment to admire him as water streams off his body and pulls his white shorts a bit lower.

"Yeah," I answer, and she looks at me over her shoulder and grins.

"Me too," she tells Finn.

We both get into the Jacuzzi. The water, at first, is almost too hot, but as I close my eyes, my whole body relaxes. "I so need this," I say.

"Me too. Finn's been so stressed lately." I open my eyes and look at Siobhan. "Over what?" I ask.

She pushes the water away from her with a delicate arm. "His brother."

I can't stop the snort that leaves my mouth. "Which one?" I ask, and she laughs.

"Yeah, I know. It's normally Darragh, but lately it's Connor. Who I have never met. I assume you have."

A fist tightens inside my belly. "Yeah, Connor's cool. He comes across a bit dark, but he's cool." I'm smiling. Connor always reminded me of the incredible hulk. He was bigger than the other boys, but he was a force to be reckoned with. Anyone who stood in his way fell, and they fell hard.

"He misses him so much," she adds, and all I can do is nod.

The day I left my job, I drove to the cross guns for a few quiet drinks. It was there I met Connor after three years of not seeing each other. We laughed a lot, and it was like old times. He had made me promise that I wouldn't tell anyone, and I hadn't. It hadn't crossed my mind, but right now, I question if telling Finn where Connor was, would it ease him? Finn arrives back with the drinks.

"I turn my back, and you girls are lapping it up," he says, handing me a bottle of Budweiser. Siobhan gets hers delivered with a kiss.

I look away even as I smile. It's nice to see Finn happy and see him with something that's his alone and not his and Darragh's.

When I finish my drink, I leave Siobhan and Finn alone. He's sitting closer to her, and I can see it in their eyes that they need some alone time.

I pull on a dressing gown and flip-flops as I make my way across the courtyard. It's cold outside, but after the heat of the pool house, I'm not surprised.

I pause at the door when I find Shane lying on the bed, his arm covering his eyes. Moving to him slowly, I notice the soft rise and fall of his chest. He's asleep. I need to get into dry clothes. The strap of my dressing gown is pulled, and I can't stop my heart from tripping as I turn to Shane. His eyes are open and focused on me.

"Did you have a nice swim?" he asks, pulling me closer while he sits up.

"I did," I tell him with a smile.

"Finn got to see you in a swimsuit before me?"

Finn's eyes were focused on Siobhan, and she was beach ready. My emerald green one-piece along with pale skin and red hair wasn't on the most desired list.

"You had your chance," I tease as he opens the belt of my dressing gown. I don't know why it's odd, but a nervous energy zings up my spine with the idea of him seeing me, yet I don't stop him. When he has it open, his warm hands go to my hips, and I shiver at the contact.

"A good job I didn't go swimming."

Holding my breath, I fear the worst.

"I don't think we would have done much swimming."

And like that, all my worries and insecurities fly away.

My body fits perfectly onto his lap. He doesn't complain about the cold water against his skin, and the contrast of his hot body has me pushing myself closer to him. Being this close to Shane allows me to see the strain around his eyes. Dark circles ring them. My lips press against each eyelid before I kiss his nose.

"As nice as this is, I need to have a shower and warm up," I tell him, leaving one final kiss on his lips. It's hard to walk away, but I need to warm up. The shower looks nice, but the bath is what calls to me.

I strip off as I pour in a bubble bath and run the taps. It doesn't take long for the room to fill with steam. Stepping into the bath, I lie back and close my eyes.

"I've changed my mind," I call out to Shane in case he is waiting for me.

"I'm taking a bath." Colors move from behind my eyes.

"I can see that." Water sloshes over the tub and onto the floor. Opening my eyes and then narrow them at Shane. "You nearly gave me a heart attack."

He's kneeling down along the side, his arm resting on the lip of the tub. He must have gotten wet, but he doesn't seem to care.

"I want to tell you a secret." I settle down as Shane speaks and rest my head against the back of the tub again. "You're not scary when you're mad. You're sexy as hell." I want to be offended, but his words send a thrill through my body.

"I can be scary," I tell him.

"Never," he tells me. His fingers dip into the water. He grazes my arm with his fingertips, and the sensation has a heartbeat thrilling in between my legs. I focus on his arm, his tattoo that always captures my attention.

"What does it mean?" I ask before gathering a pile of bubbles in my palm and blowing them towards Shane. He swipes them away quickly with a grin.

"My tattoo?" he asks, and there is uncertainty there. He isn't looking at me now.

"If it's private, you don't have to tell me."

"It's not that it's private. I just don't think it would do you much good knowing." Now I want to know. I try to pull myself up in the bath, but Shane's fingers hold onto my arm.

"I want to know who I'm lying beside."

He laughs at my words, but his laugh is so tired and drained that my stomach churns with guilt at pushing him. But I hate not knowing every part of him.

"Okay, I'm going to tell you. But… and I mean but, no questions. No names. I'll tell you what it represents." Why is my heart pounding? I nod my head. Shane holds my eye, and that gives me confidence that what the tattoos mean can't be so bad.

"Every death that I have experienced, I get a band added." My eyes are counting the bands rapidly, and Shane moves his arms.

"Una," he warns.

"I'm only counting them," I tell him, but I know that's not enough. Who died? Is one for his mum?

The man who isn't okay from the other night. But no new ink covers his arm. The atmosphere becomes somber as I think of the man, the one who has been spinning around in my head.

"The missing boy from the north. Is he the same person as the man from the other night?" There is a wild look of panic in Shane's eyes, but when he closes them and looks back at me, it's gone.

"No, and don't ever let anyone hear you say that." He's taken my face in his hands, his words soft, and I nod.

"I won't," I tell him.

He relaxes back down along the side of the bath. We are both silent. I'm studying him as he stares at the water, and there is such a sadness there that my heart hurts. It's funny to feel such pain for someone else.

"What's bothering you?" I ask him, thinking there is no way he will actually tell me. But I can't ask. His gaze flickers up to me, and he reminds me of a cute puppy with his big brown eyes.

He exhales heavily before speaking. "Connor. I can't find him, and we need him home." I look away from Shane. I had promised Connor I wouldn't, but that was before.

"If you knew where he was, what would you do?" Shane tilts his head and sits up a bit straighter.

"I'd ask him to come home. We need him."

"Did he run away?" I ask.

"No. Una, do you know something?"

"I know where Connor is," I tell him, and his eyes widen like it's a miracle. Laughter bubbles up from his throat, confusing me, but when he looks at me, the light in his eyes has me smiling.

"I've been searching for him for a while. Is he far away?" Now that Shane is looking happier, I can use this to my advantage.

"The information will come at a price," I tell him with a smirk. I squeal as Shane jumps into the bath fully clothed. I think most of the water is now on the floor, but I can't stop the laughter.

"What the hell, Shane," I say, but he's moving over me, his lips getting closer.

"Name your price," he tells me, not an inch from my lips.

"You," I tell him, and he pays in full.

CHAPTER TWENTY FIVE

SHANE

I'm lying, gazing at her as she sleeps, and it's more beautiful now being this close. How many years had I watched her from the shadows? Her long stretches are pulling the quilt down slightly, showcasing the curve of her breast through her cream-colored, silky nightdress.

The desire to see her eyes has me running my fingers along her jawline. She stirs under my touch. Her lids half open, and a goofy smile coats her face. "Good morning," she tells me, becoming more alert.

"Is breá liom tú," I tell her I love her before kissing her puffy pink lips.

"Tá mé i ngrá leat freisin." Her words have me smiling.

"I didn't know you spoke Irish so well."

She leans in and kisses my arm. "It's a phrase I know well, along with, póg mo thóin," Now she's giggling, and I can't help pulling back the covers and doing what she asked. Kissing her perfect arse.

She's still giggling when I come back up and kiss her. "I have a surprise for you today," I tell her, but I'm nervous. Today, I want her to see Deerpark Stud farm with me. I hope she loves it as much as I do.

"What should I wear?" Always such a dilemma for a woman. But with Una, she could wear anything.

"Be comfortable and wear whatever you want," I tell her with a final kiss before getting out of bed. She's still smiling as she gets dressed, and I can't stop myself from stealing kisses as we make our way down to breakfast. Mary has pancakes ready as I had requested the night before.

"Thank you, Mary," I say, and she looks at me twice. I hear you're welcome as we sit down.

"I'm going to get fat with all these pancakes," Una warns. The navy and cream sleeveless swing dress she is wearing makes her look sexy yet innocent. "Even fat, you would be adorable," I tell her as Mary places the pancakes in front of us.

***

I've taken the Cadillac again today, knowing that it's Una's favorite. She's rubbing it and making small noises as she checks it out, and I'm afraid at how perfect everything is with her. I'm waiting for the other shoe to fall, always pessimistic. I push the darkness aside and steal glances of Una. Her smile is infectious, and I find myself grinning now and then.

"So where are we going?"

She's asked several times, and we are almost there. "Patience," I tell her, and she sticks out her tongue. If I wasn't driving, I know what I would do with it.

Pulling up at the large steel gates, I ring the bell. "Welcome to Deerpark Stud. Do you have an appointment?" I flicker a quick look at Una, and her eyes are darting to the large gates with the horse heads on them back to the monitor.

"Shane O Regan. I have an appointment." It takes a moment before the gates start to open.

"Please, come on in." I wait until the gates have fully opened before I drive up slowly. Letting the roof down, it gives Una a panoramic view.

I want her to love it.

VICIOUS IRISH

"Why do you have an appointment here?" she's asking, but her eyes are roaming the well-groomed fields. The old outbuildings come into view, and they have been restored. But the most stunning part is the house.

A two-story white house that's over 12,000 square feet. Not as big as the home place, but still decent. The grounds, buildings and house are in perfect condition. You could move in, in the morning if you wanted.

When I stop the car, the auctioneer greets me. "Mr. O' Reagan." He takes Una's hand and shakes it. She places her hands behind her back, looking unsure. Taking her hand, I twine our fingers together.

"There have been two more views for this place, take a look around, but I wouldn't take long making a bid." I nod not wanting to talk money in front of Una.

"What kind of money are we talking?" Una asks sweetly.

The auctioneer looks at me, and I give him a nod that I hope Una doesn't see.

"One point five million. But I would say bid two million, and the place will be yours."

Una stumbles, and I hold on to her hand tighter.

"I'll leave you both to it. You can find me in the foyer after." He leaves, and he's not even out of earshot before Una starts.

"Two million euro. Why are you looking at this place?"

"We are looking at this place," I tell her making my intentions clear.

"We," she repeats, color rising in her cheeks, and I can't help but kiss her lightly.

"We will need our own place, and Summer would be happy here."

She looks unsure, so I take both her hands. "It's an investment."

"A huge one that I can't help with," Una interrupts me.

"I know that. But you would help run the place. It's a profitable business," I tell her, and I can see her softening.

"Just two million, Shane." Her exhale ends on a laugh like she can't believe it.

"Look at the place and tell me what you think."

We walk, and I observe Una take it all in. "I mean it's perfect Shane. But I mean, it's your decision."

I squeeze her hand. "There is no more me. Only us," I tell her, and she looks so perplexed that I find myself kissing her again.

"Can you see yourself living here?" I ask her as we make our way around to the house.

"Yes." She sounds almost breathless as we stop and admire it.

"Can you see yourself having a family here?" As I say it, my heart beats a little faster. It's something I have never thought about, never thought I would have. My own family. Una turns to me, her eyes searching my face.

"Yes." I kiss her deeply this time. "I love you," I tell her before we make our way into the house.

The auctioneer, as promised, is waiting in the foyer. The moment he sees us, he stands up. I let Una wander off as I speak to him. "I'll take it," I tell him.

"There will be other bidders," he starts, but Una looks happy here.

"Two million, and I want the deal closed by the end of the week," I tell him, and he's already getting his phone out to make the call.

***

After leaving Deerpark Stud, I take Una out for food in Cabra Castle. It's close to home and serves decent food. It's the first day in a long time I can breathe. I know I still have a lot of problems, but they all seem easy to solve. Knowing where Connor is has made it all so much easier. Later tonight, I will go get him, and his first job will be finding out what that girl Ava knows and keeping an eye on her. Brian will keep his mouth shut. If he doesn't, I won't touch him. I can get Connor to do that, as well.

Moving the bodies became vital now. We needed to clear out the bog. Leaving any form of evidence around wasn't wise.

"You have to taste this pavlova. It's delicious." Una holds up a spoon to my lips filled with dessert. I take it and smile at her before breaking off a piece of my sticky toffee pudding and feeding it to her.

She moans, and I think I'll keep doing this for a while.

"So you like the house?" I ask her in between spoonfulls. She nods and smiles. The auctioneer had gotten back to me not long after leaving. The offer was accepted. The place was ours.

"Well, it's our new home." She stills for a moment, a piece of chocolate falling onto her chin. I reach across and clean it.

"Are you serious?"

I can't stop the smile. "Yes, I am," I tell her, and she squeals getting the attention of an elderly couple beside us. She's around the table and in my arms.

"I don't know what to say," she says with a look of awe on her face.

"You don't have to say anything. Just be my forever," I tell her and mean it. As long as I have Una, I'm stronger and better. Without her, that thought, I don't let form.

"I've always been your forever." Her words send a thrill through me, and I kiss her softly on her lips.

Seal it with a kiss, I can almost hear my mother whisper. I do. I seal it all in, knowing it will always be there.

Ruthless is now available on Amazon.

Fighting is all I've ever done. I've fought for my father, my brothers. I've fought for money or just for the thrill of it but now I have a new reason to fight. I must fight to keep Ava safe only this time it's not with my fists.

VI Carter has authored an intriguing, well written, and outstanding book. – 5 stars – Amazon Reviewer

If you never want to miss a new release you can sign up to my newsletter at my website.
www.authorvicarter.com

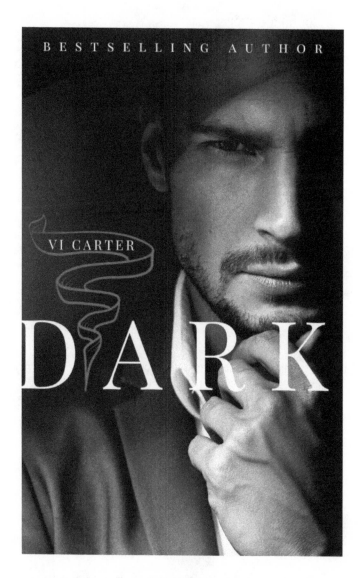

DARK

A debt is owed, and he takes me as payment.

HER

When my father runs up too much debt, I pay the price.

I've been sold.

Sold to a man who vows to break me.

A man who keeps his face hidden from me, even as his dark desires awaken mine.

It wasn't my debt to pay, but he took me, anyway.

He said he would have his payment, even if it cost me my soul.

HIM

I run the club.

If someone steps out of line, they either work for me or disappear.

VICIOUS IRISH

But when a local man runs up too much debt, I take his daughter as payment.

She is mine to do with as I please.

I will have her completely; mind, body, and soul.

Nothing would please me more than breaking her.

I didn't think I would feel for her.

I didn't think I could love again.

Now I might be the one who ends up broken.

Enjoy this book? You can make a big difference

Reviews are the most powerful tools in my arsenal when it comes to getting attention for my books. Much as I'd like to, I don't have the financial muscle of a New York publisher.

(Not yet, anyway.)

But I do have something much more powerful and effective than that, and it's something that those publishers would kill to get their hands on.

A committed and loyal bunch of readers.

Honest reviews of my book help bring them to the attention of other readers.

So if you've enjoyed this book I would be very grateful if you could spend just five minutes leaving a review.

Thank you very much!

About The Author

When Vi Carter isn't writing contemporary & dark romance books, that feature the mafia, are filled with suspense, and take you on a fast paced ride, you can find her reading her favorite authors, baking, taking photos or watching Netflix.

Married with two children, Vi divides her time between motherhood and all the other hats she wears as an Author.

She has declared herself a coffee & chocolate addict! Do not judge

Social Media Links for Vi Carter

Website: https://authorvicarter.com